THE WAY IT WAS

The Way It Was

Ian Farquhar

Foreword by

Baroness Mallalieu KC

President of the Countryside Alliance

Anthony Eyre

MOUNT ORLEANS PRESS

DISCLAIMER

Hunting within the Law

It should be noted that within this book a variety of pieces will be written about Hunting. The hunting may take place in a variety of countries whose laws now vary regarding the hunting of live quarry. There will also be historical pieces referring to hounds and hunting over the last few centuries. It should therefore be taken that any reference to hunting refers to an activity undertaken within the law of that country at that particular time. When describing hounds for example reference will be made to scent. It is not practical every time to detail whether that scent is quarry or artificial scent. Again, therefore all references to hounds' capabilities should be taken that if in a country where hunting live quarry with dogs is banned, the scent referred to will be a simulated one. For practical purposes also a hound may be referred to as having 'fox sense' an attribute which allows it to anticipate quarry behaviour. As the artificial trails also simulate quarry behaviour this trait will still be referred to as fox scent. It is not practical to differentiate between a hound from 1874 with 'fox sense' hunting a different scent to the hound descended from it which displays this quality in England in the present day. These traits therefore will be described across the ages and countries, for practical reasons as ever.

Frontispiece: IWF at Badminton. (Photo by Ray Bird)

Published in Great Britain in 2023
by Anthony Eyre, Mount Orleans Press
23 High Street, Cricklade SN6 6AP
https://anthonyeyre.com

© Ian Farquhar 2023

Ian Farquhar has asserted his right to be
identified as the author of this work in accordance with
the Copyright, Designs and Patents Act 1988.

ISBN 978-1-912945-42-9

A CIP record for this book is available
from the British Library

Printed in Malta by
Gutenberg Press

To Pammie-Jane

*For your companionship in the duration of much of this exciting
and often very enjoyable and rewarding part of my life.
I cannot thank you enough.*

Bicester days: IWF with Emma on her Shetland.

ACKNOWLEDGEMENTS

I WOULD LIKE TO thank all those who have produced photographs for inclusion in this book, and also those who have helped me with facts and memories, too many to perhaps be included but certainly not forgotten. I would like to thank Kay Gardner for her role as proof reader. It was of enormous benefit in that not only is she an author herself, but she knows Badminton and is an expert on hounds and their breeding. I would like to thank my family for putting up with me. Emma and George, Arthur and Evie who all go from strength to strength in Dorset. Victoria and Pete who have triumphed at The Holford Arms and who are now living at Happylands with Winnie, Walter and Coco and planning their future with the Quarry. Rose and George (Gemmell) recently married with George becoming a great addition to the family.

I would like to thank Jimmy Graham for his sterling help in bringing back to life many old photos so they could be included in this book. Thank you for your time Jimmy. I would also like to sincerely thank Jo Aldridge, without whose support and inspiration quite simply this book would never have got off the ground (probably to the relief of all). Jo painstakingly typed out every chapter of badly produced scribble, put it in a readable form and then helped with the syntax and the facts. Jo, you have been an absolute brick.

I would like to acknowledge Simon Dring, David Beaufort's agent, who I dealt with on a regular basis regarding the finances of the hunt and estate. Simon and myself always got on incredibly well and I am enormously grateful for his understanding of something which could have led to a tricky situation but never did. Thank you, Simon.

Lastly, I would like to thank the English foxhound whose well-being has always been at the centre of my thoughts.

Ian Farquhar
March 2023

FOREWORD

IN THE WORLD of hunting Ian Farquhar is quite simply a legend. He is the predominant hound breeder and huntsman of his generation. His story told in these memoirs goes way beyond that. This is modern history starting with an undeniably privileged upbringing and about a life lived through an era which is no more. It is told by a man with immense charm, bravery, outstanding kindness, and a sense of fun, but above all, with an all-consuming passion for an occupation of which so many have no knowledge or understanding. Ian hunted two packs of foxhounds, the Bicester for 12 seasons up to 1985 and the Beaufort until his retirement from hunting the hounds in 2011 and as Master in 2019. The results of his hound breeding are to be found today in packs throughout the United Kingdom, the United States, Canada, Australia, and Europe. But there is so much more to say. Ian is a man with an exceptional gift—an ability to command the respect and affection of both men and animals and to work together with both as a team. He knew his farming communities as friends and neighbours and did a job they needed brilliantly.

He almost certainly knew the countryside in which he hunted better than anyone else—not just from its roads and paths like the rest of us—but where each gate lead, the spinneys, the woodlands, the streams, rivers and ways across. He would know that in every village there were doors he could knock at almost any hour, and he would be welcomed. He was their friend, neighbour, and hero.

Ian talked to everyone as an equal. He did, quite literally, 'walk with kings—nor lose the common touch' as Kipling's poem describes. He also 'filled the unforgiving minute with sixty seconds worth of distance run.'

Left: IWF, Bicester years: hunting hounds on Jackie.

9

This book deserves to be read by those who want to remember a world which has changed vastly over one man's lifetime and also those who want to understand what has been lost. Life with the Captain was clearly a rollercoaster with 'bumps in the road' as he puts it, but how grateful are those of us who tried to follow in his slipstream, hanging onto the neck strap and sharing the excitement, the friendship, the sheer magic of hunting and life enhancement that it gave, for which he was responsible.

Ann Mallalieu
March 2023

CONTENTS

Michael Farquhar, Anthony Farquhar, IWF [the Author], Sir Peter Farquhar;
Turnworth, Dorset 1952.

THE BEGINNING

IT WAS ONCE explained to me that every great hunt and every story should have a beginning, a middle and an end and therefore I shall pick as my beginning my family.

The Farquhars are a Scottish Clan from Aberdeenshire. Highlanders, who boast that the red and the yellow lines in their tartan prove that they took part in 'the Fifteen' and 'the Forty Five' Jacobite rebellions. I have been told that Clan Farquhar was part of Bonnie Prince Charlie's body-guard at the Battle of Culloden and that when the Prince slipped off to the Isle of Skye with Flora Macdonald, the Clan stood firm and were slaughtered to a man—but that may be a myth. Obviously, there were bairns left at home and a branch of the family finished up in Ayrshire at Gilmilnscroft and thence to London where my father's Great Great Great Great Great Grandfather Walter, was made a Baronet in 1796 by the then Prince of Wales (the future George IV) whose apothecary he was.

My own father, Sir Peter Walter Farquhar was born in 1904 and lived mostly in London and at Shaw House, near Newbury, one of the most outstanding Elizabethan houses in the country—once Charles I's head-quarters for the Battle of Newbury—where Dad developed a love of the countryside, hounds, and horses.

It was while at Eton in 1918, at the age of 14 he was informed of the death of his father, a captain in the Royal Field Artillery, who was an ADC to Brigadier General Cator on the Western Front, killed in action a fortnight before the cessation of hostilities. The future Lord Margadale, who as John Granville Morrison was to later become Master of the South and West Wilts and Chairman of the British Field Sports' Society told me that he was standing with my father looking out of the window of their House, the one looking up Eton High Street when in the middle

13

of the afternoon a postman delivered a telegram out of normal hours. Apparently, they looked at one another and remarked, "Some poor bugger's father has copped it." About an hour later Dad was sent for by his Housemaster. Salutary stuff for a 14-year-old.

After Eton he went to the Royal Military College, Sandhurst where I believe he won the Saddle[1], joining the Scots Greys in India in 1926. Invalided out of India, he was put on half pay and went to Ireland to recuperate and whilst there hunted the Bray Harriers. He always joked that they hunted deer, hare or the fox, whichever they found first and it was surprising how often a pack of hounds would stick to the one they started with! It sounded a lot of fun, and that was where his love of hunting really took hold. He joined the 16th/5th Lancers at Tidworth and in 1927 applied for an interview with then Commanding Officer, Lt. Col. Geoffrey Brooke, later General Brooke who among other achievements founded with his wife Dorothy, the Brooke Hospital for Animals in Cairo, that to this day does so much for horses and donkeys that have fallen on hard times.

Anyway, the Adjutant asked why Dad wanted to see the Colonel, to which he replied, "A private matter." On being asked by the Colonel, "Well what do you want?" He replied, "Have I your permission to hunt the Tedworth hounds next season?"

"Thank God—for a horrible moment I thought you wanted to get married! Of course you can but you will have to do Orderly Officer on Sundays!" I just love the idea that it was perfectly acceptable for a subaltern to hunt a pack of hounds but not to get married!

A fellow officer at the time, Dick Fanshawe, also 16th/5th Lancers, was hunting mad as well, and as an amateur whipped in to the Tedworth before marrying my father's sister Ruth and taking on the mastership of the South Oxfordshire in 1937. Aunt Ruth herself hunted the South Oxfordshire during the War—more of that later—but after the War they both moved to the North Cotswold. Their younger son, Captain Brian Fanshawe, my cousin, was also to become a legend in the hunting field as a huntsman and hound breeder. Again more of that later.

The late 1920's and early 1930's are an interesting time for those who study the evolution of the modern English Foxhound. The type that had

---

1   A prize awarded to the most promising cadet of the year

The Duke of Northumberland, Sir Peter Farquhar, Ronnie Wallace, Sir Watkins Williams-Wynn and Lord Margadale—Peterborough Judges late 60's.

become fashionable at the turn of the previous century was heavy, over at the knee and at that time was dubbed the 'Shorthorn' due to its poor conformation. Two people really stand out for starting the turn around of the foxhound back to an animal of quality. The first being Sir Edward Curre who had been breeding his own hounds at Itton Court since 1896, the best of the lighter old type with an infusion of Welsh blood, and then Mr. Ikey Bell, an American who became one of his first disciples. Ikey Bell who had been dispatched to England to finish his education at Cambridge had become fascinated by the art of foxhunting and believe it or not hunted the Galway Blazers as a Cambridge undergraduate. Not much time for tutorials! Someone observed it that it must have needed quite tricky organization, "Oh no, a man on the train did my coat, and a man on the boat did my boots!" Soon, they had other disciples, the 10th Earl of Coventry, Major Bill Scott, my father, and the 10th Duke of Beaufort to name but a few. Dad always told the story that he went to Itton to see the hounds and to understand some of their Welsh ancestry when needless to say they all sat up fairly late. Next morning hounds

*Sir Peter Farquhar with 'Master'—
Judging at the Richmond Royal Horse
Show June 1952.*

were taken to a dingle, opening with a tremendous crash of music, "My word," says Dad, "What a cry!"

"You wait till they find", rejoined Sir Edward.

My father moved to the Meynell in 1931 where he met my mother, who was already married (her family the Hurts had their own pack of hounds back at Alderwasley Hall in Derbyshire). In 1934 he left the Meynell taking the Whaddon Chase, until with the threat of war looming, he rejoined the Army in 1938.

This is not a book about his personal exploits, suffice to say he was in France, was sunk on the Lancastria at Dunkirk, and more than lucky to survive, then sent to North Africa to command the 3rd Hussars, a DSO at El Alamein, then up through Italy, the Battle of Monte Cassino, and a second DSO before being sent back to England in 1944, wounded and rather disillusioned by all the killing. He sold his home, Shaw in 1944 and moved to Turnworth, in Dorset where I was born in 1945, brother Mike having arrived in 1938 and my middle brother Ant, three years later.

TURNWORTH AND OUR UPBRINGING

TURNWORTH WAS A magical place, quite a large house, Jacobean, beautifully set in its own valley with a large lawn dominated by a cedar tree, and extensive kitchen gardens behind with a farm further up the valley. The whole was surrounded by banks and woodland. I cannot remember much until the early 1950's by which time my father had got over a bout of post war depression and taken the Portman hounds, initially as Joint Master with Major Bill Scott (Uncle Bill). The story goes that he and Mum had been asked to stay at Badminton with 'Master', the 10th Duke of Beaufort who had offered Dad a horse to hunt the next day. He had replied that he never wished to go hunting again, and anyway he had not brought his kit. "Oh yes you have," said my mother, "I packed it all!" Grudgingly he acquiesced, and was duly sent on point to a corner of the Verge. Away went a fox, away went the hounds, away went Dad. He applied for the Portman that night!

We were taught to shoot by our keeper, Jack Churchill who was a charming man. We played on the farm all day, ran wild in the woods at night—no one seemed to bother—had ponies, went everywhere by bike, and rushed into the nursery every now and again to bolt down some food! The farm was fairly old fashioned with about twenty Guernseys that were still milked by hand. As children we helped with the relief milking on Sundays—if you got the hang of it was amazing how far you could send a squirt of milk straight from the teat—certainly a brother on the next-door stool was well within range! Harvesting was done by a binder which of course necessitated stooks, ricks, and a threshing machine. Hundreds of rats exploded when the ricks got low and there followed the intense excitement of sticks and terriers!

One of my early recollections is of watching the Coronation on our first television. A surprising number of house, farm, kennel and garden

Turnworth House. Painted by a German prisoner of war, Wolfgang Hartman, who was in a camp in Turnworth village. He became an acquaintance of Lady Farquhar's lady's maid and stayed in the UK after he was given a farming job by Sir Peter.

staff crammed into the Smoking Room to watch what looked like a snowstorm on the screen with the occasional glimpse of Her Majesty the Queen.

Martin Scott, Uncle Bill and Aunt Pam's son, eight months older than me, seemed to be a regular visitor. We were occasionally driven off to the kindergarten at Croft House in Dad's old Bentley driven by Spike the chauffeur, with Martin and myself in the back and two hound puppies sitting in the front. To this day I know one was called Lollipop! I would venture that Spike thought the latter two passengers rather less trouble than the former!

I inherited Brandy, my brother Ant's spaniel when he was sent to Ludgrove to board and we became inseparable. I recall going to stay with the Scotts. Aunt Pam was not as doggy as the rest of us, so Brandy was secreted into a suitcase with holes drilled into it, to ensure he wasn't left behind. Aunt Pam I recall was never very amused!

The entire family went to Scotland to Clebrig Lodge near Altnaharra, Sutherland for the month of August every year, with salmon fishing on the Naver, trout in the lochs, grouse over setters and the occasional stag

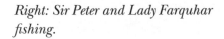

Above: Martin Scott and IWF,
Sandbanks, Dorset, 1949.

Right: Sir Peter and Lady Farquhar
fishing.

high up on Ben Klibreck if they ventured over during the night from
Loch Choire. The Lodge was on the edge of Loch Naver and had no electricity, our water coming straight from the burn, but it was still heaven.
Then it was down south at the end of the month for a fortnight's cub
hunting before going back to school. My first pony, a Shetland called
Judy, like most things was a hand-me-down from Ant. Typical of many
Shetlands she had a vile temperament and basically only did what she
wanted to do at the speed she thought fit. Her best trick, having spent
some time in Bertram Mills' Circus, was that if you stood in front of her
and raised your hand she would stand upright on her hind legs—great
fun if friends were staying! Her other foible was that if anyone got on
her even a pound heavier than she thought acceptable, she would buck
them straight off. We took her up the back stairs at Turnworth once so
she could join in the fun in the nursery. Nanny was not amused when
Judy did what every horse does when they are worried and for a small
pony it was a big one!! There was more to come, though if anyone is
thinking of taking their horse upstairs—let me put you straight—some
horses might climb stairs, but I have never known one that will walk
back down again! It took ropes, four strong men and the use of the
wider front stairs, otherwise Judy would have remained in the nursery.

Mum & IWF on Judy — 1950 Dorset Show.

Aged about nine, I graduated onto Claire, a skewbald also from Ant. Claire was bigger, faster and could jump, so proper hunting became the thing. I often loved to ride beside my father to see what he was doing with the hounds, but he had a job to do and seemed to make a habit of losing me. Perhaps it was character building.

Turnworth was always full of hunting people. Masters, huntsmen, hound breeders and the chat was often hounds. I have always been very proud of a photograph of the legendary Ikey Bell sitting in the Portman kennels with my mother and father and a small boy cross legged at the great man's feet. As a young boy I often accompanied my father and his friends to the kennels and can remember just how long seemingly intelligent and important individuals could spend looking at one or two hounds discussing at length every part of their anatomy. Yet it wasn't all hounds. We shot a lot, caught rabbits and moles, controlled anything that was considered vermin and generally spent all of our time out of doors. We had every type of pet, a tame squirrel, a jackdaw, a magpie, a hedgehog, a tortoise, masses of hamsters and a rabbit or two although maybe the most surprising was a fox cub called Vicky that my mother raised on a pipette. She had followed one of our

Sir Peter and IWF hunting with the Portman.

hunt terriers out of an earth when her eyes were not even open. The terrier, Sadie had had puppies not that long before. Vicky lived in the dog room for a year with all the other terriers (ten of them!) and by then she thought she was a dog herself. In the spring however she went missing until turning up one day on the front lawn with four cubs which she brought down to be fed every day. She had given birth under the summerhouse on the bank above the herbaceous border. My mother could still handle her, but not the cubs who steadily retreated further into the woods. She remained about all winter and had another litter next spring, but these were not nearly so tame. It did seem rather bizarre that on hunting days a whipper-in would be stationed on the lawn to safeguard Vicky, but sadly she did then get a snare around her leg, not on our farm I hasten to add. This obviously unsettled her, and she would not be caught. Then the inevitable happened and being lame she was caught by the hounds. Nature's way, but sad indeed was the loss. Country jungle drums being the way they are, it was not long before another orphan cub turned up for my mother to look after. Misty was older and so never became quite convinced she was a dog, although she did live in the house for a while.

My father was at this time very much part of the National Association of Boys' Clubs (for which later he received an OBE) and was caught up with fundraising and show business personalities who had been involved with the Boys' Clubs. Comedian Jimmy Edwards and singer Frankie Vaughan spring to mind. Frankie Vaughan was a great favourite of my mother's and not having had what you would call a rural upbringing, he was rather surprised one evening at dinner when brother Mike let out a yelp and a fox flew out from underneath the dinner table to land on the sideboard the other end of the room. Mike had taken his shoes off. He had a hole in one sock, and was wiggling his big toe which was too much for Misty who had pounced and bitten it! I have a small, sweet sketch of Misty by artist Peter Beigel but without the toe!

Turnworth had a number of cottages, three of which were occupied by families other than farm staff. Peter Beigel, lived in the Old Stable Cottage where he had his studio. He paid his rent in pictures, hounds, horses, ponies, dogs, hunting scenes and as boys we spent hours watching him paint—sadly none of his skill rubbed off on me! We had tame ducks on a pond, muscovies which were charming. One day when I was about eight or nine Peter was painting a duck, I asked him if I could buy it.

"How much can you afford?"

"Two bob," says I.

"I'll go and get it." I found half a crown and rushed back to Peter. "Will you frame it for the extra?" He did, such was the nature of the man. In another cottage was the highly decorated George Millar who had spent part of the Second World War in dangerous circumstances in Paris before being parachuted into Normandy to work for the Special Operations Executive with the Maquis, which he wrote about in a book of that name. He wrote other books, typing away in the warmth of the greenhouses in the walled garden. Jack Moore-Stevens lived in another farm cottage with his wife, she had been widowed, plus her three children, Alec, Colin, and Robyn, who we all played with, and who remained great friends.

Turnworth was sold in 1959, my father having given up the hounds that same year and we moved to a farmhouse close by; much smaller, very pretty and a great deal warmer, but not the same. Turnworth was pulled down shortly afterwards—a tragedy and the end of an era. We moved to West Kington in the Beaufort country in 1961 in time for the big snow.

*Above: Angela Meade "Tiddles" and IWF aka
Wally and Dot (middles names Walter and
Dorothy!)*
Right: IWF, first rabbit, Turnworth, Dorset.

To hark back, though now aged around seven and a half, like most small boys I thought that my education was going swimmingly. I was just beginning to get the hang of shooting not only with a .22 rifle but also with a single barrel 'poacher' 410 shotgun (you could break them in the middle and fold them up for quick concealment!) I was also beginning to get the hang of hunting, and although jumping did not come easily, following hounds did, but a real passion was taking out our own Turnworth 'pack' to hunt rabbits. We had about ten terriers, a lurcher, a spaniel and a labrador or two and our 'country' was the farm or a piece of common land close by, covered in bramble bushes and lifting with rabbits. Of course, they often went to ground, but quite a lot did not and sometimes our tally was quite respectable. I well remember my father passing us on his way home after hunting one morning. "How many did you catch Dad?" "Busy morning, three," was the answer. "Bad luck, we have caught twelve!" I am sure he was delighted but didn't seem to show it. It might have been the sight of his best labrador dog doing wheelies round a bramble bush that put him off. I repeat, I thought I was learning everything there was to be learnt or on anything that mattered anyway.

IWF, Mike Farquhar, Ant Farquhar—at home with the terriers.

Reading and writing fell into a very different category and although I sort of knew it was inevitable the shock of being sent off to boarding school on a permanent basis instead of the occasional visit to the junior school at Croft House Girls School was unsettling. Saying goodbye to Nanny and the dogs, especially my spaniel Brandy who I think missed me more than the parents, was always a tearful business. To exchange the freedom of the woods and farm for the disruption of the classroom and organised games came as quite a shock. Ludgrove, looking back was in fact a very good place if you had to be incarcerated, and I seem to remember that perhaps the other bonus was winning matches against neighbouring prep schools, rather than the promotion of academic skills. My middle brother Ant was still there for my first two years and was already showing himself to be a natural games player, seeming to excel at whatever he did. I did get into the 1st XV cricket and football, but more as a middle ranker whereas he was Captain of both. The odd thing was that I did become Troop Leader of the Ludgrove Scouts!

My eldest brother Mike had been christened 'Fishy Farquhar', whether that was because he was a very talented fisher from an early age,

Brothers Ian, Mike and Ant at home.

or whether it was the fact that it just sounded right, but nicknames stuck for all of us! Mike then became Fishy Major, Ant Fishy Minor, therefore I became Fishy Minimus! I later finished up with the moniker 'Good Scout Fish', which I wasn't too keen about. It's funny the things that make a lasting impression on a small boy.

There were prayers before supper in the Dining Room every night with a hymn—the first night of every term 'Abide With Me' was the doleful choice, not an ideal dirge for homesick little boys—'Abide With Me—sob sob—Fast Falls the Eventide—sob sob'. The last night of term saw a much more celebratory hymn—'Onward Christian Soldiers'— hurrah hurrah—Marching As to War—hurrah hurrah! Like most schools there was a doctrine of carrot and stick. If you did well in anything you were lauded, or badly, the stick! At supper on a regular basis 'Colours' were announced. "So and So Minor has been awarded Third Eleven Colours." Everyone cheered. "So and So Major has been awarded First Eleven Colours," and everyone cheered and cheered. Likewise, being appointed a Monitor or Captain of Fives or Squash, the cheers would ring out again, which of course made the recipient happy and proud and even more determined to do well. The other side of the coin of course was the stick. In those days it seemed to be fairly accepted that occasionally we were caned. I can't remember that it was particularly overdone. I can remember being beaten myself for flicking toothpaste in the communal bathroom, probably more for not ceasing when told to, rather than the act itself. Another lesson in life; know when to stop! On the subject of punishment—caning, this was the prerogative of the Headmaster, although one master always smacked you himself over his knee whether you were guilty or not. "Sir Sir it's not fair!" Smack. "Life is unfair my boy and the sooner you learn it the better!" Smack. I often think it one of the best lessons I ever had!

Ludgrove at the time was very much a games orientated school and as long as you could play cricket and kick a football you were fine and it seemed one's future was assured. It was actually a very happy school and you were only occasionally beaten. Quite a funny story on that account, was that a friend of mine who was rather prone to misbehaving was given six of the best twice in one week which did not improve the symmetry of his backside. In fact it was quite a mess and he used to let other boys have a look at it for half a Mars bar, that being the currency at the time. Some years later having joined the Brigade of Guards he had become a General and was GOC (General Officer Commanding) London District. He was standing next to the Queen on Horse Guards, when I started to laugh and the assembled company enquired what I was laughing about and were rather shocked when I blurted out that the very important Officer in the plumed hat used to sell a peep at his bottom for half a Mars bar!

Ludgrove was a very extensive school. As well as numerous games pitches, it had two fives courts, a squash court and a small golf course, as well as a mass of tiny gardens that boys were encouraged to take on. I grew a conker tree in mine, but doubt it lasted long! There were lots of plays and concerts and on the whole we were kept occupied and happy. Quite a large percentage of inmates were bound for Eton which meant taking the Entrance Exam after which you were graded as to which level you went on to, that is if you passed at all. It did come as a slight surprise to my parents when they were told it was not a foregone conclusion that their youngest son would sail through Common Entrance as his brothers had. Luckily my mother had the answer and I was put on 'the Box'. For the uninitiated the Box was an electrical apparatus run by a believer who fed in a few spots of your blood and in return the gadget would inform the operator what was wrong with the 'patient' and then send out waves to put them right. My mother put everybody and everything on the Box—family, friends, dogs, horses, hens, ducks, fox cubs, in fact any animals she came across. Also apparently given the right instructions it could make you run faster and also pass exams! So on to the Box I went, and all I can say is that I did pass the Common Entrance and did scrape into Eton Lower Fourth which was at the bottom, but at least I got there!

Eton

Much has been written about Eton in every book and article imaginable, much of it is true and it was an extraordinary and diverse school, although of course it was not a school, but a college and run on college lines. It was big, around one thousand boys who all lived in separate Houses, each overseen by a Housemaster who was in charge of education and a Dame who looked after the housekeeping. The boys there were then taught outside of their House, making their own way to Divs (divisions or lessons) which could be anywhere in the town of Eton. The facilities were second to none, any language, any degree of mathematics, plus all sciences and modern studies. These were backed up by amazing playing fields—a very professional rowing set-up on the Thames, every ball game imaginable, a School of Mechanics, thriving Arts Centre, the Corps, a pack of beagles,the gym, and the opportunity to work with local charities, its own pub 'Tap', plus a flourishing School of Dramatics. In fact you could follow just about any notion that took your fancy. Returning to the House system however, when you were put down to go there, often practically as a baby, a House could be chosen, which then normally accepted you so long as nothing changed. In my case I was down for the same House as my brothers had been in. Unfortunately the housemaster in question retired the year before I went there and his successor already had a full house, so I went on to what was known as the General List and was allocated a different House run by a master who quite frankly was not famous for running a particularly successful Tutors. He was a Beak who taught French. 'Beak' being Eton slang for a Master. He was a funny mixture for Eton, being a Quaker, a pacifist and slightly Left Wing. When he was standing on the touchline watching his boys play a match, he used to cheer for both sides so as not to be construed to be biased. I cannot say we got on particularly well. Another Eton tradition was that as generally food was not of the highest order, a group of boys of the same age would combine to cook themselves tea. There were stoves on each landing. This was called 'Messing'. I often point out how diverse Eton actually was. At one point my messing companions were James Cecil, a future Conservative Leader of the House of Lords, Johnny Grimond whose father was Leader of the Liberals, William Shawcross, son of the famous Labour QC, and Teddy Faure-Walker son of a big Hertfordshire farmer. As you can imagine we had some quite heated discussions over our burnt toast and baked beans. Mostly the fare was frugal, but occasionally one of us would come back with a pheasant or suchlike which the local Tuck shop would cook for you, plus vegetables, which made a welcome change. During the winter of the Big Freeze, 1962/63, I shot a goose in Gloucestershire in early January, took it and hung it outside my window where it remained frozen. We ate it in late March—delicious. That spring half there were no games, the pitches were all frozen. We spent two months skating on Virginia Water, a nearby lake. Going back to the beginning again, having been allocated a House it was always a relief to find that as an individual you were just tall enough to go straight into tails, whereas our shorter brethren had to put up with the ignominy of wearing 'bum freezers'—a short jacket that only went down to the waist with a large white collar around the neck. They looked as if they had come straight out of the nursery, which of course to some degree they had!

The next move on arrival was to be allocated one's first lessons. Anyone who like me just scraped into Lower Fourth will well remember the terror of being taught by Deadly Headley who as the Beak seemed to take great delight in making the lives of slightly less academic young hopefuls who found Latin incomprehensible, a misery. One of the systems in use then was that if you failed an organised written test you could be given a 'Rip' i.e. the top of your failed paper would be partially torn/ripped which you then had to take to your housemaster to be signed, with the attendant shame, before handing it back to Deadly Headley. I can still see the malicious look in his eyes, "Failed again Farquhar!" Rip Rip! Thank God I did get what was termed a 'double bunk' at the end of my first half, which promoted you up to 'removes' and away from Deadly's clutches! In the meantime life carried on—I found games relatively easy, and thankfully I saw my middle brother Anthony every now and again. He was I might add now really top of every tree—Keeper (captain) of Association Football, either in the Cricket Eleven or the Twenty-Two (the second eleven), winning the Fives and then elected to Pop, the prestigious Eton society. I did get my House Colours for the Field Game which I loved. It was a wonderful mix of soccer and rugby. You did not carry the ball, but still had a scrum, scored by kicking the ball over the back line while making physical contact with a member of the opposing team's body, not arms, and then touching it down. The goal was tiny and a Try was converted by a 'ram' of the three heaviest members of the scrum linking arms one behind the other and charging the opposition who had the ball at their feet and tried to score a goal, thuggery of the first order! I also did take up boxing which surprisingly enough I enjoyed. Reg the coach was an ex-professional needless to say, and was full of encouragement although I remember him telling me one day, "You're fast but you lack punch, hit me as hard as you can." So with all my fifteen year old skinny strength I hit him on the solar plexus as hard as I could, he did not even flinch. "See what I mean, you need to strengthen up." Easier said than done! I did box for the school a few times, but normally got knocked out when I was ahead on points. One such occasion was a match against Bloxham and years later when I was Master of the Bicester, I went for a haircut in Bicester and the owner who was working that day said, "We know each other. You are the new Master of Hounds?" I replied, "Yes and you are the bastard who knocked me out at Bloxham all those years ago!" Small world! Eton actually had a top class team then—Fiennes, Andre, Meinertzhagen, Sadler and Watson, most went on to Oxford and got Blues.

Academically I did little more than survive although I did really quite well at mathematics and sciences. I never did get Latin, but I managed to get enough O-levels to make me eligible for Sandhurst which my father, with my blessing I might add, had come to the conclusion was probably the way ahead. So it was off to the Regular Commission Board at Westbury for three days where one was faced with the most bizarre problems. How do you get your group across a chasm with only a few planks and a bit of rope none of which were long enough? The answer of course which we did not know at the time, was that there was no answer, but you were judged on your ability to make a plan and then persuade your fellows to give it a try. Another test was to give a lecture—I had been tipped off that the senior adjudicating officer was a very keen fisherman, so I gave a demonstration as to how to tie a salmon fly from scratch—anyway I passed. I have to admit my latter days at Eton were not covered in glory, but having passed the Army Exam and the RCB it was just a question of seeing your time out, which was made more convivial by falling in with an Irish crowd. We spent most of our time in Tap drinking Black and Tans (half bitter and half stout) and laughing and talking about sport. One rather memorable interlude does come to light however. We were discussing stalking in particular one afternoon, and the possibility of a MacNab when Alistair Janson joined us whose mother owned Uppat House plus Dunrobin Castle and the Sutherland Estate. We bet him that we could poach a stag off his own home ground between midnight on a Sunday in August and midnight on the Monday. George Lopes, Charlie Birkett and myself left a party on the Helmesdale to arrive at first light to walk straight on to the highest point on Uppat to start to spy. Fog, thick fog until around 9am, when a small party of stags appeared just round the corner. The chance of a long shot soon saw us burying the stag in the heather when a keeper appeared and we thought the game was up. But lo and behold he was heading slightly to our left, so we just waved, and he walked on. It transpired that he was the beat keeper furthest away from the house, whose telephone was down and when Janson had tried to warn him to be on the look out, he had not got the message. We left the stag well hidden and walked off the hill to find that Lopes had left the keys to his truck in my car the other side of the hill entailing another twelve mile hike back! Keys sorted, we loaded the stag into the truck, having dragged it away in the rain just before dark, and drove to Uppat House. We propped the head against the door, rang the bell and scarpered. As we fled, we heard the Scottish maid let out a squeal as the stag's head landed at her feet on the mat! Anyway, we had not been caught and Jansen settled the bet! It always annoys me now when I read about a MacNab Dinner or a MacNab pre-sentation or similar in the sporting press. I was always brought up that a stag, a salmon, and a brace of grouse on the same day was known as a Royal Bag, nothing wrong with that. We, my brothers and I, all achieved it at Klibreck mainly because it was possible there. But a MacNab is only a MacNab if it is poached and the landowner warned, a fact that now seems to be forgotten at all the London celebrations. Such I suppose is life.

But now to return to the progress of IWF...

ARMY DAYS

Sandhurst

I LEFT ETON ON about the 21st of December, 1963, spent Christmas at home, a few days hunting and a few days shooting, had a haircut and reported to Sandhurst on 7th January 1964. No 'Gap Year' in those days!

I was just three weeks past my 18th birthday and to be honest had no idea what to expect. I had rather old-fashioned ideas as to how Sandhurst worked mostly stemming from my father's generation: "The rough riders were very demanding and I was lucky to win the Saddle!" Whereas from a more recent generation: "Your first term will be purgatory, they try to break you to see if you are up to it." The latter was nearer the truth! "Keep your head down and don't try to buck the system," was the best advice one recent incumbent gave me, and so after I was given my third haircut in two days (I had tried to slip the barber a few bob not to be too drastic, rather childish but it had not worked ...) I kept my mouth shut and smiled! The next indication of what to expect was when Company Sergeant Major 'Dad' Pope, Grenadier Guards, lined up the new intake of Rhine Company to which I had been drafted. "I call you all 'Sir' and you call me 'Sir'. You will discover you mean it and I don't!"

Sandhurst was split into three colleges, which one you finished up in I expect was entirely random. Old College was rather grand and spacious with imposing steps and colonnades marking the impressive entrance. If the Sovereign's Parade ever appears on television there is always a shot of the Adjutant riding his horse up the steps to disappear into the interior of Old College. Mostly the individual rooms assigned to the officer cadets are large and airy and thoroughly smart. Next there was New College, built a little later, but also with good accommodation and a spacious Mess Hall and a comfortable ante room. Finally there was Victory College planned in a hurry in wartime to accommodate an influx of officer cadets, which consisted of a number of very basic Nissen huts situated at the back of New College. Rhine Company was very much in the Nissen huts with tiny little individual rooms and not much else. It did not matter much of course because you were only in your room when you were cleaning it or sleeping. Sleeping was certainly not a problem! However it wasn't too bad and there was always plenty of hot water. Victory College used the Mess Hall of New College and food was always plentiful, if you ever had time to eat it. Each Company was split into intakes, senior, intermediate, and juniors. The senior intake were mostly given a rank, Under Officer Cadet, Sergeant Cadet and Corporal, who were given the responsibility of helping to run the discipline within the Company.

The make up of the intake that I joined of Rhine Company, about 30 souls, was slightly different than I had been used to, but nothing wrong with that. In fact it was enormously refreshing—four public schoolboys, four from overseas—Nigeria, Ghana, Saudi Arabia, Ceylon and the rest Grammar and Comprehensive schools plus a couple from a military crammer. The day was pretty exhausting for the Junior Term—a 6am run with a full back pack, 7 o'clock breakfast, 8am lectures and drill till about 12.30pm, lunch if allowed off parade ground, an afternoon of military history, weapon training and more drill. Long days followed more or less along those lines. Evening was kit cleaning or "Bull." If you were lucky around 9p.m. and your kit passed inspection you were allowed to think of going to bed! That inspection was carried out by the Under Officers (cadets from the senior intake) who were normally more fierce than the permanent staff.

As a member of the Junior Intake you were not allowed off the grounds and alcohol was banned. It was therefore a breath of fresh air when having done rather well in a Company Cross Country Race, I had been asked to run for the Academy. This meant an evening out and an hour or two in the pub with the team, although one paid for it by being behind hand with the interminable kit inspections. It was not long of course before we were taken out on Barossa training ground behind the Academy on exercise and it surprised me how hopeless most of the intake were at finding their way about at night. If you turned most of them round once, they didn't even know which direction they had started from. Simple factors like moon or contours was not something they had ever come across. Playing in the dark in the Turnworth woods certainly paid dividends, as indeed being brought up with a gun and a rifle from an early age perhaps put one at an advantage when it came to the Ranges. Talking of exercises, one of the things I shall never forget is how totally miserable some of them were. Spending two nights in a slit trench in six inches of snow and freezing temperatures was merely a forerunner to the larger exercises on the Brecon Beacons later. Fine in the summer, but in midwinter they were not much fun. I well remember exercises after which I made a beeline for the hot bath before attending to my rifle and I was soon on a charge for a rusty bayonet and marched in front of the then Senior Under Officer Malcolm Ross. As it happened we had been at school together, but he was obviously slightly senior to me. He gave me two extra drills, but did wink at me before I was marched out! Years later, his wife Susie, who co-incidentally had been at school with Pammie, by then my wife, hunted with us at the Beaufort. After the first term life certainly looked up. For a start you could take back a car, which meant that you were not tied to the Academy and a modicum of social life materialised. In those early days however, drill still seemed to dominate and this is when the Guards Sergeant Majors held the whip hand. They were brilliant. On the Parade Ground they ran the show. They didn't settle for second best and were incredibly funny at the same time. Some of their jibes were predictably sexist: "You carries your rifle as you would your girlfriend." Since we had not been allowed out of barracks for three months, we had forgotten we even had a girlfriend or if we had, the girlfriend had definitely forgotten us! Rhine Company's RSM 'Dad' Pope was as good as any of them. Our 'right marker' tall and rather gangly kept marching one day after the command to halt. "Send us a postcard Mr Snowden when you are thinking of coming back." Undoubtedly, the best one I ever heard was when I had done something stupid and he shouted across the Parade Ground, "Mr Fariharkurhaaar Sir," they could never pronounce my name, "If your brains were made of fuse wire they would not fit around a canary's cock!" I had heard some good ones, but thought that took the biscuit!

As one progressed up the ladder at Sandhurst life definitely got better. Exercises were still pretty tough and uncomfortable, and drills still dominated, but that could be very rewarding. In my second year I was asked to be a whipper-in to the Draghounds. The then Captain Piers Bengough (later Lt-Col. Sir Piers Bengough, Her Majesty's Representative at Ascot) was Master and Huntsman and Martin Scott was first whipper-in. We had about eight and a half couple of bobbery hounds that were kenneled with the Staff College Beagles and hunted Wednesday afternoons and most Saturdays on arranged lines, mostly not too far from Sandhurst. It was actually enormous fun. My father let me have a horse of his, Tremoor, a real class Irish quality hunter who lived in the Commandant's stables. It did not do one's street cred any harm in that two of the stalwart supporters of the Draghounds were the Commandant, General John Mogg (later Sir John) and Colonel Bill Lithgow, College Commander. Piers Bengough, Martin Scott and myself spent hours exercising the hounds on Barossa, the training area behind Sandhurst which we all felt was more rewarding than other military tutorials. It was also great fun to run to be back hobnobbing with my childhood Dorset mate, Martin Scott. It was not long before we found ourselves going off to parties in London together, although being older than me the girls always seemed to take him more seriously! Funny things always seemed to be cropping up and I always remember one hound exercise when Bengough was riding a racehorse he had just bought—I think it was called April Rose—which he wanted to ride in the Grand Military and it kept rearing up. He turned his whip round and clocked it on the head to teach it a lesson. Obviously he caught it wrong and it went down pole-axed, and we had the unhappy situation of a stretched out horse being sniffed by eight and a half couple of hounds who were not sure what was going on, plus a distraught cavalry officer muttering, "Do get up! I'm sure you're all right?" Anyhow she did, and later both went on to acquit themselves with flying colours.

It was also about this time that I learnt I was going to be made a Senior Under Officer. It did actually make quite a big difference. To start with you had lots of braid on the lower arm of your khaki uniform, wore a Sam Brown belt and carried a sword on parade. You even held your own 'Orders' to deal with minor miscreants within the company. Shades of Malcolm Ross and the rusty bayonet! The epitome of success for every company was to become the Sovereign's Company which Rhine had done twice, once under Malcolm and again under Alistair

Stewart—more of him later. It was while we were in Libya on exercise, hunched up in a sangar (an above ground slit trench built from rocks) that the message came through that the Juniors had won the drill and therefore we had once again won the Sovereigns Company. The Sovereign's flag was accepted at my Passing Out Parade and as an SUO I had to give a few words of command. At twenty it was quite something to shout, "Sandhurst 'Shun!" (Attention!) and see a thousand cadets react in unison. My parents were there and it was a very proud moment. One of the most important decisions that any Sandhurst cadet has to make is which regiment or corps he is going to join. Some will already have a family allegiance to a particular regiment and will already be spoken for; others will make up their mind while training as a cadet. In my case I had the choice of four cavalry regiments that my father had served in at different times—the Scots Greys, the 16th/5th Lancers, the 9th/12th Lancers and the 3rd Hussars. My father advised me that the Greys were too rich! So we settled on the 9th/12th Lancers and indeed I'd already started to have uniforms made for the 9th/12th when I bumped into an old school chum Johnny Bulkeley who persuaded me to rethink. The 9th/12th were in tanks and scheduled for a long sojourn in Germany and were a skiing regiment whereas the Queen's Own Hussars were in armoured cars and looking forward to postings at Catterick, the Middle East, the Far East and were also a top polo regiment. Therefore, halfway through Sandhurst I changed. Quite an amusing anecdote. Prior to being accepted for a regiment it was customary to be interviewed. In this case I was asked to meet Colonel Sir Douglas Scott—where better than in Whites Club in St James's. He was a friend of my father and we had a drink or two before an excellent lunch—hunting, shooting, rivers in Scotland, horses, acquaintances ...

"Have a glass of port old boy!"

"Thank you Colonel."

"How's your father? I well remember ... Have another glass of port old boy?"

"Thank you Colonel."

"I must be off, things to do you know. Really enjoyed talking to you. Do tell me why you're here?"

"You're interviewing me for the Regiment, Colonel."

"Am I? OK, that will be fine. Give your father my best. Goodbye!"

So with Sandhurst behind me, and a place in the Queen's Own Hussars, it was off to Catterick to join the Regiment.

A Subaltern's Life

Most newly commissioned Subalterns would agree that the prospect of joining a group of individuals who had known each other for some time, worked and played together was a fairly daunting prospect—in that respect I was very lucky. I arrived on a Friday and was straight away asked if I had a dinner jacket with me as the Adjutant Michael Sherwin was getting married the next day. All were invited to a party after the wedding in the cellars of Sheriff Hutton Hall, the home of the bride, Sarah Legard. By the end of an hilarious night I had got to know most of the officers and was quickly made to feel welcome. It was more than a memorable evening for me however, as I met the most beautiful seventeen year old I had ever clapped my eyes on and we danced most of the night. Others kept trying to muscle in, but luckily, I was able to play the hunting card as it transpired her father was Master and Huntsman of a local pack of hounds, the Derwent and knew my family. That seemed to work in my favour. Her name was Pamela-Jane Chafer and some seven years later when we had all grown up a bit she was to become my wife.

As was the order of things after a short spell at Catterick it was off to Bovington to attend the Young Officers' Course for three months to learn how to survive in an Armoured Regiment. A month of Driving and Maintenance (D and M), when the rudiments of the workings of the combustion engine were explained, then a month on Gunnery, both in a classroom and then live firing on the ranges. Finally a month of Signals to enable armoured vehicles to keep in contact with each other. I loved Gunnery, found D and M rewarding, but found the intricacies of signals rather boring and did not do well. It was normal army practice therefore, a couple of years later that I should be made Regimental Signals Officer!

Bovington was an enormous amount of fun. It couldn't not be— Dorset is the most delightful county and a group of young men in their early twenties, newly commissioned from every cavalry regiment in the British Army were bound to go for it. You made a lot of new friends, and on my part an Irish Hussar by the name of Richard Clifford became a close buddy. We were subsequently to join forces on the polo field on many occasions. Although there was plenty to do in Dorset, London still beckoned and off we sometimes went. I can remember we were returning one night in the very early hours and as usual completely knackered through lack of sleep, we arrived in Salisbury at some traffic lights. Red Stop—Sleep—Amber—Green. Green—Amber—Red ... Still there half an hour later, another group returning from the Smoke woke us up and we all got back just in time for First Parade!

Following three months at Bovington and now in theory well prepared to become a troop leader in tanks or armoured cars, and in any theatre of war, it was off to join my regiment who had a very different job indeed. We were the 'training regiment' for the Royal Armoured Corps, which in essence meant taking on a bunch of raw recruits, putting them through their basic training and hopefully teaching them some aspects of what would be required when they passed out. It was a different role, but did have its satisfactory side. As a young officer you were put in charge of a Sergeant, or more correctly he was put in charge of you, a number of Corporals and Lance Corporals and quite a few Troopers—equivalent to a private in the infantry.

Once every three months some 60 or so recruits would arrive at Darlington Station to commence their lives as soldiers. Looking back they were an interesting bunch, bearing in mind this was still the mid 1960's, from every background and all corners of the Kingdom. Scots, Geordies, Northerners, Brummies, Londoners, Home Counties, Midlands, Welsh, Irish, West Country, and overseas. In theory they had all taken the Queen's Shilling to serve their country. The reasons were as diverse as their backgrounds. "Father was a soldier in the War," or, "Home life a mess, I wanted out before I got into too much trouble with the wrong gang." They had to pass a fairly rudimentary exam and show a certain level of fitness, but the initial discipline did come as a bit of a shock. The basic training in the early stages was left almost entirely to the NCOs and the job of the Officers was to oversee and deal with the endless personal problems, finance, family fights, pregnant girlfriends, lack of fitness, injuries, homesickness—and so on it all went. Out of the 60 you started with, about 40 actually passed out. Towards the end of the three months the role of the officers became more hands on, and we accompanied them on exercises on the local training area and got involved with weapon practice and more soldierly pursuits. It always amused me that most of them had never come across a thing called an officer before. They were frightened of and held in awe the sergeant, listened to and admired the corporals and could equate themselves to some degree with lance corporals and troopers, but could not work out the officers at all. Officers lived in a different environment spent a lot of time riding a horse—wore a slightly different uniform and were often accompanied by a dog—but on exercise hopefully seemed to know what was going on! When eventually the new intake Passed Out and then got drunk at the party afterwards, which their families and girlfriends often attended, their final shot was often the same, "One day Sarge I'm going to be like you." Then to us, "You're the best fooking officer I have ever met." Even though in most cases you were the only fooking officer they had ever met!

Off duty however, life at Catterick was very different, if you were a sportsman Yorkshire was paradise for a young man. The trout fishing in particular was of a high order, as was the shooting, both grouse and pheasant if you were lucky enough to be invited. I gravitated more to the horse and realised the wisdom of changing regiments when at the start of my first summer I was allocated two ponies, Lager and Shandy who had been purchased by the Regiment's Polo Fund. What a start that was! Both were experienced and sound. Shandy very easy and almost laid back, whereas Lager was fast and a bit of a handful, but totally brave in a ride off. Shandy was snaffle mouthed, Lager needed a gag and running reins but out on his own was un-catchable. Shandy turned on her hocks instantly, whilst Lager propped on her forehand, swinging her backside round before off she went again. I adored them both. They were to remain with me throughout my military life, before later leaving the Army and coming to the Bicester.

Horses could be kept in the regimental stables for £5 per month per horse. Sounds amazing, but a Subaltern's pay was £32 per month and there were other things to pay for! We played regularly on the aerodrome at Catterick and at Toulston and occasionally down south if you were lucky enough to be picked for an away match. The pinnacle for me at the time, was being selected for the Army Inter-Regimental team in 1967, the Blue Riband. The team comprised Charles Lockhart, Malcolm Sherwin, Ian McConnell and myself. Amazingly we won which resulted in the team being invited to go to Persia to play in a tournament against the Persian Army, bearing in mind that this was still in the days of the

29 Regimental Polo Team playing in Persia: left to right - Charles Lockhart, Malcolm Sherwin, Ian McConnell, IWF 1970

Shah. With the backup of Hugh Lovett, we joined a British Army 'exercise' for a month. We were based in Tehran not to play soldiers, but to play polo and prepare local ponies for their high profile matches. We were allocated a house, a driver, a car and sixteen very green and inexperienced ponies. We were very well looked after, including a trip to the Caspian Sea (mounds of caviar) and then stayed in Isfahan in a hotel just opposite the Great Mosque. We were able to inspect the gardens in the grounds and the four ancient stone pillars still standing, where we were told early Persians used to strike the beheaded skulls of their enemies up and down with wooden mallets, the origins of the game of polo before it spread to India. The area adjacent to the four pillars was the exact size of a modern day polo pitch.

The first game we played on our new ponies we were trounced, but then set about schooling them every day for a considerable amount of time. The second big match we played, as it happened in front of the Shah's brother, we drew. So full of confidence we arrived to play the last big match in front of an extremely large crowd and were somewhat horrified to find waiting for us a completely new set of ponies.

Schooling 'Watermark' with Brother Ant, early 60's.

"Where are the ponies?" We asked.

"They're all lame," was the reply.

"They were all right yesterday?"

"All lame!" Was the repeat. Needless to say once again we were completely trounced! However it had been a most memorable trip and we had met some very charming and pro-British high-ranking officials—we heard afterwards, following the coup against the Shah, and the arrival of the Ayatollahs that many of them were never seen again.

In the winter we hunted with the Bedale and occasionally with the Zetland. I was lucky enough that my father came up trumps having promised me a horse following Sandhurst. He purchased a five year old mare from Captain Evan Williams from the Tipperary in Ireland that had won a Bumper (a flat race run on a jumping course). She was well bred, called Watermark and I took her out at the Bedale Opening Meet, to be qualified. We jumped six rails, broke four, fell at three, when Major John Howie, the then master told me he would give me a point-to-point certificate there and then if I never brought her out again! She had cost my father £150. You wouldn't get much for that now! I spent

IWF on David Beaufort's horse 'Cuddle Up' — Berkeley Point to Point.
Won the (adjacent's) members race.

most of Christmas confined to barracks doing Orderly Officer (another story) so Watermark went back home to be brought on by Dad's groom. Our first excursion on to the racetrack was in a Novice United Services' Race at Tweseldown, her first point-to-point and mine. As I left Salisbury Plain (we were on exercise) Ian McConnell, already a great friend gave me a fiver to put on myself. I could take a bird out to dinner, and dance all night at the smartest nightclub for a fiver in those days and still have some to spare, so I never put the bet on. Coming into the last it suddenly dawned on me I could win. Prize money £30, odds 14/1, meant £70 to McConnell, loss £40 pounds, month's pay £32—not good. I remember thinking we might never win again though, so we did. She did run well again and went to the sales as we were going abroad and she fetched 1000 Guineas, so perhaps it all turned out for the better in the end.

Ian became a very close friend, and part by chance and part by organisation, we often arrived, sometimes just the two of us, in different countries—holidays—polo—duty, and it never seemed to be long before a party was in progress. Each time, Ian would soon be holding the floor, jabbering away in the local lingo to much laughter. It was only later that I discovered that he always learnt one sentence in whatever language was needed: "Take off all your clothes, my friend will pay."

Undoubtedly my best fun point-to-pointing was on a mare called Cuddle Up that belonged to David Somerset (later the 11th Duke of Beaufort). It was during the foot and mouth outbreak in 1967 when all hunting had been cancelled and the then Duke, 'Master', used to ask quite a number of locals to meet at Badminton House on a Saturday morning where he would wander about followed by his butler Leslie with a basket and a bottle or two of whisky, and the favoured few would be offered a quick tipple. At 11 o'clock the heavier hunters would be dispatched to gallop across the Park, up the Avenue to finish at Worcester Lodge, distance three miles. They were followed by the faster hunters and when they were halfway across the Park, the clean bred horses and the point-to-pointers would also be let go. Master and his entourage would then drive round to Worcester Lodge and welcome the winners. David Somerset himself used to ride a horse called Clandestine, who had raced under rules and he often asked me to take part on Clandestine's dam, Cuddle Up, who proved to be somewhat faster than expected, so we were soon upgraded to the late starters and seemed to be able to hold our own with the fast team. My father persuaded DS, as he was known in those days, to run Cuddle Up in a few point-to-points. I think I rode her eight or nine times, was brought down once at Larkhill, but other than that was never out of the frame, and at last winning at Berkeley. She was trained at Badminton by David's Polish groom, another Leslie, and when we won at Berkeley, David turned and said, "Didn't he ride that well?" The groom replied, "If the boy was any bloody good he would have won every other time!"

We had the most amazing selection of kindred spirits at Catterick, too many to go into, one of the most dangerous being Mark Price, or 'Pricey' as he was called, who led us astray on numerous occasions. I well remember him looking rather forlorn one morning at breakfast when in reply to my, "What's up with you Pricey?" Came the reply, "These are probably the happiest days of my life and I can't remember any of them!"

A lot of very funny things happened—Her Majesty Queen Elizabeth, the Queen Mother, was due to inspect the Regiment and so a full dress rehearsal parade was held the day before. I had a border terrier in those days, Mr Todhunter or Tod for short, who I had left shut in my room. Another officer running even later than me and looking for spare kit had opened my door. I recall standing there on parade when out of the corner of my eye I saw Tod sniffing about on the edge of the parade ground. All I could think was 'Please please don't!' Too late, he trotted nonchalantly across in front of everybody, passed the Commanding Officer and cocked his leg on the drum horse before trotting off again. That cost me another week's Orderly Officer! That night after a rather raucous evening in the Mess, a mattress or two went out of the window onto the flower beds below. Next morning a posse of subalterns were to be found with matchsticks and sellotape splicing flowers back onto their stems prior to the imminent arrival of Her Majesty.

The Desert, Aden and Malaya

Anyway, we all survived Catterick, more or less, before receiving orders of our next postings. Now reverting to a fully fledged armoured car regiment, we learnt that the three squadrons were to be split, one to Aden, one to Cyprus and one to Sharjah in the Persian Gulf. Most of

Fire Power Demo in Muscat, Persian Gulf, 1968.

us would have favoured Aden as the most exciting. Active service and all that. That role fell to A Squadron, C Squadron to Cyprus, potentially a lot of fun, and dear old B Squadron faced the delights of the desert, attached to the Trucial Oman Scouts. This sounded very romantic but was in fact was pretty boring in Camp except for quite lengthy exercises when the whole squadron would spend a month on a show of force round the desert forts. These included the town of Muscat and the periphery of what was known as the Empty Quarter. It was actually a fascinating area. It was before that part of the world hit oil and was still entirely primitive. The fifteen months we were there, we never drove on a tarmac road and never talked to a female or even saw one come to that. In the desert we sweated, you could fry an egg on the back decking of an armoured car by just breaking it, and in Camp we swam and ate a lot of camel and got very good at playing darts! Thank goodness in the middle, two troops of B Squadron were sent down to relieve two troops of A Squadron in Aden which was a very welcome change of venue. Some people got very excited about being on active service but compared with more recent situations it really was not very dangerous. Dear old Pricey

45

as always came up with a winner: "Fast cars and bad horses will kill more of us than the Arabs ever will!" To start with I was attached to the Paras in Aden town and then spent a time with the Argyll and Sutherland Highlanders in Crater, producing armoured back-up for Lt. Col. Colin 'Mad Mitch' Mitchell their Commanding Officer. The soldiers were as lethal as they were cracked up to be—the Arabs in Crater were terrified of them and Mad Mitch lived up to his name. It was an interesting few weeks. Brigadier, later Major General Philip Tower insisted on playing polo in Aden right up to the end and a few of us galloped up and down, guarded by Paras and Marines who were not sure that was what they wanted to be doing! My troop was the last out of Aden, taken off by HMS Fearless and I well remember thinking that sneaking out 'guns reversed' was not what my father would have been proud of. It's a small world and years later an earth stopper in the Bicester country told me we had met before—"I was the loading Sergeant on Fearless and I never forget a foxhunting name!" It was then back to Sharjah where the numbers of troops had escalated. It amused me that the new officers turned their noses up at eating camel, so being messing officer I changed the name to 'beef' curry and they wolfed it down.

After the Middle East we had a six month wait before being sent to the Far East and not knowing what to do with us, the regiment found themselves quartered at Maresfield in Sussex. Handy for London and with the ponies and grooms based at Tidworth with the Queen's Royal Irish Hussars, it was actually a very good summer indeed. Cornets (Irish Hussar subalterns) Richard Clifford and Arthur Denaro in particular became good friends.

My next posting to the Jungle Warfare School at Kota Tinggi in Malaya for two months therefore came as a bit of a shock. It apparently was the rule for the future Assistant Adjutant in Regimental Headquarters to also be Jungle Warfare Officer, but then I turned up three days late in desert kit-faded khaki shirt, light weight corduroys, desert boots and red side hat, "Sorry Colonel, the Regiment kept me in England for the finals of the Inter-Regimental Polo." This of course did not go down well to a veteran of Korea, immaculate in jungle green. "This is not a holiday camp, it's blood sweat and tears. Go and get out of your fancy dress and I'll be watching you." Watch me he did! The 30 or so officers and senior NCOs on the course were mostly Paras and Marines, Australian Special Forces, hopeful SAS recruits and Borneo veterans. The chat in the Mess over a cooling lemonade was how to cut the throat of a terrorist without making a noise, or the relevant stopping power of a different handgun. Not subjects I was well briefed in! Luckily there was the odd trip to Singapore to stay with Sir John Fuller, a Life Guard and subsequently a Master of the Avon Vale, and his charming wife Lorna. Their conversation was more along the lines one was used to; hunting, fishing, shooting, horses, girls, friends. Oh dear, were we that typecast?

The jungle was not pleasant: it was very hot and humid. The sun stayed firmly above the canopy of trees and I'm not sure which were the worst, the mosquitoes or the leeches. Leeches had a habit of getting into places that were normally out of bounds and burning them off with a cigarette round the rear end needed a buddy with a steady hand who could also be trusted. Mind you, since you both did it for each other there was an incentive to play fair! I was put in charge of a group for the final exercise and the Colonel Commandant, true to his word came to observe my lot and when we really pushed it, he did have the decency to say that perhaps the Cavalry were not quite so soft after all.

Regimental life in Singapore was good. Once again we were split into Squadrons—A Squadron Hong Kong, B Squadron Singapore plus Regimental HQ and C Squadron in Cyprus. In Singapore we were living in an airy colonial barracks close to Changi of Japanese prisoner of war fame. I then enjoyed organising training all our other soldiers in the jungle, far more rewarding than flogging through it myself! I was now Assistant Adjutant sharing an office with Lt-Col. Robin Carnegie, Commanding Officer and Captain Hugh Saunders, Adjutant, who were actually both brilliant. Robin Carnegie who we always addressed as Colonel, later became a General. Behind his back he was known as Col. Derek as he was Derek Nimmo personified.

On the sport front I had totally fallen on my feet when on being introduced to the Sultan of Johor, a total Anglophile, he asked me whether a certain Farquhar who had signed the Protectorates for the Sultans throughout Malaya on behalf of the British Government was any relation. I had never heard of him, but at very short notice he became my Great Great Grandfather. To boot, when asked, did I play polo, I immediately replied it was a passion of mine, and was duly signed up for the

47

Johor Team with six ponies for the next 15 months. How lucky was that! Tengku Mahmud the Sultan's son who ran the team was a playboy of the first order. His greatest delight was to take his friends after polo down to Singapore, only just over the causeway to enjoy the delights of the first air-conditioned hotel, the Mandarin, and the accompanying floor shows.

Prior to going to the Far East my father had paid off my overdraft accrued over the summer in England, stopping my allowance, with the rejoinder, "You can go abroad and live off your pay!" Therefore cash was short. The polo being taken care of by the Sultan of Johor was a considerable relief, but other funds were necessary. Two opportunities materialised. Firstly some of the officers suggested we ran a roulette wheel and others advocated setting up a mobile discotheque. We did both and in theory they worked hand in hand—gambling and dancing. We had a double ended roulette table made by a local Chinese carpenter and we went to Macau to buy a proper wheel. That was a trip in itself, however we got it all together and since it was mobile we played in Clubs and Officers' Messes all over the region. Two of us acted as the centre croupiers, two other mates worked the ends. Our Paymaster did the finances. We won every time we played except once at the Singapore Polo Club when we were persuaded to double our maximum stake on any one bet and played for three hours instead of two. In the first hour we did hit 14 low blacks running and cleaned up, but then hit a more predictable wheel and for the next two hours watched that evening's profit and the previous year's profit slide away to the hard gambling Chinese.

The mobile discotheque had turntables, loudspeakers, psychedelic lights that flashed in time to the music, and a speaker system that Michael Hewitson (also a B Squadron subaltern) and myself used as disc jockeys to introduce the records. We had a steady supply from England, all the latest Top Ten hits often before they arrived in the Far East, and fancy dress shirts Carnaby Street style, the attire that was all the rage among the young at the time. The discotheque was a great success and we were asked to play at a lot of the local sporting clubs; we were even flown out to Indonesia to play at a very important local princely celebration!

Mike and myself used to pack the disco paraphernalia into a long wheel based Army Land Rover, often accompanied by a couple of female helpers before heading off to Malaya or somewhere, surprisingly with

Tiny Borneo ponies—Hong Kong polo.

no questions asked. We did however provide our own petrol! Singapore continued to be a lot of fun. When not in the jungle we waterskied and of course played polo. I did get involved with the local flat racing stables and for my sins was dispatched to Kuala Lumpur to ride the favourite in a six furlong handicap. If anyone thinks a steeplechase is frightening, try a short distance flat race, absolutely as fast as you can go from start to finish and tight round bends in a total huddle. Anyway I was beaten a head by a 56 year-old woman. Not good for the street cred in the Mess, even though I did try to point out that she was the sister of the well known trainer Ryan Price.

The Far East did have its other moments. A trip to Vietnam with an Australian captain, obviously no frontline stuff because as Brits we were banned, but just being in Hanoi was an eye-opener. The cleanliness of the city, the sheer number of American GIs in uniform and the fact that all the locals travelled by scooter with the most beautiful girls all dressed in white, riding sidesaddle pillion was out of the ordinary. Hong Kong was also riveting, bearing in mind this was still the mid 1960's. The difference between Hong Kong itself, skyscrapers and money as opposed to the New Territories—Chinese pig farms and local cheap bars where everything could be bartered was very striking. Our boys were stationed by an aerodrome in the New Territories where occasionally they were asked to assist the local Hong Kong police by providing armoured cars and back up to help deal with a Chinese riot, but other than that life was fairly peaceful. When there we did play polo on tiny little Borneo ponies, they were so small I remember one tall officer getting into the saddle by putting his leg over without even taking the other one off the ground! I took an under the neck shot and accidentally tripped my pony up by getting my right leg between its fore legs. I will never forget seeing Jimmy Edwards, the larger-than-life English comedian climb aboard a pony, all twenty stone of him without the pony turning a hair, goodness they were tough.

Back to Singapore the steady round of uncomfortable forays into the jungle was much outweighed by life at Selangor Barracks, with hilarious evenings provided by the street vendors in Bugis Street. The best Chinese meal you could ever wish to eat cooked on a wok balanced on the back of a bicycle and transferred to a trestle table. This overseen by the presence of the stunningly beautiful transvestite hookers that plied their trade in that particular area. They were mostly Eurasian and the giveaway was a pronounced Adam's Apple and large wrists, apparently they did catch a sailor or two!

Having been there for some time we eventually got a spot of leave and a fellow officer Philip Gay came up with the scheme to hire a yawl, a two masted sailing boat, quite serious and comfortable, with a small outboard motor to sail around the Tioman Islands off the east coast of Malaya, which was totally idyllic and where in fact South Pacific was filmed. They were mostly uninhabited, with the most beautiful lagoons full of tropical fish and we thought we had gone to heaven. Having mastered the art of island-hopping, the plan was then to venture further out into the Indian Ocean. Not being equipped with radios or anything sophisticated like that, the fact that a typhoon was heading just north of our supposedly sedate path did alter the equilibrium somewhat when our handheld wire wind gauge went from Force Five—quite exciting, to Force Ten—terrifying. Our 'crew' retired downstairs and sat huddled together when the foresail blew out and cups and plates started to fly about the galley. At this stage I did ask Philip if he had experienced this sort of storm before when he was skippering a boat in the Fastnet

Bugis Street, Singapore: IWF and Dick Gainsford blending in.

Race, at which point he did admit that he had not been skipper, but a deckhand. Marvellous! Thankfully the storm blew itself out and we limped back to the mainland where we were greeted by a Malayan Navy patrol boat with Tengku Mahmoud on board who had just promoted himself to an Admiral. He insisted we accompanied him to the ward-room, where exhausted by a near miss at sea, we were soon the worse for wear. Eventually back on our boat we motored to a nearby creek and anchored up, the plan being to display a riding light which for some reason did not materialise. We awoke next morning to find that the tide had gone out and we were slightly aground. The reason for no light became apparent, an empty box of matches that now surrounded a hurricane lamp with the wick turned down.

Before the trip Col. Robin had had the odd chat with me as to my future. A nine month posting to the French Cavalry School at Samour was quite an appealing option, although friends who had done that course before did say it had so altered their style of riding that their ability across country had suffered. Another option was to try for the SAS which a number of compatriots had gone for, which indeed I thought would be a challenge. However then he mentioned that the Regiment had been asked to put a name forward to be an Equerry to H.M. Queen Elizabeth, the Queen Mother, who was our Colonel in Chief. The regiments that Her Majesty was Colonel in Chief of, namely the Queen's Own Hussars, the 9th/12th Lancers, the Queen's Dragoon Guards and the Black Watch all took it in turn to provide an Equerry for two years and it was our turn. I had met Queen Elizabeth on occasions before, fishing in Scotland and at Badminton and the chance of serving her as an Equerry was an unbelievable opportunity. As we disembarked from our trip in the South China Seas I already knew that the next venture was to be as a shirt and tie courtier in England. The wonderful difference between the pompous and the bizarre was illustrated when Philip and myself arrived back in the Mess dressed in kikoys, our skins pretty dark—and in my case sporting an extremely unattractive Dago moustache—holding Percy a pet python, or at least Philip was … There we were met by our new Adjutant, in fact a super bloke, who was wearing a freshly tailored white colonial lightweight suit, shirt and tie and panama hat, muttering to himself, "Oh my God, I see the officers have gone native!"

To explain the presence of Percy? We had caught him in a chicken pen, run by the Chinese cook behind the Mess, where he had slithered in, eaten a chicken and was unable to slither out again. We had a cage built for him where he lived on the veranda of the Mess kept company by two gerbils in case he felt hungry. He would occasionally come for a walk, he didn't bite as long as you picked him up just behind the head, but since he was nine foot long it was unwise to handle him without an accomplice because if he started to squeeze your arm it took two of you to untangle him. The Chinese Mess waiters hated him as did our Mess dogs. One day he escaped and finished up in the engine of Mike Cunningham's new Triumph TR. It was only when the engine was left running and got too hot that he decided to come out. He didn't eat for three months and when I returned to England he still had not. How long a chicken lasted seemed surprising although the lump in his stomach was steadily subsiding.

After a few more months in Singapore it was back to England to a desk job as UK Adjutant at Maresfield in Sussex, where a regimental skeleton staff still operated. It was sad to leave the Far East where I had made some very good friends outside of the Army, although I must admit it was not sad to say goodbye to the jungle. The jungle was not a pleasant place to operate in and I have stated before the heat and humidity and lack of sunshine were not particularly conducive to a feeling of physical well-being and the ever present leeches and mosquitoes did get tiresome! However it was an experience not to be missed. The eerie screeching of monkeys that went on all night, the phenomenal brightness of a firefly in the total blackness of a jungle night and the amazing size and colour of the butterflies across an occasional clearing that allowed some sunlight to perforate through the thick jungle canopy were beautiful to behold. Outsiders often queried the dangers of snakes. Yes, it was off-putting to hear the plop of a snake falling into the water beside you when traversing a swamp area, then seeing its head bobbing about rather too close for comfort as it swam away, but it was somewhat comforting to be reminded that more people were killed in Malaya by being hit on the head by a falling coconut than by being bitten by a snake!

I personally was also not sad to replace waterskiing with hunting as a winter occupation in off duty hours, and the social scene in London was rather more invigorating than the slightly repetitive forays into that one newly opened nightclub in down town Singapore. It was always fairly salutary though when one had been abroad for eighteen months or so to pitch up at a party to be met with the normal quip, "Haven't seen you for a bit—a good tan—have you been on holiday?" One of the best ports of call after a time away in order to get back in the swim again was one of the regular drinks evenings at Tite Street where two old chums, Antony Brassey and Anthony Spink, both ex Scots Greys, held open house. Antony Brassey known as just 'Brass', in particular became a great friend. In time he would become my best man and then subsequently my Chairman at the Duke of Beaufort's Hunt, when he took over that role from his father Colonel Hugh Brassey, later Sir Hugh on being knighted. Brass and myself often attended the same London dinner parties and I recall one evening, when at the end of the meal everybody started clearing up he stayed firmly put until finally getting to his feet and announcing loudly, "I think I ought to show willing." 'Willing,' I might add, subsequently received numerous telephone calls and even the odd letter!

Most of the winter back in England also gave me the opportunity to get in a bit of hunting with the Beaufort. My parents sometimes had an available horse, and also for some reason quite a few Badminton hunt horses came my way. Not that I was in any way a capable nagsman. I never saw a stride in my life, but occasionally a nappy whipper-in's horse needed getting out. One in particular I remember, a big black brute that flatly refused to go anywhere without a lead, not much good to do a job on, but never went lame and jumped like a stag.

Equerry to HM Queen Elizabeth, the Queen Mother

T HE TIME AT Maresfield gave me a breathing space to prepare for London. One of the things about being a soldier was that you were always provided with accommodation, sometimes a very comfortable officers' mess, or maybe sometimes a tent, but a roof was always on offer. There are two great attributes about the Army; in barracks there was always plenty of food and hot water! As an Equerry you found you your own accommodation, and even in those days London was relatively expensive. Luckily I met a previously mentioned school friend, George Lopes who happened to say that he shared digs in Wharton Street, very central, and that one of the group was leaving London so there might be a room spare. This was just what the doctor ordered. The house belonged to Richard Cookson, an old family friend from Northumberland. George himself, and James Barclay who was working for the family bank were the other tenants. Not much cooking went on. A cooker did arrive shortly after I did, but still had not been wired in by the time I left almost two years later!

One or two other requirements needed attending to. A couple of smart suits, together with a steady supply of stiff collars and shoes without holes were also *de rigueur*, so with all this fixed it was off to Clarence House. Like most things in that sort of environment little was left to chance, and a very efficient handover was necessary. The outgoing Equerry was a Queen's Dragoon Guards officer, Richard Jenkins, whom I already knew from living in Gloucestershire. He could not have been more friendly and helpful. Her Majesty Queen Elizabeth the Queen Mother's Household certainly made me feel welcome and comprised of Lt.-Col. Sir Martin Gilliat, Private Secretary, and Captain Alastair Aird,

Assistant Private Secretary, who were in the front line as it were with day to day organisation. Lord Adam Gordon who was Comptroller of the Household, Major Sir Ralph Anstruther Bt, Treasurer, and Major John Griffin, Press Secretary were all also Equerries, alongside a number of others who filled various roles. Then there were the Women of the Bedchamber, one of whom was always in attendance, basically taking it in turns for a fortnightly stint—Lady Jean Rankin, the Honourable Mrs Olivia Mulholland, Ruth Lady Fermoy and Mrs Frances Campbell-Preston. There was also a powerful crew of Extra Women of the Bedchamber who were called upon for particular engagements. As a new Equerry, I shared an office with Alastair Aird an ex 9th Lancer who had filled the same role as a soldier before me.

The first thing one did realise was that whereas it was a very friendly job, it was totally unlike any other. Straight away it was obvious that a certain amount of protocol needed learning and although not complicated it was best to get it right. The 'Boss' was Her Majesty Queen Elizabeth the Queen Mother, perfectly charming, but at times one did have to remind oneself that she had been Queen of England at a time when England basically seemed to rule the world. To return to the protocol, when as a member of the Household you first encountered the Queen Mother in the morning, you stood slightly to attention and bowed your head from the neck downwards. No extravagant gestures, "Good Morning Your Majesty." Then for the rest of the day it was just "Ma'am." I obviously remember my first day. As previously explained, I had met Queen Elizabeth, as we referred to her amongst ourselves, on quite a number of occasions, yet I was still somewhat nervous when she said, "Ian how nice to see you. Come and sit next to me, I want to hear all about what's going on at Badminton!"

One or two other things happened in the first week which made me aware I was in a slightly different environment. Once I walked up to Jermyn Street to buy a shirt and as I was coming back down St James's Street with the shirt in a New and Lingwood bag, I saw Sir Ralph Anstruther coming towards me complete with monocle, Brigade of Guards tie and overcoat. He walked past me as if I did not exist. Just half an hour later I was summoned to his office and very firmly informed that Her Majesty's Household did not carry parcels in London! And that if by chance I shopped anywhere where they did not deliver, an orderly would collect instead!

HM Queen Elizabeth the Queen Mother: Thurso visit—IWF with Lady Fermoy.

The Queen Mother coming out of Wick Church: LtR: Lt Col Sir Martin Gilliat, Lady Fermoy, IWF and Pammie-Jane, the Vicar & Her Majesty.

Another incident that happened to work very much to my advantage also brought out the difference in regard to protocol. When very early on I found myself discussing with Queen Elizabeth whether there was any chance of playing polo or not, (I still had some ponies), I mentioned that I'd had a letter from the Ministry signed by a clerk that they were looking into the possibility of the Regiment sending me a soldier batman to look after me. Actually, of course, I needed a groom to look after the horses! Queen Elizabeth needless to say totally understood and simply suggested that I sent a message straight away. In fact, I then wrote a letter, admittedly on Clarence House notepaper, to the General in charge of that department. A missive arrived the next morning delivered by courier and personally signed by the General in question saying a priority signal had been sent to my Regiment. Corporal Manger my groom arrived two days later!

Living in London was very different from anything I've ever come across before. I was based in an office in Clarence House just off the Mall. If there were no engagements on a given day then it was a fairly leisurely start and I would get into the office around 10 am. If Queen Elizabeth was in London, then stiff white collars were the order of the day but if not, we were allowed to wear a soft shirt. Again, when Queen Elizabeth was in London then the Household normally all had lunch together, sometimes with guests. Food on these occasions was quite frankly out of this world and it certainly wasn't a dry house! Queen Elizabeth was often out of London for the weekend at Royal Lodge so most of us had weekends off. I personally was spoilt, as in the summer I tended to play polo and in the winter went hunting!

The military equerry's job was obviously to deal with any military engagements, but in the early 70s there were probably less of them than in previous generations, and therefore one did get involved with other engagements of a non-military nature. As a junior there was only a certain number of these that one was allowed to be let loose on, but of course they were all fascinating and very rewarding.

The degree of respect which individuals showed when actually faced with 'the Boss' was phenomenal. Indeed, on occasions some would even change their stance. I well remember going on a recce to a factory in Birmingham when the head trade union guy stated very firmly that he had no truck with the Royal Family and he would have to think about whether he was going to attend the line up. However, on the day there he was on the end of the line in an immaculate brand-new suit with his shoes so shiny that they could have been polished by the local army barracks, and when congratulated by Queen Elizabeth for looking after the men so well, he was heard to respond, "We do our best Your Majesty, it's such an honour to have you here today." At another factory in Birmingham a chap to be presented did let drop to me that he had been a mess waiter on Britannia after the War. Her Majesty did stop and say to him, "I'm sure we've met before. Was it Britannia?" Following on behind it was delightful to hear him turn to his mate, "That's the most amazing woman I've ever met, she remembered me from all those years ago. I would die for her tomorrow!"

One of the biggest pleasures of engagements such as these was that on occasion we used to stay on the Royal Train. Queen Elizabeth obviously had her own compartment adjacent to that of the lady-in-waiting, with a very comfortable sitting room and dining room. Other bedrooms were further down the passage, proper beds, sheets and adjacent bathrooms with the intriguing fact that the rims of the baths turned inwards to prevent the water splashing out as the train moved along! We normally parked up in a siding for dinner, and indeed probably for the night. One of the standing jokes of these trips was Queen Elizabeth declaring after dinner, "We must have a glass of Railway port!" Next morning when one went for a walk before breakfast I always felt slightly sorry for the British Rail Police staff who had been standing guard all night. For me one of the sadnesses of my time was that we never did a trip on Britannia although every year we did go back on board for a drink with the Royal Family when they had called in for lunch at the Castle of Mey.

Most of the summer however was based in London with letters to write on behalf of Her Majesty and occasional engagements, continually meeting and dealing with a fascinating array of people who called in to see Queen Elizabeth. I was rather surprised on one lowish key engagement to find myself sitting next to Margaret Thatcher who was then Shadow Minister of Education at a luncheon at Lancaster House, after she had attended a discussion on modern education. She turned to me and said, "Where did you go to school?" I found myself having to mutter, "Eton." It wasn't entirely surprising that she spent the rest of lunch talking to the person on her left!

Back to the razzmatazz of a fairly wild bachelor establishment in Walton Street—too much gambling, whisky, parties and no shortage of girls. A 10am start might seem luxurious, but it still came round rather too quickly! I was able to escape to the Polo—mostly at Cirencester, but also quite often at Tidworth. Shandy and Lager were still with me. Both ponies were very happy to be back in England and looked after by Corporal Manger. We won a lot of matches!

Undoubtedly for me one of the biggest pleasures of the year was the trips to Scotland, firstly to Birkhall, at the time, the Queen Mother's house on the Balmoral Estate, for the fishing, normally in May. Sometimes also a spring trip to the Castle of Mey in Caithness and then a time-honoured trip back to Mey in August to chase the elusive grouse that were still in residence. This again was followed by another visit to Birkhall. As a junior equerry I was also lucky enough to get the Mey trips and then the lower key autumn shooting and fishing on the Dee if the weather was playing ball. I often used to think that mine must have been one of the most enviable jobs in the world. Sending out guns and rods, and then being able to join in oneself was an enormous privilege. Occasionally outsiders would say that it must be quite difficult to put it all together, but of course the truth was that the staff who mostly had been there for years certainly did not need any interference from a two-bit boy who had just arrived. The chauffeurs knew the game backwards and tended to move around with Queen Elizabeth. Mr Pearl, the Birkhall keeper and Mr Cameron, the Castle of Mey keeper were experts in their field, both were brilliant as well as being charming. The lowland shooting for the latter part of the stay at Birkhall was without any question the most fun shooting I was lucky enough to ever come across. Not big bags, a small number of guns and an enormous variety of game. Those elusive grouse in Caithness were considerably harder work, but equally rewarding.

One of the pleasures to all of these trips was that the same staff from Clarence House used to accompany the Queen Mother, and hearing William Tallon, her Page accompanied by Reg the footman roaring with laughter night after night after a fairly extensive day was an eye-opener. Another side to the enjoyment of these sporting excursions was of course they were always broken up by an outdoor picnic lunch. There were normally tables and chairs set up by Queen Elizabeth and her Lady in Waiting ready for the return of those that had been on the hill. There were some wonderfully bizarre moments. I remember well a day when the midges became so bad they were almost unbearable. I have a photograph of such an occasion on the gravel outside Cameron's house at Mey, when a large bracken and heather fire was burning merrily underneath the lunch table with everybody sitting around coughing and spluttering, but at least free from the midges. Needless to say Queen Elizabeth was at the end of the table, her old green hat pulled well down, carrying on as if nothing untoward had happened at all.

Generally speaking the guest list remained fairly static. At Birkhall it was made up mainly of the more serious shooters such as the Earl and Countess of Dalhousie, Commander and Lady Doris Vyner (Lady Doris had been a childhood friend of Queen Elizabeth) and Lord Elphinstone amongst others. The guests at the Castle of Mey on the other hand tended to be a younger crowd made up of ex-equerries and previous members of the Household. The dinner parties were inclined to be extremely convivial, although if there were no non-local guests, and being so far north, with the light evenings the fishers were often dispatched for a last cast or two before bedtime. After dinner at Mey the story was somewhat different, either dancing reels to a wind up gramophone or more often a fiendishly competitive game of racing demon. Queen Elizabeth herself was extremely proficient at cards, though it was certainly understood by the Household that to come close was fun, but to win more than very occasionally was always followed by the observation from Sir Martin Gilliatt, Private Secretary, "Steady old boy just remember the train leaves for the South at Georgemas Junction tomorrow morning at 8:30!"

There were quite a number of other amusing occasions. I remember one evening we had all gone into the next door room to play cards, leaving Lord Elphinstone talking to the local Scottish Presbyterian Minister's wife. When asked on our return if she had been alright she replied, "Thank you, Your Majesty. I have been having wonderful intercourse on the sofa with Lord Elphinstone"!

Sometimes the joke was against oneself. One year there being more cars than chauffeurs I was asked to drive Queen Elizabeth's own long wheelbase Ford which was used in Scotland south. After a morning's cub hunting with the Meynell on the way down I was somewhat horrified to be woken early next morning by the apparently panic stricken

Master of the Meynell, namely Dermot Kelly. "I'm afraid we really have overdone it this time, last night after you went to bed we got carried away and gave Queen Elizabeth's car a new coat of paint." It appeared they were not joking and parked on the driveway was a very different looking vehicle from the one that had been left there the night before. It was sometime after searching Yellow Pages to see if I could get a car re-sprayed by Tuesday morning that they came clean, sluiced it with a hose removing the sham emulsion and restoring the car it to its former splendour. Phew!

One of the most interesting things about working at Clarence House was the sheer professionalism of everybody there, both members of the Household and domestic staff—things simply did not go wrong. However, I did manage myself on one occasion to completely miss out on an engagement. The Queen Mother was due to visit the RAF at Little Rissington and as it was a Services engagement, being a military equerry, about a month beforehand I was dispatched to fix up the programme. As her Equerry I was to accompany Her Majesty together with a Lady-in-Waiting. We were due to leave Clarence House early on a Monday morning to drive to London Airport to catch a Queens Flight to Little Rissington. In fact I had returned to London in good time on the Sunday evening and had elected to go to bed quite early! I woke next morning and was shaving in what I thought was in plenty of time to get to work when I suddenly realised in horror that we were leaving rather earlier than normal and I had not got time to get to Clarence House and into uniform before the cars left—Panic! I even tried to hire a helicopter to no avail! Instead I spent a miserable day in London and nobody appeared to want to talk to me! I envisaged being sent back to my Regiment in disgrace! I did manage to persuade William Tallon, Her Majesty's Page who was slightly more on my side to ask Queen Elizabeth if I could see her when she returned, to apologise. I heard the cars arrive and received a message shortly afterwards that I could go upstairs to her private drawing room. She was sitting in an armchair, feet up on a footstool. Expecting my life come to an end, all I could do was mutter how sorry I was. It was a mark of the kindness and thoughtfulness of that great lady, that all she said was it been a tiring day and I did I have a problem waking up in the morning? With that she reached underneath her chair and pulled out an alarm clock that she had already asked one of the housemaids to purchase. It is something I treasure, and still have to this day. Even though we were upstairs on the second floor had I been asked in that moment to jump out of the window, I would have done so, willingly with a smile on my face.

One of the most interesting elements of the job was the sheer diversity of events, in particular participating in Investitures when Queen Elizabeth was standing in for the Queen. The ceremony would take place in the Ballroom at Buckingham Palace with those receiving an Honour being held in a line over to the right and their families sitting in chairs in the centre. Queen Elizabeth would be standing on a dais in front of the relatives of those about to be invested. If my memory is right, Knighthoods were dealt with first, then the Victorian Order followed by the Military Medals and then British Empire Medals, OBE and MBE. An equerry would be issued with a list of those to be presented whose names would be announced as they left the line up, and it was their job to quietly let Her Majesty know what each had achieved. One was always slightly nervous that the order might be different from the paperwork and in error would mutter, "Drains Newcastle Ma'am," instead of, "Saving lives at sea!" Amongst other numerous exciting moments was a visit to a nuclear submarine at Rosyth. All rather different from normal London duties, although it was impressive at the speed with which the Metropolitan Police would get a Royal entourage through the traffic. Cars halted at every crossroads on the way to an engagement.

I must admit that at the time I was entirely spoilt, being let off to hunt and play polo pretty regularly unless we had a definite engagement. While in London during the winter I did try and ride in the odd point-to-point. At one stage I was lent a hunter chaser that had belonged to Jim Joel and had been re-allocated by Charles Radcliffe, famous for re-homing horses that had failed on the track. He was called Dumble and was very fast, but was a bit apt not to take off! I rode him five times and fell on each occasion. I then made the mistake of entering him for the Past and Present Military Race at Sandown. If I had been less fearful of being called a coward I would definitely have scratched! We hit the first of the Railway Fences all ends up, but finished third, being pipped from second place by Andrew Parker-Bowles riding The Fossa who had just been round Aintree. Rather a different class!

Back in London at Clarence House during the summer there were

Peter Gifford, IWF, Mrs Pinky, Ian McConnell and Richard Clifford—Mrs Pinky's Specials 1970

numerous unforgettable alfresco lunches in the garden, the table laid underneath the trees, sometimes just with the Household and at other times with members of the Royal Family together with a diverse array of friends, many from the worlds of racing and the theatre.

Polo and More Hunting Connections

So, as I have explained, being lucky enough to have most week-ends off, there could be regular polo at Tidworth and Cirencester during the summer, and hunting in the winter would follow, initially in Gloucestershire and then in Derbyshire with the Meynell. There I normally stayed at Cubley Lodge, with Dad's brother Uncle Mike and his wife Aunt Nance and my cousins Daphne and Angela ('Tiddles'). Daffer's and Tiddles were, and still are, the sisters I never had, enormous fun, a guinea a minute and too many stories to tell. The Master and huntsman of the Meynell at that time was Captain Dermot Kelly. His determination to 'get on' and enthusiasm revitalised in me the love of 'the Chase'. Also at that time the polo was going rather well. One of the funniest teams without any doubt was that of Ian McConnell, Richard Clifford, myself and local farmer Pete Gifford. We called ourselves

Hugh Pitman, Andrew Parker Bowles, IWF, Bruce Gordon and HRH the
Prince of Wales in Nairobi, Kenya, 1971.

Mrs Pinky's Specials after the revitalising brew that Mrs Pinky, wife of the
Cirencester Polo Club Bar Manager used to mix every Sunday morning
following some of our rather late nights. It was a yellow concoction and
certainly seemed to spur on the game! By some miracle at Cirencester
Park we won the medium goal as a team, and were asked to go to
Sotogrande that New Year to celebrate the inaugural matches of their
new polo club. It seemed the less we slept the better we played. I recall
the first match when we lined up in front of one of our hosts from the
Domecq sherry family who asked, "Who is the Captain of your team?"
To which Pete Gifford replied, "There are three effing captains in this
team but I am the boss!"

Another very memorable trip was being selected to represent the
Army in a team that went to Kenya in 1971. The team consisted of
Hugh Pitman, Andrew Parker-Bowles both in the Household Cavalry
(Blues), myself and Bruce Gordon, both Hussars. To become acclima-
tised Hugh and his wife Rosemary, plus Andrew and his wife Camilla,
Bruce and myself all stayed in a house on the coast at Killifi. Lucky us. By
a quirk of fate I was asked to dinner by the then Lady Delamere of White
Mischief fame (Lord Errol, Delves Broughton and all that). What I can

remember was, even then as an older woman she had the most piercing blue eyes of anybody I have ever come across. She was kind enough to suggest I had a day's fishing marlin on one of her boats that were always named 'Bear' this or 'Bear' that. I was allocated 'White Bear' and at one stage we ran into a shoal of marlin and suddenly had six on at the same moment. Needless to say there were so many lines running that they all crossed each other, and we finished up landing none of them! After that we went up country and stayed with mostly local farmers and played at all the different clubs. One amusing interlude was when Bruce Gordon and myself thought we would raid the neighbouring house where Pitman and Parker-Bowles were staying. We found a couple of lion skins and thought we would give them a fright. All that happened was that as we were going across the lawn, the owner released a couple of Ridgebacks, so when Parker-Bowles and Pitman came out to see what the excitement was, we were sitting up a tree!

I still have the photograph at home of the four of us playing in the finals in Nairobi joined by the then young Prince of Wales. Funny how the lives intertwined—they would all later hunt with me at the Beaufort.

It was during my latter time in London that I came across Pammie-Jane Chafer again and we used to go to Northumberland fairly regularly to stay with the Cooksons, although I was myself mainly hunting in Derbyshire with Dermot Kelly at the Meynell.

German Winter 1972

Returning to Hohne, the winters were not so good unless you were a skier which I most definitely was not! There was not too much to do and we still rode most days. I now had an ex-chaser of Queen Elizabeth's that she had given me called Artist's Son who was a lovely ride, quite strong and totally sound, but just did not win races. I did take him out with the local German draghounds on a few occasions, which to be honest was not a great success. As soon as they set off it was not long before I hit the front. I didn't get muddled up with the hounds, but passed a rather livid looking German who had a lot of tassels on his arm. When we stopped at the end of the first run, I was given a glass of pretty filthy schnapps, and admonished for passing the Hassles as apparently that was taboo. When we set off for the next run—or lines as they called them—the same thing happened. Again stopped I did get some more schnapps, but things were definitely frosty. The third line, the same again. Final stop. No schnapps! It was not intentional, he was just a very keen English thoroughbred chaser!

The weather could turn incredibly cold, and at one stage I think it went down to about -30, but being the British Army they still took great glee in often sending us out—good training! It was so cold that we had to keep the tanks running all night otherwise they would have literally frozen up. With the hatches closed and the engine running, for us it was nearly bearable. However we did feel sorry for the infantry huddled up outside. I had never served in tanks before and I must say their power and ability to cross country was pretty phenomenal. At times in those days exercises were to a degree still played for real and going across country. Hedges, spinneys and using barns as cover was all rather exciting stuff although it did not endear the British Army to the German farmers, even if they did get compensation.

We did at times come across the Russians, which was in theory why we were all there, and all I can say is that the ones that I met just roared with laughter and drank copious amounts of vodka, although I am sure in a different environment they could have been slightly less friendly.

After the boredom of a German winter it was a great relief in the spring to take a week's leave and go home. Pammie-Jane came to stay and in the middle of the week we went out to dinner and when we got back I suggested we go down to the stables and see the puppies. Neither of us now can remember whether they were a litter of lurcher or hound puppies. I still think they were lurchers out of a bitch of Mary Beaufort's (Duchess) called Misty by my dog Beckett that I had bought from the Badminton bus driver. Anyway, I suddenly plucked up courage and asked her to marry me, and rather to my amazement she said yes! I waited for her next morning before breakfast and said, "Did you mean what you said?" All she replied was, "You will find that I don't change my mind!" We told my parents who were delighted, so I returned to Germany a very happy man. With all of that to look forward to the summer was really quite fun. I actually enjoyed the soldiering and one trip in particular sticks in my memory. The Squadron of which I was second-in-command was scheduled to go to southern Germany (Bavaria) for three weeks to exercise with the Americans, who were stationed in the south not far from Munich. A great friend, Mike Cunningham was also in B Squadron

IWF and Pammie-Jane

and we discovered that the exercise coincided with the Munich Polo Festival. We decided to take a few days off. Our Squadron leader, Teddy Bagnall accompanied the tanks which went by rail on flatbeds, and I was in charge of the road party. We fixed up the Regimental horsebox, loaded it with a couple of grooms and enough ponies, and set off in convoy. It was a long way, and we stayed overnight at an American camp on the way down. A charming American officer met us and pointed out the soldiers' accommodation, announcing that since he was married to an English girl, Mike and myself could stay with him. He was somewhat surprised however when we unloaded six ponies and asked if there was a grass area where we could tether them for the night!

"What the hell have you got those for?"

"They are very useful to pull the tanks out if they get bogged."

"What a good idea I must tell my Colonel."

I think he did believe us!

The exercise was an eye-opener, at every briefing I went to as a lowly

Our Wedding Day 1972.

Captain I was surrounded by American Generals who were charming, but very concerned that the Brits did not get enough fresh rations in the field. It was hot, but the delivery of fresh ice cream was obviously quite a major issue. Anyway it all seemed to go quite well and Mike and myself were extremely pleased when Pammie-Jane and Mike's wife to be, Virginia, also very beautiful and charming, both arrived. We decamped to the Four Seasons in Munich for three days where we were very well looked after both in the hotel and on the polo ground. The day after the final match the girls left for England, the ponies and grooms made their own way back to Hohne and we were back in a tank.

About then I was once again asked to represent the Army, this time in India for the month of November, something I had always been very keen to do. I suggested to Pammie that we went together, at which point I was very firmly told that we were getting married in November. I muttered couldn't we somehow do both? This was met with a firm 'No!' My old mate Richard Clifford went to India, and we got married on the

18th of November 1972. As is customary I did have a couple of bachelor 'Do's', one in the Mess at Hohne and one in London. For the one in Hohne I plied them with what I called Clarence House Martinis, which may explain why the evening finished with the ponies being brought out of the stables, ridden bareback up the Mess steps and then jumped down a line of sofas, out of the French windows, a couple of garden hedges and round again. On our wedding day Pammie did enquire where the scar on my forehead came from?

"I fell over a sofa in the Mess."

"I see... Wobbly on your feet again I suppose?"

"No on a horse actually!"

The London 'Do' was not much better. Both my brothers were there, as was Antony Brassey my Best Man, and quite a number of friends. The evening was going to plan until I stopped for a pee in a deserted street off the Kings Road, when suddenly it wasn't deserted, and I found myself first in a police car and then behind bars in Chelsea Police Station! A little over the top I thought, but at least I had a cast iron alibi as to where I was on my bachelor night!

We got married at five pm, black tie and evening dresses after a days hunting with Pammie's father Charles, master and huntsman of the Derwent. On the way to the meet he did say, "If I have a bad fall get David (Lord) Westbury to give her away." A couple of hours later his normally very careful old horse Bert turned a circle and I thought we might need Westbury after all. Charles however picked himself up and was fine. Elsie, Pammie's mother was never one to do things by half; she had Joe Loss and his Band playing in the church and around six hundred sat down for dinner—quite an evening.

It is funny how a chance conversation can totally alter the course of life. During the reception I was chatting to Alec Bond who had been at Cirencester with brother Mike, and who at the time was one of the Field Masters for the Bicester. He asked me if I was going to stay in the Army or had I considered going into hunting? It transpired that the Bicester were in a muddle, and were looking for a Master as they were being run by a Committee at the time—never satisfactory in my view—and had cut back from four days a week to three, being short of funds and organisation. After dinner and dancing Pammie and myself were packed off to the pub at Coxwold where we were staying, and decided on the way that there was no harm in looking into it. We rang the Bicester Chairman Jimmy Lane Fox the next morning from London Airport on our way to Kenya.

Honeymoon and Return to Germany

Life is never as smooth as you think it's going to be, and even our honeymoon had the odd hiccup, with Pammie complaining on the first morning that the long 'plank' of wood (the boom) that kept flying across the very small sailing dinghy we had hired was trying to knock her out! When I had taken her sailing I naturally thought I had mastered small boats, but of course I had not. However we survived. Later in the afternoon she went to sleep in the open thinking that being a little over-cast there was no danger from too much sun. The answer was of course that the ultraviolet rays were still getting through and she suffered third-degree burns to her legs. This was not funny, and she took three days to recover. Before we left Kilifi we did go and have a drink with a young London contingent who had just arrived when I heard Pammie say in reply to, "Have you had a good time?" With, "Actually I spent the last three days on my back in bed with my legs in the air!"

You can imagine the looks that I got! We then went up-country to go on safari with my cousin Robin Hurt who took us down to the Maasai Mara with his top team. In those days he ran shooting safaris, and still does, as well as photographic. I had no desire to shoot anything exotic, although I did account for a few buck and a buffalo. The hunters always say that buffalo are the most dangerous of them all and a wounded one will hide and lie in wait and then charge. They also take quite a lot of killing and mine was s looking menacing even after two rounds of 404. Robin was most insistent that we approached from behind for the final shot, and did not go round the front at any price.

One funny incident—after lunch one day—we were in a very comfortable tented camp—Robin and myself went for a swim in the creek, and after a while Pammie came to join us, doing a very gentle breaststroke. Then she looked up and saw one of Robin's guides standing on the point with a rifle

"What is he doing?"

"Keeping a look out for crocodiles!"

A jet propelled Mrs Farquhar was back on land within seconds! Anyway we had had an amazing time and returned to Heathrow all too soon.

As arranged, we called Jimmy Lane Fox on arrival and fixed up to see him before setting off for Hohne and a new married quarter. Jimmy and his wife Anne were both charming and Jimmy was fairly persuasive. As we left he indicated he would need an answer soon as he had other options up his sleeve, which I knew he did not. He had not founded and made a great success of estate agents Lane Fox and Partners without achieving his aims. I think he thought he probably had us signed up, and of course he was not far wrong. On the way back to Hohne, we endlessly discussed the pros and cons.

I seem to remember how Pammie in the end summed it up saying that she didn't want to spend years moving from army quarter to army quarter. What she wanted was a base for the horses and the dogs and anyway we were both born into hunting families and loved it, and even if we ran out of money after a couple of years and it was not working, at least we would have had a crack.

We found our quarter, a fairly nondescript flat in Hohne town and rescued Beckett, who was so delighted to see me he made me feel rather guilty for leaving him, not that there had ever been much option. I also collected the few possessions I had in my room in the Mess, pictures et cetera and we settled into married life. I had been to see the Colonel as soon as we got back and informed him that I wanted to leave, and that the plan was to be at the Bicester by May 1st. He was good to enough to say that he was sorry and that he had hoped I was in for the long haul, but he quite understood. I do not think he was totally surprised.

One of the only sports we got up to was to go coursing with Beckett with a lamp at night on the ranges at the back of the camp. One night we had caught a deer, but I knew we had been seen by the local forest ranger who took that sort of thing very seriously. Thank goodness I twigged. We haunched up the deer that night. I gave Beckett back to Neville there and then, and next morning fixed up for another friend to take him back to England the same day. Just as well, as when I was in the Camp next morning, a German policeman arrived at the flat and demanded to be given the 'hund' to be taken away to be shot. Pammie said there was no dog, and no deer and see what was he on about? Not being best pleased he decided to ask her a lot of questions—age, name, occupation, what does your husband do? He was dressed in a long black leather coat and Pammie was getting a bit rattled. His parting shot as he left, when she said she looked after her husband, who was an officer, was, "You have no job, no kinde? In Germany the husband works, the wife works, the children work, in England nobody works!" He might have had a point, but it was hardly his place to say so! I was sorry I was not there. Probably just as well! I must say it did nothing to enhance Pammie's love of Germany. We did stagger on through the winter and recall a very good weekend tobogganing in the mountains with Jeremy Phipps, a most amusing man who later joined the SAS, finished up a General and married the brilliant painter Susan Crawford. He did come and stay for Christmas and made us laugh a lot.

All in all, we were pleased to get back to England to prepare to move to Stratton Audley for me to take up the sole mastership of the Bicester. One of the things that very soon became apparent was the way that friends readily offered their help and advice. My application to become a member of the Masters of Foxhounds' Association which required a proposer and a seconder was soon dealt with. The 10th Duke of Beaufort 'Master' as proposer and Captain R. E. Wallace as seconder—not a bad start!

Both Ronnie and also my old childhood and Sandhurst chum, Martin Scott asked us to stay that April. 'Scottie' as Martin was to become universally known, or 'Uncle Scottie' to my children in the future, thought it best to lay down what in his opinion the ground lines should be for an MFH. The result was a very late night at the Tiverton kennel cottage, a bucket full of booze and an early start to collect a few stinking carcasses. This was followed by a quick lesson in skinning the said stinking carcasses, then a full English breakfast cooked by Mrs Scott as a prelude to a prolonged visit to see the hounds, and of course a detailed lesson in their breeding!

Captain Wallace was a little more circumspect. An excellent dinner party at Mounsey, with Rosie his wife in flying form and looking a million dollars, and Ronnie at his most informative and charming. Being undoubtedly aware that his charisma was weaker in the north than in the south, he suspected that as a Yorkshire girl, Pammie needed his full attention. His final masterstroke was to escort her up to bed and personally fill her hot water bottle. When I arrived not long afterwards, all I got was, what a charming man Ronnie was, so thoughtful and kind!

As stated, the Chairman was Jimmy Lane Fox, and the Hunt Secretary was Captain John Harding. Once again by a quirk of fate, he had at one stage been in my Regiment, in his case the 3rd Hussars. John was an incredibly kind and thoughtful man who hated any form of trouble or confrontation; he was always so effusively apologetic with angry farmers that they normally finished up feeling sorry for him! Then of course there was Bryan Pheasey, who was hunting hounds at that time, he was one of the most wonderful men I was ever lucky enough to have at my side. His family were equally brilliant, Nora his wife, his children— David the eldest—and Julie and Carol were all delightful. Colin Day was kennelman and he and Marie his wife also became great friends. We were so lucky to go into such an efficient and happy set up.

The Hunt had lent us the stud groom's cottage tacked on to the end of the stables. It had a sitting room with a bow window looking out over the hounds' grass yard, a dining room, storeroom and minute kitchen with a very ancient Rayburn. This provided hot water, needed stoking twice a day and went out at the drop of a hat, but was not too bad when it worked. Upstairs a bedroom also looking out over the grass yard, spare room, box room and a bathroom about the same size as the kitchen. Certainly not a palace, but we were as happy as Larry. I just loved it in the summer when you could lie in bed at night and hear the hounds singing. Normally around three a.m. one hound would start to sing. Not an anguished howl, but the sort of sound that wolves make, slowly and steadily the whole pack joined in, alto, soprano, tenor and bass. All were there, and the pack would sing in unison for ten to fifteen minutes before it would slowly die away. To me it beat any music I have ever heard.

On the subject of horses, we had spent quite a lot of effort during the summer trying to put together enough to get by on. Back during the previous winter we had been to see Bert Cleminson, who had a very large dealer's yard just outside York, with over a hundred horses stabled in old converted cattle sheds. Bert ran the show heading the buying and selling. One of his brothers did the rough riding. In the past he had lent Pammie a few green horses and a very good pony, something he often did, always taking them back when he thought they were ready to move on. He also had that arrangement for years with Colonel Neil Foster, the then master of the Grafton, an exceptional horseman, Weedon-trained and a martinet of a Field Master. Sadly Bert died that winter, so it was back to the drawing board. Pammie's father kindly gave her Spooker, a brave and honest horse which she generously passed on to me. He

Bryan Pheasey, IWF and Charles Wheeler

pulled like a train, so was perfect for an inadequate pilot like myself trying to hunt hounds! I might add that he loved hounds and would fall over himself rather than tread on one. I had my two rather indifferent point-to-pointers, augmented by a little 16hh mare called Bonnie, given to me by my mother. Although Bonnie was getting on a bit, she was the most lovely ride, perfectly capable of jumping anything I wanted to in those early days. I also bought a chestnut—though I never liked chestnuts much I will admit—from a charming lady in the Beaufort country, by the name of Rosemary Donner, who was retiring from hunting. He was called Kelly, and would jump anything, but used to kick hounds at the Meet, so I only got on him after we had moved off, changing horses with whoever had ridden him on. It was only a little later that we were introduced to Dr Tom Connors from Leicestershire who became a firm friend and the producer of practically all our horses.

THE BICESTER

T HE FIRST BICESTER summer was to prove a reliable pattern for summers for the next 45 seasons. As the years rolled by, it always made me smile when one actually finished hunting that there were often a number who used to say, 'Three months of holiday now, what will you do with yourself?' The answer was, and is, that there was always enough going on to keep you busy. In fact in some ways the winter was more peaceful, because on at least four or five days a week, you knew exactly what was planned, and it was written in stone. The summers on the other hand were more sociable, and a classic example at the Bicester was the Hunt's Clay Pigeon Shooting Club. There were about ten or twelve evenings organised to take place at subscribers' houses up and down the country, when about 40, each evening, mostly farmers, would meet at around six pm to shoot individually for a cash prize, or a bottle or two of whisky. The Secretary, Diana Hodgson, Miles Gosling's sister ran the administration with a rod of iron. God help any poor individual who was brave enough to disagree with her! The other members would round on them, and they very soon learnt the error of their ways. At the end of June, if my memory serves me right, there would be a final shoot at Kirtlington hosted by Mr and Mrs Alan Budgett, when after a number of rounds the finalists were called forward to shoot for the Budgett Cup. Make no mistake about it, to win the Budgett Cup was a feather in anybody's cap. For a young master it was a golden opportunity to meet a large number of the farming and shooting community in the most congenial surroundings. I was lucky that I could shoot well enough not to disgrace myself, but not too well to threaten the Club favourites! It was also an enjoyable opportunity to meet the Budgett family. Alan owned the Kirtlington Estate in partnership with his racehorse trainer brother Arthur, who ran the racing side,

76

with Alan overseeing the farms and the Kirtlington Polo Club. Arthur and Alan had jointly owned a mare called Windmill Girl who had two foals by different sires. Both won the Derby, Morston and Blakeney, beat that! Mrs Budgett was wonderfully kind, but not to be trifled with, and the two Budgett daughters, a little younger than us, but not much, were in the future with their husbands, to play such a big part in our lives, and the fortunes of the Hunt; Heather as a great friend, future master and hound breeder, and Sally as my joint master, as well as being an enormously popular Field Master.

Another summer pastime also raised its head: needless to say, polo. I had bought Shandy and Lager out of the Regimental Pony Polo Fund, they had both been with me for some years, and now found themselves at Stratton Audley. Although both were getting on a bit they were still totally sound and it seemed rather stupid not to give them an outing at Kirtlington. Also as it happened, I was still in Her Majesty's pay until July and was merely on 'retirement leave' for a couple of months. Therefore I was still eligible to play in the Inter Regimental in England, the final match being held in June at Tidworth. Still stationed in the UK were Charlie Lockhart, Mike Cunningham and myself; not too bad a team. Anyway we won, and were then faced with having to play the BAOR winners for the United Services' Cup. The Blues had won in Germany and were a stronger team than us, Hugh Pitman, Andrew Parker Bowles, plus an old mate of mine from school called Nick Cooper, together with Brian Lockhart. Inter Regimental matches were always played without bringing into account the handicap system, and so we started off minus a goal or two that would normally have been our due. On the day, Hugh Pitman gave a large lunch party at his then house not far from Windsor, with just about every senior soldier in southern England and a strong contingent of retired polo players from both regiments, plus most of the Guards Polo Club officials, as that was the match venue for the occasion. It was a hot day summer's day and Pammie and myself, not wishing to leave them at home had taken all three lurchers. We let them out for a run in Hugh's garden and off they scampered, eventually coming back looking very pleased with themselves. We discovered why when Hugh threw open his dining room door, and announced, 'Lunch. Field Marshall, everyone, Rosemary has got some rather good beef'. The windows were open and the five large plates that had been piled high with beef were miraculously empty. Hugh was incandescent with rage and poor Rosemary was dispatched to the kitchen where she found some chicken and some tins of spam! We arrived at Smith's Lawn to be greeted by marquees, bands, bars and a large crowd who had come to see the Household Cavalry triumph. As the first ball was thrown in, I could not stop myself shouting 'Bloody good beef that Hugh!' A wild swipe and a clean miss and we were on our way. Every time it looked as though things were going in their favour, another mention of the beef ensured tempers were soon lost, team playing went out of the window, and we won! A fitting finale to my Regimental Polo! The dogs got another good supper when we arrived back at Stratton Audley, not beef as we thought they had probably had enough of that for one day. They had certainly won us the match. Another plus from my point of view was that as this last match was in August, I was signed on again, on some pretext for a further three months, the result being I was back once more on the Army payroll for a short time!

Early Days

All of that was marginally in the future, because when we arrived Kennel Cottage was not quite ready; the Hunt had organised that it should be painted properly for the first time in many years. Luckily Miles Gosling (as Captain Miles Gosling, he had hunted the hounds and been a master in the early and 1950s) came to our rescue, and fixed up for us to stay with his mother, Mrs Helen Combe, who lived in a Gosling house in the village. Helen was one of the sisters of a famous triumvirate of daughters of Lord Percy St. Maur and his wife the Hon Violet White who were christened Helen, Lettice and Lucia and all being quite powerful were soon known as Hell Let Loose! Helen, was completely wonderful, very kind, very funny and delightfully outspoken, and since she was only a two minute bicycle ride from the kennels I was able to be on time at 6:30 am on May 1st. I worked in the kennels every morning unless something else important cropped up, and did that all summer. The first job each morning was to wash down the yards which were not a pretty sight after a whole pack of hounds had spent the night there! As soon as we began to move the occupants of one of the lodges into the grass yard, and they said hello as they went past, I knew I had taken the right decision and felt perfectly at home. Bryan Pheasey made me laugh straight away the first morning by having a word with a new boy, whose first morning it also was, making sure it was within my hearing. "Rule One. Keep all doors and your mouth shut!" Very sound advice as there was a job to be done and no-one wanted a lot of prattle or stupid questions!

As soon as the yards were clean and the fresh straw had replaced the old, the hounds minus the hot bitches were all mixed together and we would all clamber on board the somewhat dilapidated kennel bicycles and off we would go round the lanes adjacent to Stratton Audley. Bryan and myself would go in front, with Johnny Kennelly bringing up the rear pushing on the stragglers. I went with Bryan in order to learn the ropes, and what he taught me then stuck with me for the rest of my hunting life. Although in time I was probably less regimented than Bryan. He would keep all the hounds closely up-together with us in front through the villages, and then would let them run on when we left the village, and close them up again when we entered another. He would shout at the culprits if they were getting too far in front when they were free, and pull them back if he thought they were in danger of getting out of control. Later on, when I was hunting them myself full time, if I had the staff as we entered a village, it was the second whipper-in's job to either cycle, or when we were on horses, to ride past us to get to the front of the pack and make sure that no hounds overtook him until we were clear the village. He would then drop back and let the hounds run on again. Likewise, if we encountered a car coming towards us, or indeed if one wanted to get past from behind, we would all pull up and put the entire pack over to the left-hand side of the road. The same would happen for a walker, although we would try to execute that movement without stopping, unless they had a dog with them in which case the operation would be rigorously enforced. This was not because the hounds were in danger of hunting another dog, but the puppies in particular were always very inquisitive, and a single dog was often pretty over awed by the sheer number of a pack of hounds. The word of command to get them onto the side of the road was simply 'Hold Over' probably with a whip held out and the lash hanging down to indicate they should not go over to the right hand side. This would have been drummed into them as puppies at a very early age, on foot and on hound exercise, when they would have been coupled up to an older hound who knew the word of command. The uninitiated might be rather surprised that a huntsman would call any dog that is not a hound, a cur dog. The word cur could sound detrimental, but in fact a dog could have won every field trial championship in the country, and have a pedigree a mile long, but in a huntsman's language he still a cur dog. I will deal with the question of the training of hounds in greater detail later on.

To continue with the mornings hound exercise, as soon as hounds returned to kennels in the summer, the dogs and bitches would be split up, and the two lots would then be fed. In the Bicester which was a fairly big dairy country in those days, there was nearly always plenty of flesh, so all the hounds were fed purely on raw meat. Bryan did not necessarily feed every day but would add a light meal for any that needed it, whereas later on at the Beaufort we fed every day, and of the two systems I am very much in favour of the latter.

There was one downside to the whole early morning procedure, as a newly arrived couple we were out to supper most evenings, and I have to admit I often arrived at the kennels at 6:30am with a shortage of sleep and a slight hangover. The effect of clearing up a sea of dog shit did sometimes have an adverse effect! I don't think I have ever so regularly lost the previous night's supper, but there you are!

As soon as we had finished with the hounds, I would leave Bryan and his team to deal with the flesh collection and skinning. It had always been traditional for the huntsman/kennel huntsman to have the skin money, some of which he gave to the second whipper-in if he had one. The kennelman had the fat money which sounds rather strange, but a diligent kennelman would cut off lumps of fat from the carcass and throw them into a bin which would go off to be rendered down into pure fat. Some of this I might add, would go into the cosmetics industry, and I used to have great fun when showing people round the kennels, to point out a stinking barrel of untreated fat and telling the ladies present that this is where their lipstick came from; it always raised a grimace or two! In fact the skin money and to a lesser degree the fat money greatly enhanced the wages of hunt staff who historically would only get agricultural wage, and would supplement that with their perks—in some hunt countries to a considerable tune.

After breakfast it was time to concentrate on other duties, the biggest to start with was to get to know the farmers. I probably was not as organised as some, as I used to just drive round and drop in. On wet days and in the evening there was probably a better chance of finding someone about. Nowadays, I believe that everybody uses a mobile telephone and books an appointment, but in those days most farmers just had one telephone, often hanging up on the wall in a draughty passage somewhere near the kitchen, and anyway it was the importance of personal contact that I was such a believer in. Nevertheless, getting round the farmers was an enjoyable and rewarding business and so many of them became great friends. It's amazing how times change. Then, if you visited quite a lot of farmers especially in the evening, you were ushered into the front parlour, and 'the Wife' would be sent off to find whisky, glasses, and water. You would discuss what ever needed discussing and then maybe 'the Wife' was allowed back to be properly introduced, and if she was lucky was also given a drink. Can you imagine that happening now? There would be war

The first summer was fairly hectic, which was something one had to get used to and certainly was never going to change. The Puppy Show and Hound Show season was also quite an eye-opener. I had never imagined that really quite knowledgeable and intelligent people could spend quite so long looking at hounds, or indeed just one hound, discussing its conformation, its head, its neck, its shoulders, back, hind legs, front legs, feet, movement at a trot and a gallop, and every other attribute you can think of. I have to admit it was not long before I joined the club!

Every master new or old is always slightly nervous about their Puppy Show, even more so for their first one. A happy and successful Puppy Show is to some degree an indication of a happy and successful Hunt. Our first Puppy Show was on the time honoured date of the first Wednesday in June. Bryan obviously had the hounds in good nick, and we had already had quite a number of evenings with guests, to help practice the young hounds. Bryan and myself had also put together a list of individual hounds and groups that we wanted to show people after tea. As judges, I had asked the 10th Duke of Beaufort ('Master') and Captain Ronnie Wallace, who was also a neighbouring master at the Heythrop. We were lucky as you could not get two more famous judges from anywhere in the country. A large tent had been erected just opposite the Kennel Cottage in the hound paddock, and Pammie surpassed herself by providing eggs drumkilbo, a concoction of lobster, prawns, tomatoes, and eggs etc for the starter, followed by some cold meat, for the lunch beforehand for about forty guests. Most puppy show lunches consist of the judges and their wives, together with a number of local adjacent masters, family and close friends and a few local landowners. The puppy walkers, plus some farmers and often a mass of other helpers are usually asked to the Tea and there would probably be prize-giving and speeches. Thank goodness, our first seemed to go all right, and everybody was very jolly after a drink in Bryan and Nora's house—another tradition long recognised up and down the country.

Shortly after this we started cub hunting, you were still allowed to call it that back in the 70s. Bryan Pheasey had the first morning as I was only going to hunt hounds part time. My own first morning I will never forget. We met at Sheepcote Hill on the Waddesdon Estate which belonged to the Rothschilds. The first covert I drew was a little tiny spinney adjacent to the larger wood. I arrived and shouted 'Leu in There,' and was so frightened that the hounds would just sit and look at me, I jumped off my horse, ran in and proceeded to draw every stinging nettle that was there very laboriously. We then adjourned to the bigger wood where hounds did hunt round rather nicely, but without catching anything. Still it was a start. My father and mother had come up. My father's only observation was, "Not too bad, horn blowing atrocious, but your voice is promising!"

The next time I was hunting hounds myself, my cousin Angela ('Tiddles') came to stay and we found her a horse. We drew the Bucknell Spinneys, one rather unadventurous cub went round and round, and after really quite a long time sat down in a nettle patch and duly paid the price. I was over the moon, but was rather disappointed that no one else seemed remotely interested. I then found out that as soon as I had caught my first fox, Tiddles had been bucked off and left for dead, and so as normal she was very much the centre of attention! I should not have been surprised as she has been doing that all her life!

When I was not hunting hounds I had to do field-mastering, which actually of course was a very good discipline. I have often thought that every aspiring amateur huntsman, as well as working in kennels for a spell, should also do a stint as a Field Master so that they have a good understanding of what that office entails. I also feel strongly that joint masters of a pack with a professional huntsman who have been given the

Ian & Pammie-Jane at Bicester Hunt Ball.

responsibility of overseeing the kennels, should at the very least spend a week or two working in kennels with the professional, so that they are conversant as to what the job entails.

During the course of that summer, we were obviously talking to a great number of the Bicester hunting fraternity and it is sad to relate that we were often regaled with tales of how the country became split into factions. It was an eye-opener to me that a normal pro-hunting community could fall out to such a degree. When we arrived we just tried to get on with everybody and pick the most capable individuals for any appointments regardless of which camp they were in. It amused me looking back, when I was told very firmly by some of the hierarchy that there were three individuals that I should beware of at all costs. One became Hunt Treasurer, another a prominent Field Master and the third, one of our greatest friends. A story that was often repeated was that at the Annual General Meeting in the village hall, it was completely packed with the two factions either side of the central aisle,

IWF on Harold—Bicester 1979

none of them speaking to one another. Apparently one very inebriated London subscriber rather dominated the meeting by shouting, 'All we want is sport' every time anybody said anything, until he was asked to leave by the Chairman, escorted out and the doors closed. At which point the windows round the hall would suddenly fly open, and the same face would reappear once again shouting, 'All we want is sport!' The Chairman had to take the rather unprecedented step of allocating £10 from Hunt funds entrusted to a sound committee member with the instructions to take said 'friend' down to the pub and finish him off! I was obviously not there as it was before my time, but I have always thought of that meeting as a yardstick—that a successful AGM is when only those making reports are present and preferably very few others!

That first summer at the Bicester was also memorable for the unfortunate fact that after six weeks or so, by which time we were in the Kennel Cottage, Pammie contracted glandular fever and retired home to Yorkshire to be looked after by her family, considerably better than by me! Luckily Liz Gosling and her housekeeper Audrey came to my rescue and used to come and tidy up the cottage, do some laundry and provide the occasional meal in the evening. Bryan Pheasey also insisted that I had breakfast every morning with him and Nora after hound exercise. Talk about falling on your feet! As that summer progressed it was a relief when a rejuvenated Pammie returned from Yorkshire, and we could start to plan the commencement of the start of the season. It was in fact Bryan's suggestion that since we were both hunting and therefore had two packs fit and in work, that we should hunt them both out on a Saturday, one in the north of the country and the other in the south and that we could alternate each week. It actually worked well and was the greatest fun. Bryan took the kennel horsebox and two horses, and Pammie and myself took the other pack, and a couple of horses all in two trailers. No jealousy, but maybe a little good-natured banter ensued when we got back to the kennels. There was no question in those days of a quick telephone call to see how the other others were faring, but all would be revealed when we got back to base. There was however a certain amount of one-upmanship in our own camp as to who knew more about the job of hunting hounds. Pammie had whipped in to her father for a number of years, and I was new to the game, so quite a lot of advice was forthcoming. Probably perfectly deserved, but nevertheless slightly disconcerting. I can remember early on coming to the conclusion that the sooner Mrs Farquhar was elevated to the role of a Field Master and I had a whipper-in who did not answer back, the better! Anyway we only had the two packs out on the same day during cub hunting and once we got going in the main Season Bryan whipped-in to me and was more than helpful.

On the whole our first Season went reasonably well, and the country appeared willing to forget the old petty disagreements and pull together. A number of other factors did strike me early on, one of the first being that I was very much a new boy when it came to the hounds. I could see that they were basically a well-behaved pack, and good in the field, and Bryan for his part hunted them extremely sympathetically. To my mind however they did just lack that bit of extra drive, as well as the accuracy that sets out a top pack from an adequate one. One pleasing realisation when it came down to it, was that hounds seemed to like me, and if hounds genuinely like and respect a huntsman, there is every chance of capitalising on that to mould a really effective team. In my view, hounds of every type have an inherent genetic trait that requires direction and trust, coupled with a sense of freedom. The Bicester hounds then had been bred on fairly orthodox post-war lines using the established type popular in those days—ie without using modern outcrosses.

Bicester Early Days of the Welsh Outcross and Sir Newton Rycroft

Another legacy that I inherited, was from former master and hunts-man Tony Younghusband and his ability to cross the country. By all accounts he was good, not just good, but unbeatable. He was one of those totally fearless horsemen that horses went for, regardless of their age or experience. He could cross the country just as effectively on a green four year-old as on a more experienced animal. For somebody like myself, who, remember had never seen a stride into a fence, follow-ing that was rather a tall order!

Times have a tendency to change and that first year at the Bicester was no exception. I expect few will have any recollection that 1974 saw one of the early mini recessions; the finances of most hunts are normally somewhat precarious and the Bicester was not alone in this. Jimmy Lane-Fox, Hunt Chairman, had always been on the ball in that direction, and I remember him suggesting that an outside injection of cash was needed. He asked if I had met Roy Strudwick who had just started hunting with us, and who was making a fortune with his property company Royco, building houses. I replied that I had in fact met Roy in rather amusing circumstances out hunting the previous season. I was hunting hounds when suddenly a loose horse had passed me going like the wind with its reins hanging down, and stirrup irons flapping, closely followed by another horse with a rider in the saddle and a passenger sitting behind riding pillion with his arms round the pilot. At that point an Irish voice rang out, 'Morning Master is it all right if we go on to catch that horse?' In the saddle was a character I was to get to know very well, Vince Kilkenny, and the pillion rider was none other than our man of property from London's East End, Roy Strudwick. Later, I asked them both back for a drink at the Kennel Cottage and straight away Roy said he would be delighted to help as he had come to the conclusion that going hunting was the best fun he had had for years, and he could not get enough of it. He became joint master on 1st May, 1974 and remained

Right: Vince Kilkenny

in office for the next four years. Great fun and a tremendous help financially which was a godsend when most of our neighbours were cutting back, and we were able to keep going full bore, increasing our subscription list with the obvious benefits all round.

Vince Kilkenny in the meantime became a legend, fearless and capable on a horse, a guinea a minute on foot or mounted, with a capacity for alcohol that was second to none. Brought up in Ireland, hence the horses, and with a history of the knuckle fighting in the pubs, Vincent arrived in London to work the 'on the lump' putting in fittings on building sites. The story goes, that one morning when Roy Strudwick's building empire was just taking off, he was rung to be told that he had better get down to one of his sites quickly as his foreman was lying in the bottom of a trench and every time he tried to get up a belligerent Irishman punched him again and put him back down. Strudwick would recount the story that he asked Kilkenny why he had it in for the foreman, and the answer came back that he was, 'An ignorant fokker who did not know his job!' Seeing that the foreman had not got a lot of work left in him for the rest of the day, Roy offered Vince the job. Vince replied that he would not take the job, but he would take a contract. As Royko expanded, so did Vince's side of the business, and he soon had over a hundred Irish lads working for him, so was full of money and therefore horses. He was a hard man across country, more so on himself than his mounts who all seemed to go brilliantly. It was not many years before I produced a system whereby I always took somebody with me to facilitate

Portman Kennels—Ikey Bell with my parents and a young IWF, 1952.

a speedy passage whilst hunting and that roll soon fell to Vince, resulting in quite a number of bizarre situations. One might have been given
an inkling of that when very early on one day, at Stratton Audley, a bit
of a party ensued at Kennel Cottage. Mrs Farquhar came into the sitting
room (the only room) saying, 'For Christ's sake go and sort out Vince,'
who was systematically beating the life out of one of our doors with his
bare fist. When asked what the hell he thought he was doing, he simply
replied, 'I've got to t'ump something, I like all you bastards in there!' It
was a little unorthodox at times, but goodness we had a lot of fun even
if it did make some of the Establishment raise their eyebrows at times!

To return to the hounds, at the beginning of the 1974-1975 season,
I was starting to look for a different magical potion to fire up the performance of what in fairness was already a perfectly workable pack. I
was largely taking advice from my father and also Ronnie Wallace, as
to what to use of the bloodlines current at the time, and continually
badgering my father regarding the success of his foray into the Welsh
outcross on the advice of Mr Ikey Bell and others pre-war. His answer

was quite simple, Yes, it could be time for another injection of Welsh blood, and undoubtedly the man to talk to was Sir Newton Rycroft Bt., Master of the New Forest. Sir Newton was a most intriguing man and soon became a great friend, and as far as I was concerned, my guru on Welsh blood. A Wykehamist, hence the analytical and brilliant brain, he certainly was not fearful of experimenting outside of the box. He had already made his name by breeding and hunting one of the best packs of beagles that have ever graced our shires, namely the Dummer in the Cotswolds, that he had started in 1939, and nurtured until 1963. Some would say that Newton could be a little eccentric, but he was passionate about nature and an authority on birds, as well as hounds. I have always loved the tale that during the Second World War, he was sent into Crete undercover to send back information as to the lie of the land prior to the invasion. However after the Allies had landed, he had thought his role superfluous, and so took himself off to the hills with a pair of binoculars and wearing an old pair of corduroys. When challenged, as to who the hell he was, and what was he doing up there he replied, 'Major Sir Newton Rycroft, British Intelligence, I'm looking for a sterna maxima'. This, being a type of tern, might have been lost on an American sergeant—and did not stave off his arrest for spying until his credentials could be checked. He was in fact mentioned in dispatches for special services in the Balkans, and later awarded the Order of the Phoenix by Greece. The first time I met him he had already gone a long way down the line of producing a new Welsh outcross in New Forest Medyg '69. Medyg was a well put together dog, possibly a little short in front, maybe lacking a good neck, but obviously exceptional in his work. That could be construed as just the opinion of his breeder, but there is one thing absolutely certain, Sir Newton was never ever persuaded by personal aggrandisement or the opinion of others. He was only interested in the improvement of the foxhound. Medyg was by Plas Machynlleth Miller '63, a pure Welsh dog that had been recommended to him by Harry Roberts, who had bred the Plas Machynlleth. Harry was as knowledgeable on the Welsh hound as anybody and very much listened to by Sir Newton as his informant on what was going on in the hound world in the Principality. Medyg's mother was a New Forest bitch called Traffic '65, who as it happened went back to Old Berkshire Playfair '60, bred by Major Bill Scott, Martin's father, and therefore was full of all the

Pammie-Jane on Arabella—Bicester 1974.

best Portman blood. 'Uncle' Bill and my father had been very much in cahoots on the Welsh bloodlines as well as for a while being joint masters. By the time I used Medyg at the Bicester in 1974, he was already being talked about, although it was not until 1976 that he was used at the Beaufort, producing amongst others Monmouth '77, who not only won his puppy show, but later went on to win Peterborough, which of course in some people's minds put him on the map. However, not wishing to tell tales out of school, I do recall being told that although 'Master' was delighted that he had used Medyg, he was not quite so sure at the time that he was in favour of rough coats. He was very much aware that there was still an aversion to 'wool' in the show ring and apparently Brian Gupwell was ordered to draft any puppies that looked if they were going to be hairy—the foibles of fashion!

To continue with the Rycroft influence, having decided to branch out and use Medyg, and also having spent quite a bit of time in the New Forest Kennels, I was very flattered that Newton suggested that we should join him for a visit to the Vale of Clettwr in Carmarthenshire on an exploratory mission to look for a follow-up to the Plas Machynlleth blood. This I might add was also the advice of Harry Roberts, who I did meet on a couple of occasions. He informed Newton that Trevor Jones, the master and huntsman of the Clettwr had bred a highly effective pack of Welsh hounds that were doing a good job with fox control in predominantly a sheep farming country. So towards the end of that summer, Newton accompanied by my father, Pammie and myself, set off for Wales with Dad driving. We were slightly held up when crossing the moor on the way to Pencader. Newton suddenly shouted, 'Stop' leaping out of the car, and disappeared. He had seen a red kite, fairly rare in those days and he was determined to get a closer look. We were late therefore to meet Trevor at Blaenpant to be taken to the kennels, which as it transpired were on an old isolated farm down a very rough track. The house was derelict, and hounds lived in a basic stone barn. It was surprisingly quiet when we arrived, the reason becoming apparent when Trevor discovered a hole in the back wall. The hounds had dug themselves out during the night, and we then could hear them hunting in the valley below! Trevor did not seem too perturbed, and started to blow his horn. Before long the majority were back, probably thinking it was time for some grub. After careful inspection we settled on one of the larger bitches, fairly rough coated and mainly white with one black blob on her flank, who as it happened had not gone hunting as she was in season, and was therefore kennelled in a different part of the barn. Trevor agreed with Newton that he would lend her for a year or two, and off we set back to West Kington with Fairy, as that was her name, in the back of Dad's car. 'Just remember the washing up liquid boyo'. On the way home Newton suddenly turned to me, and said he thought it would be a good idea if I took her back to the Bicester to try her out in a more galloping country than the New Forest; no thanks to me, but that is how I acquired Fairy who was to found her own dynasty in the foxhound world. On our return, as she was in season we put her overnight in one of Dad's garages. Her head was poking out of the bottom next morning where she had tried to chew her way out, luckily unsuccessfully. She was put to a Beaufort stallion hound, Gimcrack '70, and so it was that in the 1975 Bicester entry that there were two litters of a Welsh outcross, New Forest Medyg to a Bicester bitch, along with the Fairy litter. Out of interest, the other litters that year were by a College Valley dog, Bellman '70, two others by Beaufort dogs, together with two litters by Portman Pilot '71.

Sir Newton's philosophy on the theory of genetics when pairing two hounds together, which I might add he spent many hours enlarging on, was in fact little different from that pioneered by Ikey Bell, in conjunction with my father, plus Lord Coventry, Bill Scott, Gordon Foster and others before the Second World War. The theory was, and is in fact quite simple. On one hand, capitalise on the power of line breeding, and on the other utilise the benefits derived from new blood using an outcross. By line breeding we mean using the same blood lines on both sides of the pedigree i.e. both the male and the female in a number of subsequent generations, with the aim of generating a type that in itself produces consistency not only in conformation, but also in ability both athletically and mentally. When I say using the same blood in subsequent generations, this can be taken to quite a strong degree, and some pedigrees in the fifth and sixth generations can as an exception contain the same hound name up to eight or so times out of a total of thirty two or going back further to sixty four. This can be perfectly acceptable, with the underlying proviso that the lines you are using are sound in the first place. The extensive use of line breeding will undoubtedly increase the chances of bringing out the qualities that you are looking for, but in reverse can also multiply any underlying faults. Another generally accepted guideline in the use of line breeding, is that the same blood should not normally go closer than grandparent on one side, and great grand parent on another in any particular mating. To continue with the theory however, it is probably also generally accepted that too small a gene pool will eventually run out of steam, and thereby affect performance. This is where the use of the outcross comes in. It of course applies to humans as well! Again there are two main aims to bear in mind, when contemplating an outcross. Firstly that you are looking for a change of blood without losing quality, and secondly seeking a significant change in mental attitude to the job in question. With luck therefore you can achieve your aim with no loss of physical conformation whilst also stimulating the determination factor, drive, and scenting ability which hopefully is enhanced by what is known as hybrid vigour, which can be invaluable. One might wonder if the theory being relatively so simple, why the implementation can take so many hours of deep discussion. The answer being that the interpretation on the relative worth of anyone blood line that requires analysing is a matter of opinion, and therefore takes time. Hence the hours disciples of the foxhound spend discussing the pros and cons of particular lines can be considerable and Newton was no exception. I have a drawer full of letters from him, some pages long and some just a few lines, mostly on hounds, but occasionally on people. I once read that an individual who wrote letters starting with a steady hand, but then interspersed the writing with capitals and italics, different coloured pens, covering random parts of the page, showed signs of a brilliance bordering on insanity. Newton did all of this! However, he was enormously good company, and certainly a great benefit in the evolution of the modern day foxhound.

This might sound as if Newton was the only person worth listening to in those days; he was a breath of fresh air, but there were many others. Undoubtedly the most influential then was Captain Ronnie Wallace, who as Chairman of the Masters of Foxhounds Association, as well as being master and huntsman of the Heythrop, was at the top of his game. His knowledge and understanding of hound pedigrees was prodigious, although probably more as a consolidator rather than an innovator. He was always thoroughly in favour of looking outside of the box, but possibly not with the Welsh hound in mind. It was a shame in retrospect that he and Rycroft were at loggerheads as they both had a great deal to offer. Ronnie had got to the stage where he thought he was top dog, and did not like the fact that Newton had got a ball rolling that he, Ronnie, was not in control of—control being the operative word. Some of Newton's remarks in his letters about Ronnie were both vitriolic, and also at times funny, but nevertheless it was a shame as it therefore took some time for the Welsh outcross to reassert itself. This was an even bigger pity as the success of the Heythrop in particular was very much based on the Portman blood, which of course went straight back to Meynell Pageant '35 and the early Welsh outcrosses.

On the other hand, Ronnie was incredibly kind and supportive of me in those early Bicester years and indeed later, and having a few days with him in those first few seasons was extremely beneficial. He was an exceptional organiser, and without question a very good huntsman. I took on board two lessons, firstly never leave any stone unturned to discover where your fox has gone, and secondly if in doubt keep going forward in a quiet way. You might strike lucky, but few followers would ever know! As well as being a neighbour and a help with the hounds, he was in those days always looking ahead. He was the catalyst and fundraiser behind organising Dr David MacDonald, Head of Zoology at Oxford University to look into the effect of earth stopping on the badger. It was just after the League Against Cruel Sports began to argue in the national press that earth stopping had an adverse effect on the well-being of the badger population. Of course this was despite the fact that the badger numerically, although being sold as a delightful harmless nocturnal creature that could do no wrong, was getting out of control causing problems to the farming industry particularly over tuberculosis, as well as decimating bees and hedgehogs. For three years David MacDonald headed a scientific survey that was eventually peer reviewed. The groundwork for this was being carried out by a delightful recently qualified university zoology graduate called Ian Lindsay who lived in a bothy on our farm. I always greatly admired David MacDonald who would never be drawn as to whether he was pro or anti-hunting, but always just left it, that as a scientist he believed purely in evidence. I did have cause in time to call on that evidence when at the Beaufort, but we will deal with that later.

Another farsighted move that Ronnie instigated was to ask Edmund Vestey to carry out a detailed report on the machinations as to how each sporting body operated; all forms of hunting with dogs, the shooting organisations, as well as all the fishing disciplines. I was asked to sit on it as the MFHA representative, and I must say it was most enlightening. I remember for instance, the different attitudes taken by the three fishing groups, the coarse fishers, the deep sea anglers, and the Salmon and Trout Association, and being surprised that already the thinking of some was tainted by old prejudices. One of my most vivid memories was sitting in Fishmongers' Hall with the life size portrait by Annigoni of Her Majesty the Queen looking down on us.

After really quite a lot of detailed work our recommendations were that it was time to split the responsibility of the various hunting organisations, leaving the internal running of hunting to the MFHA on one hand, and setting up a press and political wing running alongside, but separate from the MFHA on the other. The report was probably before its time as far as the hierarchy was concerned. Ronnie Wallace made a point of coming to see me to talk about the Paper, and sitting in the bay window looking down our mill stream at Twyford said, 'I don't think we need to alter things at the moment, we can still control the situation in the corridors of power'. The report was side-lined. In this of course he was right as they did control the situation for the next twenty or so years although of course we eventually lost. I personally have always felt that this was partially due to allowing our enemies time to get ahead in the Press battle.

Bicester Fairy and Farmer

We were now progressing with our new Welsh blood at the Bicester. The Medyg line was steadily proving its worth with an outstanding litter from the 1975 entry, Medley and her siblings plus another very good family in the 1976 entry, by Medyg out of Salary '72, who as it happened was by Whaddon Chase Grimston '61 whose name will appear again shortly. Fairy produced a small litter from her liaison on the way back from Wales with Beaufort Gimcrack '70 (one son Fairfax later becoming a useful stallion hound) she subsequently had made her mark in the field. Bloody-minded in kennels, at times a little argumentative with her colleagues, she was nothing other than lethal with the kennel staff who were firmly bitten if it was ever suggested that she could not be on the list of those that were drawn to go hunting, a trait I might add that she passed on to a number of her descendants. In the field she displayed all the characteristics that we were after. She had a good nose, that was to be expected, and the ability that not all smaller Welsh hounds have physically, to withstand long days in a galloping environment (hark back to Newton's comment, 'Take her to the Bicester and see how she fares in a galloping country'). Above all she had the accuracy, and the determination not to give up trying, but just to keep bloody well working out where that 'bloomin varmint' had gone! She would turn short with her fox rather than rather than fly on, and again and again in those early days you could see the main body with a bit of a head-on over run. When a fox turned short through a hedgerow, Fairy would just pause and dart through, regardless of what anybody else was up to. She got the thumbs up as far as I was concerned, and the arrangement seemed reciprocal.

Fairy then nearly suffered a catastrophe. One day we had been hunting in the much favoured Bicester Thursday country, grass and big hedges, and believe me some of them were big, when on our way to box up after a fairly high octane day, Bryan announced that we were one short and that it was Fairy. We boxed up the others, blew for a time, but no sign of her, and went back to the kennels; sometimes telephone calls would come through with a bit of information, but nothing. After a bite of tea, now pitch dark, Pammie, Bryan and myself went back to Wotton Underwood to a covert called Rushbeds which had a railway line running through it; not a mainline but still used, which we had clipped the edges of just before we had finished. We parked on the bridge, left Pammie in the car as liaison, and armed with torches we entered the covert, Bryan going east down the line, and I went west. Anybody who has been on a railway line in the dark when a train at whatever speed comes through knows that it is a fairly awesome occurrence. So it was with a mixture of relief and foreboding, that further down the track I heard a whimpering and saw a little white bundle beside the line, Fairy. She had been incredibly lucky, a train had hit her on the side of her head and had removed a part of one ear and left a nasty gash on her neck. She had obviously been concussed and had bled quite a bit, but miraculously had escaped any other serious injury. Bryan who had drawn a blank going the other way had joined me and together we carried her back to the car. She was wrapped in a blanket, placed on Pammie's lap and taken back to Kennel Cottage. Bryan cleaned the wound, gave her some painkillers and a rather the worst for wear foxhound was left on another clean blanket in front of the Rayburn. As is so often the case, I can still see the trust in her eyes to this day. She had obviously had quite a smack, but just lying in the warm for ten days or so, and eating sparingly she began improving and made a full recovery except for a slightly wonky head carriage and a re-arranged ear. She was soon back hunting and maybe the rest had done her good, as she came into season and this time we put her to one of our own dogs, Bicester Freshman '73, a smaller, but beautifully balanced dog that both Bryan and myself rated—his grandsire was once again Whaddon Chase Grimston '61. Without harking back too much to the importance of line breeding, coupled with the input of

Brian Fanshawe and Farmer '76

the outcross, Grimston had in my view the best genes possible coursing through his veins. Portman Wizard '65 and Portman Grossman '52 on his dam's side and the best of the Beaufort through Garter '55, also full of the cream of that era, Four Burrow, Whaddon, and even a touch of Carlow. It is not entirely surprising therefore that the Freshman/Fairy litter produced one of the most spectacular hounds I was ever lucky enough to be associated with, Bicester Farmer '76. Maybe that proves the point of the importance of both well thought out line breeding with the careful planning of the right outcross.

Farmer's progress through life was not without its initial hiccup. So keen was I to pass on the Fairy bloodline that I gave him as a whelp to my brother-in-law Neil Ewart who was married to Sammie's sister Sally. Neil was hunting the Derwent, the pack that my father-in-law Charles Chafer had supported and run for three decades. Farmer was walked at Elleron where food and freedom were in plentiful supply, which of course is all a puppy needs, plus a little company and love, both of which he had. It was not his fault that he had been originally christened Farquhar, and

97

Charles Chafer & Mum (Lady Farquhar) IWF & PJF Wedding 1972

he was far too busy hunting the Elleron woods by night and sleeping in his favourite rosebed by day, (a thorn between two roses) and no need to worry about anything so trivial as a name. Fate as always came to play its part. Neil gave up the Derwent prior to moving to the Radnor, leaving Farquhar in Yorkshire where he was going to be hunted by Colonel the Hon Nick Crossley, a splendid chap and a great friend, but who I knew was not fond of Welsh hounds. Farquhar came back to the Bicester still a puppy and was renamed Farmer. I was not going to have a hound called Farquhar as can you imagine the licence for a whipper-in shouting, "Farquhar you bloody idiot!" As I have said, he was brilliant and was a lynchpin to the Fairy dynasty.

Harking back to start of the 75/76 season, again it was an exciting time as not only were the hounds shaping up, but we had a new terrierman in the guise of local farmer, Frank Tutt. Our professional terrierman, and his wife Anne who had been stud groom, had moved back to Wales; Anne is still always on the gate of Builth Wells Hound Show. Frank had a small farm near Gawcot not far from the kennels, and

IWF with Frank Tutt, terrier man

being semi-retired offered his services as terrierman free if we helped out with some petrol. Frank was a totally delightful character and a true countrymen, and understood the ways of foxes. In some ways he was also a very private individual, minded his own business and expected others to do likewise. In the seven or so years he did terrierman for me, I never once had a clue what he was up to! He loved hunting and had a great respect for the animal fox, and although he accepted that they needed controlling, he had at one stage been a successful sheep farmer, he would never condone anything he felt was underhand. He never had a bath, washed in clear water, and would take Pammie in his old Land Rover, both when she was expecting, and then with the children when they were very young. He was as mindful of them as if they were his own. Frank brought home to me the importance of a good terrierman, who was at one with the fox population and to the sport. He was very much his own man, and I remember going to see if I could find him one Monday in the summer, to be informed by his wife that he was not at home, and that she didn't know quite where he was. He had left the house on the previous Friday saying that he was going out to get some fish. He returned home the following Friday with a van full of the fish he had caught off the south coast—"I told you I was going to get some fish and here they are!"

That year we bought Twyford Mill, just upstream from the village of Twyford. It was an idyllic situation surrounded by the mill sluice and the adjoining leet. The old millers living quarters were reasonably intact, but the mill itself had not being touched, so fairly extensive work was required. The millstream ran under the newly renovated sitting room which was stunning, until one winter in a flood the water built up against the back of the house and proceeded to force its way through the wall. A barrier of railway sleepers carefully placed did negate the problem, but the sound of sizzling from the fire, and the sight of jets of water coming from electricity sockets either side of the mantelpiece was alarming, let alone the four inches of water over the new carpet. I have felt sorry for those suffering flood damage ever since.

In 1976 we also purchased Manor Farm, Hillesden about a mile away, a slightly rundown dairy farm of about four hundred acres, with a view to start milking in the autumn. Alec Bond who had been largely instrumental in us going to the Bicester in the first place had sadly broken his back in a point-to-point the spring before we arrived. He was my saving-grace farming wise, and nursed me through the planning stages, together with guidance regarding all the problems thrown up with starting a farm business. I was also lucky in that first summer, as a neighbouring farmer and friend, David Jeffries advised me on the buying of cows and indeed it was a mate of his, Richard Smith who came on board as farm foreman—he quite simply was a legend and could turn his hand to anything.

As I'm sure anybody about then will remember, 1976 was the hottest summer on record. The sun was relentless, the grass turned brown and crops withered. Because we were just preparing to start milking and therefore still buying down-calvers, we did have a little bit of grass to fill up a vile contraption called a Ricco Tower—a silo used for storing grass. It jammed permanently.

That summer, being light on capital and short of machinery we made literally thousands of small bales of hay with a flat eight system and escalator plus using pitchforks in the searing heat. I will confess I never ever wanted to see another bale of hay again, but at least I was reasonably fit by the end of summer. I will also never forget the sight that year of sheep and cattle literally roaming down the roads and across the countryside just to try and find something to eat. Shortly after an indifferent harvest, which I might add was completely finished well before the end of July, I took hounds to a Pony Club rally, and said that we would draw a nearby covert because it was clear of corn; not a hound spoke so we did not start hunting again until the end of August. I well recall the day that September, hacking up the road at Marston St Lawrence after a meet with John Sumner early in the morning when it started to rain, I took my hat off to savour the drops and turned round to the followers saying, 'Thank God for that!'

On the hound front, at that time there were of course other packs and breeders that had been in the ascendancy other than just the Beaufort, Heythrop and then the New Forest; for instance the Eridge through the influence of Major Bob Field-Marsham were another orthodox option, and as already mentioned the College Valley for those seeking a Fell input; a favoured choice of theirs at that time was probably through their Bellman '70 who was possibly slightly more substantial than some of his kind, but had the quality the pack was so famous for. Their founder Sir Alfred Goodson had great foresight when it came to accounting for a fox in that tough mountainous terrain and indeed, he had only started the pack in the first place to convince the local sheep farmers that this was a more effective way to control the fox than just through the trap, the snare, or the gun. His successor, Martin Letts, who had married into the family was also of that opinion and kept the concept going, therefore the skill of their hounds was very much tied to their ability to move well. I personally always thought that Martin had as good an eye for quality in a hound as anybody in the country.

Also, at that time I went back to the Meynell blood in Latimer '73, and then a slightly new strain from the Tynedale through their Linkboy '72. In that 1977 entry we also had a number of 'woolies' by Fairy's brother, Falcon '73 who did just show a slight inclination for independence! This might have fostered one of Bryan's better remarks when one afternoon at Doddershall. He had been absent for some time, and on his return in reply to my, "Where the hell have you been Bryan?" Came the response "Getting your bloody sheep dogs out of Finemere Wood!"

As regards the broader picture 1978 was a time of change; Roy

Strudwick decided that farming in Buckinghamshire was not exactly what he had imagined it to be and left for Ireland and the Kilkenny. So, after a period of intensive frost that year it was decided that I would be joined in the mastership by Clive Preston and resulted in his taking on the job of Saturday Field Master. His family had long been associated with the hunt. Sally Nicholson, as aforementioned a Budgett sister, also became a joint master and took on field mastering in her area. She grew more capable as every day progressed and what farmer could but melt when faced with her charm. Her husband Jamie also made his name by joining in the fray mounted on a singular minded conveyance that elected not to like narrow hunt jumps with poached ground, and therefore would just pull out and jump three strands of wire instead! Our team was augmented by Rosemary Barlow who filled a vital role as fundraiser and entertainments officer, a role she has subsequently done so brilliantly for the Horse Trials Support Group and British Eventing.

Another factor at the time that was creeping into my thinking regarding hounds and their breeding, was the arrival at the North Cotswold of my cousin Captain Brian Fanshawe, son of my father's youngest sister Aunt Ruth who had been married to Brian's father, Dick, another capable horseman and huntsman. Brian, following an eminent career as a cavalry soldier 9th/12th Lancers and as a highly regarded amateur rider both in point-to-points and under rules, had also been a popular master and huntsman in Warwickshire before moving to the Galway Blazers in Ireland. They still talk to this day of the sport that Brian, backed by his wife Libby produced. Pammie and I had a day with him in that amazing grass and wall country. In my mind's eye I can still see (it was even before glasses or contact lenses!) the fox jumping a wall about half a mile in front of us, then hounds and then Fanshawe—as one Irishman put it, "All knees and nose"—and then all of us ...magic. A good day's hunting was capped off by a visit to Murphy's Bar, a famous watering hole overlooking Galway Bay after a 'settler' of a bottle or two of port, donated by an old school friend who went by the name of Petersham who we had stayed with the night before. The port was christened by Fanshawe 'Portersham's Pete', and this was the prelude to a lot of Guinness and rather too many oysters. Two other factors made the night memorable. Murphy himself had died the night before and was dressed in his best clothes accepting condolences whilst propped up in a high-backed chair upstairs in the bedroom. "Good man yerself!" So down the hatch went another libation, followed as well by the fact that Pammie had eaten one bad oyster and was not at all well. To this day the sniff of an oyster and you say goodbye to Mrs Farquhar for at least twenty-four hours!

During his time in Ireland Brian rekindled his friendship with one of life's great legends Captain Evan Williams. A Welshman, with a name like Williams what else, Evan had made his name as a jockey aged 24 by winning the Grand National in 1937 on a horse called Royal Mail. After moving to Ireland, he trained both on the Flat and over fences before hunting the Tipperary Foxhounds from 1953 to 1971; it probably helped that his delightful wife Jill had inherited a little backing from America so together they set up what became a very hospitable, by then 'Irish style' household at Knockaney. He was great friend of my father's, and very much in the post-war camp with others regarding hound breeding. He also had the racing link with Fanshawe and back in Brian's Warwickshire days Evan had persuaded Brian to go for the Carlow 'ST' line through Carlow Stylish '63 that he, Evan, had given to George Fairbairn at the Tynedale (Stamina '73). That bloodline then later re-emerged through North Cotswold Stanway '76 but more of that to follow.

I make no apologies for banging on about these pedigrees, as in fact they are what makes the foxhound so exceptional today. The Carlow blood was, and is, highly prized, the Carlow then in effect being a private pack owned by the redoubtable Mrs Hall (sadly the pack was disbanded on her death). She was known simply as 'the Missus'. She was a regular visitor to Badminton especially during the Horse Trials, where her generous form always liberally clad in tweed was often photographed in the company of HM the Queen.

Fanshawe had many amusing tales of his time in Ireland and one in particular has always tickled my rather perverse sense of humour. Leaving the Irish Foxhound Association Hound Show either at Clonmel or maybe more recently at Stradbally, and accompanied by other hound grandees, the boot of the hatch back filled with just about every piece of silver from the day open to inspection, they were pulled over by a Garda sergeant checking to seek whether they had been on a heist or not.

"And now would you gentlemen be telling me where you had been?"

"A dog show."

"A dog show, is it? Well tell me your names before I be checking your papers, and your name Sir?"

"Waterford."

"Waterford is it right, and you Sir?"

"Kildare."

"Kildare is it now?" And then yours Sir?"

"Tyrone."

Finally, to Fanshawe; "And I suppose you'll be telling me you are the Mayor of Dublin!!"

"No just Master of the Galway!"

Having ascertained they were all actually who they said they were, he apparently saluted, muttering,

"I think I am out of my depth here and you'd best be on your way!!"

March 6th 1977 heralded another important moment in our lives, when our eldest daughter Emma Elizabeth was born at the Radcliffe in Oxford. This was a considerable blessing, as only a year before, in the middle of the night I had made a worried call to our wise, local hunting doctor and friend Richard Stephenson, which resulted in an emergency dash to the same hospital and an operation in the early hours for an ectopic pregnancy performed by Douglas Ellis, at the time one of the best gynaecologists in the land, who had left a top job in London for Oxford in order to also go hunting!

Maybe that was a sign that the Gods were smiling. Twyford Mill stayed dry, the cows started to milk well, and slowly but surely the hounds seemed to thrive and undoubtedly we appeared to be entering a period of really quite exceptional sport.

The Bicester country generally seemed to be very much on side; farming was doing well, the EEC wheat bonanza, which sadly meant the death knell for many small family grass farms right the way through the Midlands, at that time was putting a smile on the faces of most of the arable guys. The Milk Marketing Board who thank goodness were still in control, ensured that dairy farming paid, and were even expanding the cheese industry. Sheep were in demand and even the beef market was thriving. On the field mastering front, as well as the changes already mentioned, Arthur Illsley, who ran a horse yard and a small farm at Quainton, stepped up to the mark to take on the demanding task of

Thursday Field Master. Thursdays in the Bicester by then had acquired a certain reputation—still a lot of grass, big hedges mostly with a ditch and some wire, but crossable—together with a very forward going crowd who seemed to take great delight in trying to outdo each other. Arthur was more than up for all of this, and he soon made a name for himself. Tony Meyrick, another farmer and passionate foxhunter field mastered most Tuesdays, plus other days if the need arose. In retrospect he probably lived too close to the kennels. It was on my way home after hunting, and for some inexplicable reason my car seemed just to take over and turn left up his drive resulting in a dangerous combination of a bottle of whisky and a complete obsession on both our parts to tease out and put to bed as to why we ever lost a fox. The surprising thing being of course, that whereas we caught quite a few, marked some to ground, and on occasion had to stop hounds because of farming patterns—lambing maybe, or urbanisation—we got to the stage where we actually lost very few foxes. At the time it always surprised me how often, when asking some other huntsman what had happened they would just shrug and say they had run out of smell. Wouldn't have suited our bill!

Tony was a useful horseman, we had played polo together in earlier days and I was stupid enough one day to tell him his farm was a shambles and difficult to cross. The reply, "Bring your lurchers over and a horse and we will ride round." A hare and ten fences later, I had to admit, OK not so bad after all. Tony was without doubt one of the best fieldmasters and a good friend to us. One day before I left the Bicester, he was being driven home from Stoneleigh by his grain merchant, when they had a bad head on accident. He was taken to Warwick Hospital where he lay unconscious for some months, on every life support machine going, jaundiced and critically ill. I remember being asked to visit him together with his son Tim, when we were told he was being moved to the Radcliffe, but that he might not make the journey. His wife Carole of course just remarked, "He will, he always does." He did survive, but even the Radcliffe could not bring him round initially; I was even asked to go into the intensive care unit which unfortunately I already knew rather too well, and blow the horn in his ear to try to trigger some reaction, rather bizarre. Maybe not because of the horn, but he did eventually regain consciousness and a few years later he was back on a horse and hunting with me at the Beaufort.

Still on the subject of fieldmasters, another change transpired about that time in the northern part of the country. Peter Houghton Brown had a fall, and when I asked him if he was okay he replied, "No, I've just taken two decisions. I will never ride this horse again, and I will never do fieldmaster again." He stayed true to his word. The result being that Mrs Farquhar stepped into the breach and took over his patch.

With the farm in good nick, the kennel staff as professional a team as you could wish for, a dedicated terrier man, a stable full of quite frankly some pretty top-class horses, and the new batch of puppies some augmented by the Welsh outcross, beginning to really shine, it was perhaps not surprising to enter what I can only describe as an exceptional era that I was lucky enough to be part of, great fun and enormously rewarding.

As a hound breeder I had maybe ventured outside of the box, but now turned my attention to the conduct of a day's hunting. The accepted format in those days quite simply, was that whippers-in were considered useful at pushing hounds up when trotting about and assisting with riot. I could never understand the logic of when in a covert or at any other crucial stage of a hunt, as a huntsman if you had not got a whipper-in with you, that when hounds for instance split or were misbehaving, by the time you had to call for help it was often too late. If you had your man standing with you it was a case of: "I'll stay with these; you stop the others." Job done. I think I proved this in spades later at the Beaufort especially with my then whipper-in Paul Hardwick.

If you haven't got a resident whipper-in then use somebody else but the role is better done by somebody who knows the hounds well. However, an enthusiastic amateur can be of enormous benefit. In that role at the Bicester two individuals in particular come to mind. One being James Delahooke. Probably one of the best bloodstock agents and buyers of yearlings in the country he was also very well mounted. He had cottoned on to the role and tempo of a hunt and knew what it was all about. Another factor that soon struck home was the importance of information. It was fine for a huntsman to have helpers with him at close quarters, but the ability of a knowledgeable rider who sank the wind and who only appeared with news of a sighting was invaluable. By then I also had the assistance of Ben Burton whose father farmed a considerable acreage at Wormleighton on the Spencer Estate. Ben subsequently hunted the East Dulverton before taking over as master and huntsman of the Zctland in the nineties. At the time he was working on the farm and therefore was able to go hunting every day that he could. At the meet I used to tell him the vague draw, and point out that I did not want to see him until he knew something useful. It was often an hour or more and then he would suddenly materialise with a hat up on the skyline perhaps a mile or more away and you were back on again. I was always intrigued, but generally speaking most foxes having done maybe a circuit of their home patch would then make themselves scarce, but nearly always downwind. This I have always assumed is because being hunters themselves, they know that the hunter finds it easier to pursue the hunted with its scent coming back at him on the wind, rather than the scent being blown away from him down the wind.

Amusingly, I recall as a boy my father always being very conscious of the wind and it was a bit of a family joke when an aspiring keen young amateur huntsman had once asked my mother, "Does Sir Peter always carry a handkerchief in order to know the direction of the wind?" My mother replied "No it's just to wipe the drip off the end of his nose!"

Returning to the 1979/80 season the hounds were flying. My father had always indoctrinated in me that when reporting or talking about a hunt, whereas hounds might run for some distance in a circular way, that there was no such thing as a point of under five miles. It was fairly exceptional that in the 1979/80 season therefore to score just over twenty five points of over five miles, four of over six miles, and three of over seven. Sadly no one was keeping an exact record at the time. From memory however, one or two days do stand out. Meeting at Marston St Lawrence with a touch of frost coming out of the ground and therefore a tricky scent, hounds scored a slow five mile point into the Grafton country past Halse and beyond. Returning to Cockley Brake they ran somewhat faster before finishing up at Whistley Wood, about the same distance. Hacking back and changing horses, the last hunt from Warden Hill now took us at a fast pace for six and a half miles nearly to Everdon not far from the home of Captain and Mrs Dick Hawkins, then joint masters of the Grafton, who joined us on foot as we were boxing up, inquiring as to what the hell we were doing spending the entire day in their country! Not a bad day's hunting!

That season continued apace. Brought up reading and occasionally listening to tales about some of the great huntsmen pre and post the

Second World War, I understood that the highest accolade any hound could achieve was that he or she was 'non-change'. By that of course, I mean that once they had locked onto a particular fox or come to that any other type of quarry, that whatever happened they would not deviate, and come hell or high water would stay true to that line, a tall order at any time and increasingly so, as other distractions crept in. Over the years I did have a number of hounds who were pretty dependable, but I think to be honest I only ever had one that genuinely would not change, and that was Bicester Farmer '76. I will relate just one incident. Early on that year we had a day at Otmoor, when finding in Shabbington Wood, our pilot left and ran to Whitecross Green, a long thin wood, around hundred acres to the east of the moor, in fact a wild boggy area that had been used as a bombing training ground during the war. Hounds were running well and up together. As we approached the wood a fresh fox jumped up from a patch of tussocks just in front of the pack. Well, off they went and why not, except for one, Farmer, who just stood there and watched them go, looked round and then put his head down, "Woof Woof" and continued to hunt the fox he had started out with. Around the wood they went, seventeen couple in full cry, and Farmer with his very notable deep voice all by himself. They passed yards apart twice at the top end of the wood, and I said to Tony Pilgrim the whipper-in, "You stick with Farmer and let me know what he gets up to." Fifteen minutes or so later he came galloping back to inform me that Farmer had just left the bottom corner and was going towards Murcot. We collected the main body of the pack and put them on behind Farmer. They caught their fox a mile or so further on, not a word of a lie.

By then we were having regular swap days with Brian Fanshawe and the North Cotswold; that year he lent me North Cotswold Stanway '76, and I still think that both Stanway and Farmer were as good a pair of dogs you could ever wish to come across.

It was a memorable season in other ways as Mrs Farquhar was back in the van with Frank Tutt, and Victoria was born on Sunday 30th December at the Radcliffe. Pammie, somewhat miffed that she had missed out on a fairly high octane season was soon back on a horse in early March; we met at the Nut Tree, for a day from Murcot once again, intending to have a steady woodland day with just a few followers. We unboxed with Keith and Diane Haynes and were trotting to the meet when my horse Snoopy,

IWF riding Snoopy with the Bicester—Muswell Hill, 1980.

a brilliant ex-Grade A showjumper who was legendary, went lame. He had come from a friend of Bryan Pheasey's who kept showjumpers and who liked to farm them out as hunters at the end of their careers. As it happened, Bryan that day was riding another of his called Xerox, also ex-Grade A and real quality. Pammie was on a cob of hers, Grey Sombrero who took some handling, but who could jump. Rather unkindly, but with not much option I got onto Xerox and told Bryan to take Snoopy back to the kennels and then re-join us in the wood. The terrier boys had bolted a fox from the stick pile at the back of the pub; an hour and a half later we stopped the hounds just inside the Heythrop country by the main railway line at Enslow, a seven and a half mile point. Not a bad baptism of fire for Mrs F! After a long hack back, Bryan rejoined us and Pammie retired. Bryan and myself then drew across Otmoor and the hounds picked up a line and yet again after an hour and a bit we stopped them by the crematorium on the outskirts of Oxford. A seven and a half mile point, and a five and a half mile point, and only two foxes hunted that day.

The sport had been so good that year that a consortium banded together and decided that this needed to be chronicled. The ringleaders, John Howard Jones and Chubb Castle with Heather Tyler acting as illustrator and advisor started the Bicester Hunt News. This would correlate and record each day's hunting, and other notable happenings for the Hun, and continued for the next five years.

On a personal front we were incredibly lucky to be invited by Queen Elizabeth, the Queen Mother to stay each year at the Castle of Mey for a week around the 12th of August. On the shooting front we walked quite a long way behind the team of setters with Cameron the keeper, a totally charming man who was ably assisted by a rather diminutive chap known as 'the Gnome' who occasionally would overtake the shooting party like a Roman Charioteer whilst being dragged by two over enthusiastic setters determined to join in the proceedings. The party at the Castle tended to stay much the same from year to year; the Household, then consisting of Lieutenant-Colonel Sir Martin Gilliat, Private Secretary, and Ruth, Lady Fermoy, Lady in Waiting, both brilliant company. Sir Martin, an ex Royal Green Jacket and former Colditz prisoner of war was gloriously outspoken, very much a bachelor, a passionate racing man and a member of the Jockey Club. He was quite a punter in small degrees, not only with racing, but also the theatre and often backed new plays and other ventures. From the Equerry's Office the deadpan voice of an automatic horse racing results machine could usually be heard. We were all amused by the fact that as a member of the Jockey Club, Martin was banned from having a wager, but kept a well used account in the name of his housekeeper, Mrs Haggard!

Ruth Fermoy, was totally delightful, I think in a different life she could have been an international pianist in her own right. She later became well-known as the grandmother of Diana, Princess of Wales. Another regular guest amongst others was Air Vice-Marshal Sir Edward Fielden, his nickname was 'Mouse' perhaps because of his whiskery moustache; he could often be seen marching about with a twelve bore looking for something, to coin his phrase, "Give it a whiff!" Mouse had commanded the Queens Flight and in fact had earlier flown Edward VIII out of the country when he abdicated. Of the younger generation and one of the favourites, was Ashe Wyndham, charm personified, ex Irish Guards and a former equerry. I have to admit he rather annoyingly shot and certainly fished rather better than me! He was also best mate to Queen Elizabeth's nephew, Mikey Glamis, later Earl of Strathmore—they had been contemporaries at Eton.

A regular occurrence was the arrival of the Royal Yacht Britannia at Scrabster Harbour during Her Majesty the Queen's annual family holiday around the Western Isles. Lunch at Mey on those occasions was always a rather daunting prospect as I was often seated next to the Monarch who I might add, was as ever completely charming. She obviously realised I knew very little about anything, and seemed more than happy to talk about hunting and the genetics of the foxhound, genetics I suppose being a subject that as far as the racehorse is concerned was of course something that she really did know about! In the evening we would all be asked back to the Yacht for a quick drink. The 'Yachtsmen', as they were proud to be known, wore plimsolls in order not to have the sound of stamping feet interfering with the tranquility of Her Majesty's domain. Then, it was a mad dash back to the Castle of Mey to watch Britannia go through the Pentland Firth, with the local coastguards using up most of their annual supply of rockets and Shamooli flares from the beach at Mey in answer to the red, white and blue illuminations from the Royal Yacht and her escorting frigate.

We were very fortunate, as we normally flew to Mey in the Chafer Company single engined, four seater plane, usually piloted by a great friend of Charles Chafer's, Colin Campbell, a former WWII fighter pilot. The initial pre-landing approach at Castletown was just to clear the sheep from the runway before making the second approach. Colin always lunched at Mey when he returned to pick us up, and would sit next to Queen Elizabeth who thought he was delightful. Moving on in that vein, it came as a complete surprise when we were asked to stay at Windsor for Royal Ascot despite the fact that we were not very smart and knew nothing about racing!

We did go riding with Her Majesty down the famous Ascot course before racing, but to me the most unforgettable moment was when the Queen said to Pammie, "Would you like to come to see my litter of dorgi puppies?" (Corgi x dachshund.)

"As it happens I have this one little boy who is looking for a home?"
"Your Majesty, how delightful."

So we returned to Twyford Mill with a rather elongated brown person,

HM the King (then Prince of Wales) out with the Beaufort Hunt. (J. Minoprio)

he had a very curly tail, a definite attitude and for some extraordinary reason went by the name of Paddington. In fact he was really quite nice, and when people exclaimed, "What the hell is that!" We were able to say, "Actually he was given to us by the Queen ..."

"Isn't he charming!"

Even the biggest of the lurchers kowtowed, and the hound puppies certainly saluted and stood to attention. For some extraordinary reason we were asked back again in 1998, and I recall being given a very memorable after dinner tour conducted by the Queen and Duke of Edinburgh around the Castle, that had been recently renovated following the disastrous fire in 1992. A pre-breakfast ride also comes to mind, to catch up with Stud Groom Tony Barrett at his cottage in Windsor Great Park. Tony was one of the Badminton Barretts and as boys we would play darts and drink beer together in the King Billy pub at Nettleton.

Continuing with Royal memories, back at the Bicester we considered ourselves honoured, when asked by the Crown Equerry Sir John Miller, if we could organise a day for the then, fairly new to hunting, Prince of Wales. We met at Caulcott, not a fashionable meet and unboxed at Chetwode Manor with the Cubitts, before we then ventured off into the cream of the Bicester country—Marsh Gibbon. We had quite a

Above: Hickstead 1979: Michael Clayton and IWF on Jackie.

reasonable day, the Prince, unlike his sister the Princess Royal, who was an internationally renowned eventing rider, had tended to remain on the flat, usually on a polo pony, but being totally brave he joined in the fray and took three horrible falls that day.

Looking back to the early 1980's, the Bicester Hunt News took the place of the diary that was never written. It is salutary to read the number of really rather spectacular hunts that were scored on a surprisingly regular basis; for instance, from the 13th of December to the 27th of December, out of eight days' hunting, hounds scored five, five-mile points and one seven-and-a-half-mile point. The other two days being pretty good, and again in February in another eight days hounds scored three five-mile points and a six-and-a-half-mile point. There were obviously other hunts during that time, but to have such consecutive long hunts was fairly exceptional. The diary of those days I might add, was written up by a panel and not by me, so I can vouch for the truth rather than its exaggeration. Sadly, that season Bryan had taken a bad fall in the autumn and was off for most of the year, which in a very open and fast season put quite an onus on the staff including Tony Pilgrim, a young and inexperienced whipper-in. I fed the hounds each day myself and also drew those that were to go hunting, which with the farm beginning to come together did not leave much time to spare.

One is always learning, and at the time being young and keen, I had a bee in my bonnet about hounds carrying too much weight. I had them stripped out to a greater degree than was good for them, bearing in mind that they were having very long days and running great distances. It took my father to put me right, telling me in no uncertain terms that as a young man he had made the same mistake, and that to have hounds too light was not only bad for their constitution, but also affected their energy levels. I remember him pointing out in a letter (he only wrote me three in my entire life) that without a strong back, the powerhouse is lacking and both speed and stamina will suffer in the long run. As always, he was correct. Fat hounds are an anathema (so too are fat horses) but that also includes hounds that are too thin, so up went the grub and so did their well-being!

The seventies were a challenging time for many reasons, one of them being the start in 1974 of what is now a popular and regular hunt pastime, namely Team Chasing. Douglas Bunn started the idea at Hickstead, at what he termed the All England Jumping Course, when he asked teams of four to take part in a cross-country event. There must have been some twenty teams from all sections of horse sports, and masters of foxhounds were invited to enter. That first year the team consisted of Dick Woodhouse, from the Portman, who had in fact just won the Foxhunters at Cheltenham, Brian Fanshawe then at the North Cotswold, another good race rider, and Robert Campbell from the Garth and South Berks, a capable showjumper in his pre-hunting days, plus myself. The event was held at Easter and was televised and there was a lot of kudos at stake. It snowed the night before, which then melted after first light. The going quite frankly was horrendous and the fences big. We all walked the course before the briefing, and such was the nervous tension amongst mostly very capable horsemen and horsewomen you could hear a pin drop. I always felt that the other three in our masters' team were in a league above me, but I did have the advantage of riding a really exceptional horse, a mare called Jackie who was actually a Bicester Hunt Horse normally ridden by Bryan. She went round that day as though she was taking part in a children's hunter trial. The rules were that you had to get three out of the four home and the time of the last of the three dictated the order as far as prizes were concerned. We all completed pretty well in a bunch with no falls, and I think came second or maybe that was a year later. Two things I do remember vividly however, was the sheer relief of surviving and the resultant cacophony of noise at the prize giving after a welcome glass was more akin to a murmuration of starlings! Another memory of that day was of the Royal Horse Artillery, the King's Troop riding their slightly smaller and cobby gun horses and between them notching up falls into double figures. We, the Masters' Team did take part for a number of years, with subsequently Michael Clayton, although not an MFH, replacing Campbell who had retired from hunting hounds.

America

1981 saw the start of what was to be the forerunner of numerous wonderfully enjoyable and entertaining trips, namely of being asked to judge the Virginia Hound Show in America. The doyen of hound shows that side of the Atlantic in those days, was himself a formidable judge of all canines, a charming gentleman by the name of Bill Brainard. The other two visiting judges with myself were Thady Ryan of Scarteen fame from Ireland, and Captain Simon Clarke then at the South and West Wilts. We stayed with Jimmy and Sue Young and met numerous fascinating people, many of whom were to become great friends. That first trip Ben Hardaway comes straight to mind. Ben made a big impression wherever he was, as did Jack McDonald from the London Hunt in Canada, and Bill Bermingham from the Hamilton Hunt, also in Canada. Amongst others who I recall from those days were Duck Martin from the Green Spring Valley, a former winner of the Maryland Hunt Cup, and Dick Webb, the Moore County to whom later I sent two Beaufort hounds in around 2005/2006. One of these was a bitch called Footloose '03 already in whelp to Founder '99. She gave birth to a large litter that was dispersed around a number of packs in the States, one of whom was lucky enough to land at the Live Oak in Florida with Marty and Daphne Wood (more of them later). At the last count, the progeny from Footloose had reached seven hundred and twenty-six descendants and climbing! Another impressive individual out there then was Sherman P Haight from the Litchfield VA, and it was probably not a coincidence that all the above became Presidents of the American MFHA. One more master who also became a good friend was Judy Greenhalgh, a long-term master of the Blue Ridge overlooking the grassy Virginia plains and Shenandoah valley. Judy also had a house in the Cotswolds and came to see us every year, and like myself was another disciple of the Vale of Clettwr Fairy blood.

Our next trip was somewhat different as I was asked to judge at the Kentucky Hound Show, and we stayed with Dr Jim Holliday who had visited us the year before for a day's hunting. Jim was a very high-powered surgeon who had taken a year off to run the first World Eventing Championships. He was a delightful host and Kentucky we found mesmerising—mile after mile of immaculate white railed paddocks. Although knowing very little about flat racehorses, it was memorable to go to Claiborne for a guided tour and to see Secretariat, Sir Ivor and Nijinsky all in adjoining boxes. Pammie was very struck by Secretariat in particular. We were also taken to see the then up and coming Lyphard at Gainsway Farm, Lexington. At 15.2hh, I thought he was a bit of a pony, but he too went on to sire a number of important horses.

We were picked up from Kentucky by Ben Hardaway who flew us down to Atlanta in his 'Lil ol' jet'. All the way down he kept banging on about his hounds, "The steadiest pack of fox dogs in the whole of the United States of Ah-meric-aa", in his southern drawl.

As soon as we arrived at his home, horses materialised and Tot Goodwin, then the Midlands black whipper-in, plus a mass of hounds of all shapes and sizes and creeds arrived. There was yet more mention of the "steadiest pack of foxhounds in the whole of the United States of America"—and then we set off into some forestry keeping to the tracks. To give Ben his due, a couple of deer crossed our path without mishap. "What did I tell you..." And the oration once again was repeated. In fact, all was going to plan until a girl arrived in front of us mounted on a skittish thoroughbred horse, accompanied by a borzoi which took one look at the hounds, then set off at great speed for home on the outskirts of Columbus. The hounds decided to join in the fun and despite the efforts of Tot, plus Ben's other whipper-in, to get ahead of them using pistols loaded with pepper shot (to me another rather novel practice) they had both run out of pellets long before the borzoi and the "steadiest pack of foxhounds" arrived at Columbus. As you can imagine there was a certain amount of leg pulling that night at dinner. Not to be put off by the whole proceedings however, Ben still had me roaring with laughter when he suddenly pointed to his wife Sarah and announced

"Ian, you see Sarah my wife sitting at the other end of the table, let me tell you something, I have ridden every sort of horse imaginable, good ones, bad ones, buckers, kickers, I have been in boats in terrific storms, I went all the way through France in the Armoured Cavalry as aide to General Manton S. Eddy—we were blown up, shot at, and Sarah is the only person I have ever been frightened of."

I have to admit that one of the earlier forays into a neighbouring country was not entirely without a little organisation from the word go. I had always wanted to get over the railway line, main road, and canal that formed the boundary with the Heythrop. So one evening, after an uplifting day around Stratton Audley, those present (still celebrating in the Kennel Cottage) and still in hunting clothes, namely myself, Mrs Farquhar, Heather Budgett, (later Tylor) Vince Kilkenny and a friend of his by the delightful name of Slim O'Callaghan, decided that since it was the night of the Heythrop Hunt Ball, it was a good opportunity to give our neighbours the chance to have a closer look at some proper foxhounds. Down to the kennels we went, to collect half a dozen of our woolly new Welsh outcrosses which were rather frowned on in some quarters. Then it was off to Blenheim where dinner was still in progress. We just had time to hear one senior Heythrop lady shrieking, "Whose cur dogs are these?" Bicester Farmer was at this point eyeing up her beef bourguignon—before we ourselves were thrown out on our ears by some burly bouncers. Two of us, minus our rather muddy red coats were allowed back in to retrieve our charges, and slightly crestfallen we made our way back over the border. Our escapade however did end on a good note, when a week later, the Duke of Marlborough joined us for a fun day's hunting at Marston St Lawrence. At tea afterwards with our host John Sumner, the Duke leant across, "Ian, I hear you finished up at Blenheim last Saturday must've been rather a good hunt?"

Burbling into my whisky I think I muttered, "Yes." Then turning to Pammie he enquired, "And were you in on it?"

"Yes," she mumbled.

"And how did you get across the river and canal?"

"Luckily we found a bridge," we ventured.

"How fortuitous," said Marlborough with a twinkle, and what a good egg we thought he was. He hunted quite a bit with us afterwards, and also at Badminton, and often pulled my leg.

On the subject of swap days, it would be too time-consuming to quantify every detail, but there were some memorable moments. After Brian Fanshawe arrived at the North Cotswold in 1975, he brought his hounds to us most years, and vice versa we returned to them. Being cousins there was always a bit of a needle which mostly I have to admit he seemed to win. Few huntsman were better across country than he, and the day he brought his hounds to meet at Twyford Mill, as it happened on my birthday in mid December, he scored a very good day indeed in the most appallingly wet conditions. The day ended with the North Cotswold secretary, Mrs Robinson completely disappearing under water in the brook that surrounded the Mill. Her stirrup leathers and irons resurfaced when they dug it out two years later! A day in the North Cotswold vale country also sticks in my mind, when after a particularly difficult morning in brussel sprouts, we got away well in the afternoon. We were heading for the best of their grass playground, when the mare I was riding—normally consistent—never rose an inch at a fence going back into the pasture where the field were waiting. I found myself on the ground still holding the bridle when hounds came back past me just behind a hare. So much for one's reputation! I did however even the score somewhat, when we took hounds to the Cottesmore quite a few years later.

A well documented trip to the Vale of Clettwr in 1980, was much enjoyed and a number of Fairy descendants gave the Bicester support-ers who braved it on horses a somewhat different aspect of what a day's hunting could entail. After a prolonged meet, the Field Master shouted, "Follow me," and proceeded to go to flat out round the perimeter of the small enclosure that we had met in, leaping three or four sets of rails that had been erected specially 'To make the visitors feel at home!' We then drew a patch of forestry, and found a brace straight away, whereupon hounds split and both lots disappeared out the other end. We never saw hide nor hair of them again that day! When we eventually collected them up later, it transpired that one lot had had a five and a half mile point and caught their fox, with the others marking to ground about the same distance away, in the opposite direction. Frustration gave way to elation, as the singing proclaimed what a brilliant day it had been, with all of the nine whippers-in, that had set off from the meet in different directions, sparks flying, to different vantage point, recounting what they had seen as hounds went by. In all fairness Trevor Jones's hounds did acquit themselves well on their return match, which of course was why Sir Newton had picked them in the first place.

Season 1981/82, although it had started on a record high then proved rather disastrous for me personally. In early December after a fun day shooting at Middleton Stoney with Jim Norman, I called in for a quick drink with John and Heather Tylor. It had snowed whilst I was there and I thought I knew the road fairly well, but I never realised that the other side of the main Oxford road and opposite their drive, was a track that continued in a straight line. In the dark and with the white of the snow, I gaily sailed out into the path of an articulated truck. I had broken numerous bones before, but nothing prepared me for this, a smashed hip, and every rib on the right hand side, plus my collarbone broken and more damage lower down in my back. Luckily I have no recollection of even leaving the Tylors who were more than a little fazed when the lorry driver called in to say, "I have just killed someone coming out of your drive!" A week in Intensive Care in the Radcliffe, with an epidural of straight morphine into the spine was the initial outcome and the pain therefore was minimal, but when I continuously grumbled to Pammie that I was perfectly okay, and when could I be allowed out to go hunting, she told them to take out the epidural. That certainly put me back in my box! There is always a funny side to any situation and when our very popular and good friend, Hunt Secretary Brigadier Nigel Birkbeck called to see me, and I pleaded for a cigarette, he said, "No I cannot bear to see the smoke wafting out of your punctured lung and into the drain jar beside the bed!" I do remember that I was also buoyed by the daily enquiry from Clarence House for a bulletin.

Eventually I was allowed home and permitted two morphine pills a day, they lasted about three hours each. I used to take one about 6pm to get me through the early part of the evening when friends tended to call, and then another around 3am to get through the rest of the night. The time between, and during the day was just sheer agony. Walking was out of the question, but after six weeks or so I was determined to begin to get going, and to try to reach a different telegraph pole further up the drive every few days. Bryan as thoughtful as ever, often came in with glowing and very uplifting reports as to how well the hounds were going. Pammie then took me to Antigua for a month where the sun and sea water worked wonders. In the past, on occasions I have been rather envious of the chap in the wheelchair being fast tracked into the aeroplane, but when in that predicament myself, I soon decided that being able to walk was a much better bet. My eldest brother Michael, and his wife Veronica, (known as Wong), came and joined us for the last fortnight. By which time the swimming, a no-go to start with, was definitely improving, as was the increase in weight that had dropped below nine stone at one point. Once home at the end of March, I did get on a horse and walk to the meet and was thrilled how complimentary everybody was about the sport they had enjoyed when the weather had cleared, and how well the hounds had gone, and what a star Bryan was.

That summer it was business as usual although sadly Frank Tutt elected to take a back seat as he was not well. All too soon it became apparent that this was an ongoing situation, and we were going to lose an integral member of our team as well as a very good friend. One door shuts and another opens, and by a complete stroke of luck in August, Frank Houghton Brown then only seventeen, and having been informed that perhaps his presence at Stowe School was no longer to his benefit, nor perhaps the school's either, was slightly at a loss. Being passionate about terrier work and hunting he agreed to come and help as an understudy. Rather like a private soldier he arrived at Twyford Mill in the clothes he stood up in, but with Mrs F as quartermaster, a visit to the local farm store, one pair of boots, three pairs of socks, two pairs of trousers, three shirts, and two jumpers to augment the old long overcoat from Oxfam, already part of his uniform, was the order of the day. The next arrival was Jack, the imaginatively named terrier that had belonged to Stuart Jeffries who tragically had suffered a farming accident with a front loader and a heap of corn, and was in a coma. Stuart—brother of David who was such a help to me with the cows—had taken on the family farm at Mollington, part of which was the venue for our point-to-point. He had also been phenomenal in his ability to keep up with hounds, carrying his spade, still in his old pair of wellies, with Jack at heel. He was just as capable on a horse I might add. Sadly he never recovered from his accident and so Jack remained with Frank.

Before continuing with the exploits of Frank and Jack, I must hark back to our involvement with Stowe School. In autumn some years before, a meet of the Stowe Beagles to be held at Twyford Mill had been organised by Brian Fanshawe's eldest son James. This would in

IWF on Black Jack: portrait by Tristram Lewis awarded to me on my retirement.

Hounds: Plaintiff, Tradesman, Artemis and Famous. Painted by Nina Colemore.

Sir Peter Farquhar hunting hounds in Portman Vale, by Peter Biegel.

Above: James Meade (my godson), Brother Mike, Tiddles Meade and IWF.

Right: IWF and Victoria on Nighty. (Photo by John Minoprio)

Above: the Beaufort Five: five consecutive years winning at Peterborough Hound Show—Gamecock, Bailey, Bombardier, Whipsnade, & Palmer.
Painted by Neil Forster.

Left: Snoopy the Horse, painted by Heather Budgett.

A Welsh foxhound.

future become an annual fixture. James of course subsequently became a successful racehorse trainer in Newmarket. Fanshawe that day being joined by Adrian Dangar and Frank, as future Stowe Beagle masters. I cannot recall whose watch it was on, but one afternoon does ring bells as unwisely I left the schoolboys in the care of an inexperienced young schoolmaster. Mrs F was cooking them bacon and eggs for tea, with a supply of just beer, when I was called back to the farm to deal with a broken combine. I was not away for long, but in the meantime the youngsters had found the whisky and were in fairly riotous form. All would probably have been okay if one of the younger ones had not been sick in the hood of the duffle coat of the unfortunate schoolmaster who was driving them home, which was hanging over the back of his seat! The culprit did make me laugh a week later however, when he turned up at a local hunt quiz with the Stowe team and offered to buy me a drink. When I said, "Don't be stupid you're at school, I'll get you one," with an impish grin he brandished a fistful of fivers and declared that he had plenty of money, as he had just sold his brother's stamp collection! I often wonder what became of him, jail or fortune?

That summer we started on horses earlier than usual as I was keen to get as fit as possible, still being slightly nervous as to how the rather bent body was going to stand up to the rigours of long days in the saddle. Looking back, I was very fortunate that Pammie generously gave me her best horse Monday, so-called as he came from the Monday country. She was right, he was definitely one of the best I ever sat on, and over the years we had some pretty good ones. He did have the most expansive jump, and was totally brave, although as is often the case, goodness on occasions he could buck and especially at the start of the season, he could put a big one in!

It was the beginning in many ways of the hounds providing another red letter season. I can still recall the enormous feeling of relief, when early on in September, not on Monday I might add, the horse I was riding never rose an inch over some pretty inconsequential rails and we turned a circle. Somebody who witnessed it queried why I was jumping up and down laughing, "It's the first fall since the accident, my ribs are still together!"

Early in that season, a day of definite note was when we took the bitches to the Cottesmore country on the 29th November. We met at Braunston in the best of their grass country. It was one of those days that was always going to be high profile and luckily it just went like clockwork from start to finish. Well mostly! We found straight away at the back of the village, the mounted Field was under the command of Jos Hanbury, probably one of the most able individuals across country of all times, a legend, and a joint master and fieldmaster at the time. Brian Fanshawe said, "Follow me," and promptly jumped a hedge off the road, whereupon his horse caught the top of a new wire fence on the landing side, fell and galloped off. I caught up with it and returned to Brian who didn't even say thank you, merely, "Why the hell did you do that when your hounds are running?"

"Because you know the country and I've never been here before in my life," was my reply!

When we caught up not long afterwards, the whole pack had run into a litter in a hedgerow which literally exploded with foxes and suddenly we had about four different little parties all close up behind their own particular fox. I did turn to Brian and say, "What the f…k do we do now?" Brian in his wisdom simply said, "That's the way we want to go, we have got plenty of whippers-in just keep going." Which is what we did, and only about a couple of minutes later we were flying into the best of the Cottesmore country with all hounds on. I am in fear of over egging the pudding, but Michael Clayton wrote the day up in his Foxford article for Horse and Hound thus;

"Brilliant away win for the Bicester in Leicestershire" was the head-line: "This could be war," said one senior foxhunter with a disarming smile as he surveyed the combined field. The visiting pack produced one of the most scintillating days foxhunting I can recall, across the cream of the Cottesmore country. Those who failed to sit down and ride hard immediately would have found it difficult to get into the action for the first exhilarating burst over some of the finest country in the Midlands. I calculated the first run at 70 minutes with hounds running over nine miles, and a furthest point of 4 1/2 miles. Another hunt of eighty two minutes with hounds running some twelve miles, was more than enough jumping of obstacles of all shapes and sizes to satisfy the most ardent equestrian."

Mrs Farquhar still maintains that despite three falls all off actually very good horses, but pushing the boundaries, it was probably the best days hunting she ever had. I think I have had better, but not many, and it was certainly a memorable day. I was in retrospect paid one of the

Bicester Hunt visiting the Cottesmore.

biggest compliments of all times by two Leicestershire swells, who after the first two hunts were hacking back to change horses, each riding either side of Ben Burton senior (father of young Ben) and one of the twenty five or so Bicester supporters, mostly farmers, that had come up for the day. One swell saying to the other, "That was as good a morning as I can ever remember."

"Same for me old boy, fantastic."

"Well, what do you make these woolly hounds of Farquhar's then?"

"Haven't been close enough to see them yet!"

Christopher Hodgson, later Chairman of the Bicester reminded me recently of one of his own memories of the day when Lady Margaret Fortescue, a most enchanting, but formidable sidesaddle Leicestershire lady, who was kicked in a gateway, turned round to the culprit, "Will you kindly take your horrible provincial horse back home where you and it belong." Only to get the rejoinder from the unfortunate guilty party, "Sorry Margaret, but actually you know me, I have subscribed to the Cottesmore for the last ten years!"

Oh the fun of it! The day ended rather ignominiously for me personally, the light was fading and hounds had come to their noses We were only hunting slowly and I jumped a fence with a bit of a drop finishing up round my horse's ears, who seeing the Field or what remained of them, ambled slowly across, and put his head down to eat grass, at which point I fell off! I remember Brian looking down at me saying, "I think this would be a good moment to call it a day." So we returned to have tea hosted by the aforementioned Jos Hanbury at Burley on the Hill, with myself so proud of my little Bicester 'woollies' who had proved themselves beyond measure.

I have copied a day that same season from the *Bicester News*, written from the perspective of four different scribes, of one good hunt which I found entertaining and include it here as follows;

A Terrifying Experience

My first and unfortunately lasting recollection of the Day from Doddershall House is one of sheer sustained terror. I rode a horse I had not previously sat on, but I had been confidently assured it would "jump the moon or higher".

I set sail with this information firmly fixed in my undoubting mind. As hounds began to run with the first fox of the day, rather than wait to jump a log in a boggy place, I remembered a set of rails in a corner to the left which would clear me of the queue. The horse never hesitated in his approach, neither did he rise. Every part of his anatomy below the chest hit the rails hard. In the absence of super-glue I was catapulted into several inches of flood water waiting on the other side of the fence. When reunited I decided that even the best of our four legged friends can occasionally err, so I contin-ued more or less undaunted.

Having negotiated the intervening fences fairly satisfactorily we galloped towards John Adams' from the direction of Doddershall House. At a good pace we approached another set of rails with a small ditch in front. Perhaps the horse has a 'wheels up' button, if so I failed to press it. Never have I seen timber fly so high or so far. Fortunately I did not have to report the damage to the Secretary, he was just behind, saw what I had done and was able to walk through the gap behind me. Work for George Chambers!

Despite increased circumspection as to the obstacles negotiated the part-nership again came apart at another set of rails further on. Again reunited with my less than careful steed we proceeded with even more caution, but the hounds were in full cry and really flying. Needs must—certainly 'the pace was too good to enquire'. We left behind us several more obstacles vibrating from the impact and eventually reached the end of an undoubtedly spectac-ular hunt. Returning the horse to his box, I dismounted with shaking knees (and a wet jacket). His owner enquired how I had fared. I couldn't say that

it had been a truly memorable day, but that I did not feel the horse and I
were quite compatible.

I also hark back with a smile to another account from the same magazine appertaining to a day in March, when we met at the apply named
Fox and Hounds in Bridestowe, Devon by invitation of the Spooners
and West Dartmoor. Hounds scored a copy book hunt straight away to
account for their fox well onto the moor after a fast twenty five minutes
running without a check. Then another hunt ensued and to quote from
the *Bicester News*: 'While this hunt was in progress, a single hound performed a notable feat. This hound was Comical '81, a third season bitch
out of Cowslip '78 whose dam was a sister to our stallion hound, Farmer
'76 making her a third generation daughter from the Welsh foundation
of Vale of Clettwr Fairy. Comical swung right-handed amongst some
sheep just after finding, and was then seen to pause and turn a fresh fox,
which she had the speed and drive to catch and kill unaided by herself
within the space of about half a mile'.

As it happened, she caught her fox in full sight of most of the foot followers who were still watching from the pub garden. By the time we returned in
the evening, one hound short, we were delighted to find a very fat Comical
asleep in front of the fire, farting and snoring, full of pie and mash, with the
fox laid out on the bar counter! A fairly uproarious stay at the Two Bridges
Hotel cemented a friendship with the Spooners, that had the spin-off some
years later when they enquired if I knew of a young man who might be
prepared to take on their mastership. Adrian Dangar came to mind, and
a round peg found a round hole. As previously mentioned I already knew
from his studying days as a co-conspirator with Frank Houghton Brown.
When, later both were hunting hounds in the mid 1990's in Yorkshire,
Frank at the Middleton, and Adrian at the Sinnington, I remember thinking that without doubt they were two of the best amateurs of the decade,
and indeed they were for many decades to come.

Sadly for the Bicester both lady joint masters, Rosemary Barlow and
Sally Nicholson retired, leaving Clive Preston and myself. Clive was to
see me through, but remained a master and subsequently Chairman for
many years. Few individuals did more for the Bicester than Clive Preston.

On the sport front things continued to flourish, and as terrierman
Frank Houghton Brown began to really find his feet, which was just as

well, as a motorbike, a car and a licence, soon became things of the past! Anybody who maintains that a dedicated and fit young man with a terrier and a spade cannot produce wonders without transport needed to take a leaf out of Frank's book. In fairness, initially he learnt a great deal from Denny Green who used to join us from the Warwickshire country, but his own ability to get himself round the country finding food and a billet was considerable, whilst at the same time consistently doing his job. A delight to witness. I recall dropping him off at Brill one Wednesday morning—we met there on Thursdays—and by chance driving past Brill Hill later that afternoon. A lonesome figure could be seen on the skyline in the familiar trademark long overcoat and old brown hat, leaping up and down as a fox pursued by Jack came down the hill from a large earth. While on the subject, Denny Green was without doubt one of the most knowledgeable foxhunters I've ever been lucky enough to know. A past master with a terrier, but what many who knew him never really appreciated in his early days was that he was as good on a young horse as anybody. Brian Fanshawe, when he left the Warwickshire and went to the Galway Blazers, had asked Denny to go with him as his Kennel Huntsman, but Denny said he was happy where he was! When he later married Charmian Jackson from Exmoor, together they made the most charming, delightful and knowledgeable couple you could ever wish to meet.

As far as family life was concerned, our youngest daughter Rose was born that September. She was actually christened Roseanne, Victoria's second name also being Rose, but Mrs F was adamant that we could not have two daughters called Rose, this debate only came to light during the christening in front of the font, I lost! Rose, as she is universally known was thankfully at home when my mother came to see her. Rose was the last of her grandchildren and at least my mother had a chance to meet her, as sadly shortly afterwards my mother died following a heart attack on the drive at West Kington whilst taking the dogs for a walk. There is always a bizarre side to any story and at her funeral in West Kington Church, 'Master' the 10th Duke gave the address, and had three pages of notes, but being of a certain age read page one, turned it over and read page two, turned the page again and re-read page one before finally ending with page three. Not a murmur was heard, nor eyebrow raised, oh to be a Duke—goodness my mother would have been amused!

That autumn on the farm we had the best harvest ever, genuinely averaging just under two and a half tons an acre, not quite East Anglia, but not bad for the Midlands. With milk at 22p per litre we were actually making money with the cows and also the corn, but even our accountant remarked that this was just as well to balance the purchase of horses! Although farming seemed to be in favour—there was even a move for the creation of an National Cheese to utilise the milk surplus—and wheat was at £145 a ton in November 1983, sadly this state of affairs was not to last. What we later realised is that we were being hoodwinked by the European economy. It is interesting to note that at that time I could fill up my car seven times for the price of 1 ton of wheat.

Another factor at that time was that we had just borrowed what was in those days quite a large amount of money to purchase the tenancy of about another two hundred acres around Twyford Mill. In good faith we had taken it out on an agreement under the Farm and Horticultural Development scheme (FHDS) to go from 100 to 200 cows. A new milking parlour, extra cubicles and a new self feeding double ended silage clamp, plus extra sheds for young stock was quite a major project for a smallish family farm. We did most of it in-house. Not me I hasten to add, but Richard Smith who was brilliant and greatly helped by Adrian Tutt who farmed next door. He was Frank Tutt's nephew who we had just sadly lost. Just before we completed the work, the Government Milk Quota System was introduced and every farm was given a quota using their 1983 milk sales. We were one year too late, and just got a quota for one hundred cows and not two hundred. I went to a tribunal in London and like many others lost. Shortly afterwards a man from the Ministry came to sign off our completed FHDS agreement, "So where is the extra quota?" I asked."Different department, goodbye," was the blunt reply. The Government decision to renege on what we had thought was a watertight contract was financially and indeed morally upsetting. At the time it was also made worse by the changing face of the countryside. Easy subsidies to take out hedgerows, drain fields and grow corn was resulting in whole farms going under the plough. In 1973 the Bicester country was 65 to 70 percent grass—cows, beef and sheep—but by 1983 it was 65 to 70 percent plough. The 158 acre family farm next to ours for instance had been one hundred percent grass—twelve fields with wet corners, hedgerows, full of trees and wildlife. It was purchased by a neighbouring corn baron and became one field. These two factors coupled maybe with the need for a change led to us beginning to put the word around about looking for pastures new. The possibility of more purist hunting might have been a consideration and a farm in the north would tip the scale. The first to contact us was George Fairbairn from the Tynedale. George was a good friend of the Chafer family, and indeed I had used his bloodlines before with Tynedale Linkboy 72 to good effect. I had also been particularly impressed by the strength of the backs of the pack generally. Pammie and myself ventured up to Northumberland whilst staying in Yorkshire that summer and were very enamoured and taken by the wildness and beauty of the country so decided to investigate further. After more discussions and lunch with Fairbairn at his club in St James's, we agreed we were on. We were not surprised therefore when the advert appeared in the Horse and Hound requesting applications for a Master/ Huntsman for the Tynedale for the coming season (standard practice). However we were surprised when I rang Colonel Neil Speke, the Chairman, to be told that he himself had not put the advert in. He had promised the present incumbent two years, and would not dream of going back on his word, but if in the future things changed he would get in touch. When I asked George what the hell was going on, he implied that he was going to take over as Chairman, sack the present mastership and that the majority of the committee were behind him. I did reply along the lines that we did not condone that sort of a deal but would keep in touch.

Life is so often a lottery as shortly afterwards, 'Master' the 10th Duke of Beaufort died, changing the ball game at Badminton.

Before moving on however I must pause to recount one or two of the happenings enormously entertaining to myself and many others that seemed to be a fairly regular occurrence at that time. One of the most seriously amusing individuals I have ever met was the Hon. Robert Corbett. Bobby, as he was universally known, or Mr Bobby to his staff who adored him, was a younger son of Lord Rowallan of Rowallan Castle in Ayrshire, who himself at one stage was Chief Scout. I think we first met Bobby when he was master of the Eglinton Foxhounds, a role he fulfilled with aplomb. He was one of the few of my friends who gained a distinction to Oxford— he was bright. Possibly however, the brainpower over-ruled the work ethic, and after surviving half a term and writing half a book he retired! He was then persuaded that he ought to get a job and a friend who played rather

'Master' and Mary, 10th Duke and Duchess of Beaufort

an important role in Hong Kong, (a Tai-pan no less I believe) gave him a job in London. Bobby duly went to the office, thought that this was just the ticket and so rang up a few friends to invite them to lunch—at the Savoy obviously. At about 4pm he rang his new employer's wife to ask if she would be kind enough to remind him the address of where he worked!

I could write a whole book about Bobby. His brain worked so fast that he only ever got half a sentence out before he was onto the next one. Quite a lot of people never understood a single word he said. He talked at great speed in staccato interjected with, "Brace up—Brace up," if he thought you were flagging. A knowledgeable gardener, he knew the Latin name of every flower or shrub, and with a completely photographic memory knew the pedigree of every hound or person he came across. At times his sense of humour was quite wicked as on occasion he took delight in relaying the real pedigree of a person rather than the pedigree on a birth certificate! Somehow, he always seemed to know. When his tranche of Rowallan money ran a bit thin, his two converted

Pammie-Jane on the Queen Mother's horse Inch Arran.

crofts on the estate, with a garden famous for just its cow parsley was suddenly superseded by a larger house and wonderful herbaceous borders,
it was then rumoured that the second inheritance from a tennis grandee
had saved the day. It may have only been a coincidence that his mother
in her day had herself been a famous player at Wimbledon also winning
the Scottish Championships at one stage with her sister.

Another quick story about Bobby at the time goes like this. Rather
surprisingly Queen Elizabeth, the Queen Mother had asked us to stay at
Royal Lodge for the King George VI race meeting. Also invited was his
great friend Sir Houston Shaw Stewart (MC, Korea aged 19), the pair
both famous imbibers. They made a slight error by pausing in Windsor
at the Black Bull to get themselves in form, probably not realising that
later there would be numerous, none too small martinis in the pipeline.

By the time he went to change, dear Bobby was well trained. His face was red and bumpy at the best of times, so a quick shave was not a good idea and the remedy to stem the flow of blood from the numerous cuts with little bits of loo paper (there being no cotton wool at hand) did not enhance the situation. At dinner with a gathering of a number of influential Jockey Club members, our friend found himself sitting next to his hostess. Thinking that perhaps things were not going entirely smoothly he grabbed a sherry decanter, swallowed a good measure, and promptly fell asleep. Queen Elizabeth, completely unfazed simply tapped the table and announced very quietly, "Dear Bobby he works so hard, we must let him sleep." So for the early half of dinner, we all talked in whispers while Corbett, his face, still dotted with loo paper and an ever-increasing blood stain seeping over a white dinner shirt snored happily. Halfway through the main course he awoke to a proclamation from our hostess, "Welcome back Bobby," and we all then resumed talking normally!

That year we were very honoured when the Queen Mother came by herself to lunch at Twyford Mill driven by her chauffeur Barty. We also asked Miles and Liz Gosling, John Sumner, and Hugo and Carol Bevan, all friends involved in the racing world and also good fun. I recall we had oeuf drumkilbo and being a Sunday, roast beef. Following lunch, we went down to the kennels to see the hounds and then the horses. We also asked Anthony Webber to give a demonstration of how he set about massaging a horse's back, which was very popular. Despite the fact it rained steadily, our guest did not seem at all perturbed returning to Royal Lodge in fine form. The date was May 1st and Charles Wheeler who had just been given the job of second whipper-in announced that he had not expected to be introduced to the Queen Mother on his first day at work!

Another change that year was that Alastair Stewart gave up being Hunt Secretary to go and hunt the Sinnington as master, and Jock Beasley took his place.

As previously mentioned, 'Master' the 10th Duke of Beaufort had sadly recently died, the dukedom being inherited by his cousin David Somerset. David was in constant contact with my father as to the way ahead, and seemed to be in favour of my joining him in the Beaufort mastership to fill a void. Despite the sport we were having and my commitment to the farm it was a heady proposal. Initially David was in a quandary as to how we went ahead to firm up arrangements, and therefore as to how and where the responsibilities lay. I remained convinced that as I was already hunting hounds four days a week anything less was not an option. Added to this, I had always felt that a shared horn could be a recipe for factions. While this was going on Antony Brassey who had succeeded his father Col Sir Hugh as Beaufort Hunt chairman, came to see me bringing with him Christopher Hart who was on the committee and as it happened was the brother of Anthony Hart, the long-term Secretary of the Masters of Foxhounds Association. 'Brass' as previously mentioned was not only one of my oldest and longest standing friends, and together they were very persuasive.

That spring Pammie and myself went on holiday with Miles and Liz Gosling to the Sea Club in Menorca. We stayed in an old villa on the coast, that had belonged to an admiral who had died. His widow took in a number of guests who ate communally and were only accepted by recommendation. Every morning I accompanied the three stunning Gosling daughters on a walk down the beach, who insisted on going topless which was still fairly avant-garde in those days. I am not sure if it was good for my image as they insisted on calling me 'Uncle Ian' in loud voices! While we were there a telegram arrived from my father warning me that David was going to ask me to join him on my terms, and to make up my mind. So shortly after returning we said yes.

True to form about a fortnight after we had put a marker down for the Beaufort, the Tynedale got in touch to say that things had not worked out and the mastership was mine if we still wanted it. I sometimes wonder what would have happened the other way round. We would have bought a farm, hunted a wilder country and our children would have been brought up as Northerners. Altogether a rather different ball game. Such is life!

It has always been a very firm principle of the Masters of Foxhounds Association that when making changes the bigger packs should always plan the arrangements well ahead prior to the actual date of change. This was to give time for the other packs affected to make their own arrangements in good time to ensure the least possible disruption to the world of hunt countries and hunt staff. In the first instance it was easier to sort out the Beaufort, and very early on Denis Brown, long-time whipper-in announced he wanted to retire and go gardening, something he was extremely good at. It was therefore thoroughly satisfactory when he was offered the job to be in charge of the kitchen garden at Highgrove, a role he held brilliantly for

Ant Farquhar, Antony Brassey, IWF.

the rest of his life. This obviously opened up a vacancy, so I asked Charles Wheeler who was bright, energetic, and very quick thinking, especially in the hunting field, if he would like to accompany me to Badminton as second whipper-in, which he jumped at. So that was settled.

Miles Gosling as Bicester Chairman fronted a consortium to find a new master and they were delighted when Luke White, the future Lord Annaly applied and it was agreed that he would take over as master with Clive, and learn the ropes of a huntsman from Bryan, once again back in the role of schoolmaster—a part he always played so brilliantly. So that too was settled.

We entered our last season as determined as ever to end on a high and before Christmas sport was generally good. We had a fascinating visit to the David Davies country in Wales in early November, where we witnessed our hounds coping impressively with the hill country, running down to the 'in bye' before returning up to the hills, all completely unaided. The singing that evening was magical culminating in a solo from an elderly man, who shuffled into the centre of the barn where the party was held, still in his old smock and a cap that looked as if it never left his head. He sang 'Land of My Fathers' and 'Abide with Me' in one of the most perfect tenor voices I have ever heard. Apparently, he specialised in hedge-laying and had been trained in his lunch hours by Lady Davies who was hoping he would sing at the Eisteddfod, but sadly he lost his nerve.

The following day we went out with their hounds who hunted beautifully and triggered in me a desire to use some of their bloodlines in the future. The David Davies brought their own hounds back to meet at Kirtlington later in March, when Lord Davies himself hunted them, and David Jones, who we were to get to know very well in years to come, whipped in. They were accompanied that day by Lord Davies's daughter Eldrydd, then a young girl on a pony. In the future Eldrydd, when married, was to become their popular joint master on returning from Australia where she had practised as a vet. Another old friend from Builth Wells Hound Show, Neville Owen also helped whip in. Their hounds managed to catch three foxes, making the international score Wales three, England nil as we had failed to catch a Welsh fox back in November. This fact of course had to be celebrated in song by our visitors at the party that evening given by the Tylors at their stud farm.

A prolonged and very severe frost after Christmas started on 5th January, lasting until the end of the month which seriously curtailed things. Hounds were out most days, often in quite frankly appalling conditions. The versatility of hounds never ceases to amaze me and as long as there is plenty of snow their pads seem to come to no harm, in fact they seem to enjoy their changed environment! A saga that is worth repeating however was not fun, and during a surprisingly long hunt one hound went through the ice crossing the lake at Trafford House She would have drowned, if Chris Bailey helped by Bryan had not jumped off his horse, broken the ice and swum out to rescue her. Both men needed resuscitating, obviously large whiskies, and a hot bath!

Not so good however, a young bitch, Mortal '84 went missing. She was out all through the bad weather a long way from home and was viewed at times firstly in the Grafton country, then on the edge of the Pytchley before crossing into Warwickshire and circling back to the Bicester by which time she had been out for nearly seven weeks. On a number of occasions both local farmers and hunt staff had got close to her, but each time she had run off. On Monday 25th February, we were having tea with the Burtons when a message came through that a lemon hound had been seen on the old aerodrome at Chipping Warden. I jumped into my car and went straight there and could see her curled up in a hedgerow. As I approached she moved off, so I sat down in the cornfield, and continued to call her quietly. Obviously I had hunted her myself that year and also she had been walked by us at Twyford Mill. Eventually she came closer and started to circle me. I stayed still and finally she crawled up to me, sniffed and then jumped about doing a 'mad dog' whimpering all the time. She followed me back to the car jumped straight in and sat on my lap. We returned to the kennels with her licking my face all the way!

I have often noted that hounds, who through no fault of their own have occasionally been away from kennels for a period of time have always appeared to be in surprisingly good condition when reunited. They have never been accused of killing stock or anything like that, and I suspect they just basically forage around farms picking up scraps.

All hounds are special, but as a Fairy granddaughter and her mother Cowslip '79 having been much admired by Captain Evan Williams for her quality, this naturally ensured that Mortal was amongst the small number accompanying us to Badminton that spring.

After the frost, winter progressed at its normal pace. Yet another visit materialised when the Cheshire Hunt came to Doddershall Park, the historic home of Mr and Mrs Christopher Prideaux. Their huntsman, Johnny O'Shea produced a cracking old-fashioned day over the best of the Bicester grass country. I personally had first met Johnny when he whipped-in to Dermot Kelly at the Meynell back in the late 1960s. Without doubt, not only was he a very fine huntsman and impressive horseman, but also the most enormous fun. Anybody who was ever lucky enough to spend an hour or two in the company of Johnny O'Shea and his great friend Bill Lander from the Wynnstay to savour the Irish wit, plus the Scottish charm that they were both famous for, could only look back and consider themselves lucky. Few duos, on or off the stage were ever funnier, and as it happened of course, they were both superlative houndmen.

As the season began to draw to a close, I have to mention the rather bizarre episode that occurred at our final meet at Twyford Mill at the

Photograph album presentation at Trafford House Meet: Clive Preston, Liz Thame, IWF, George Thame and Pammie-Jane.

end of February. Having put the word about, that all were welcome, it was not entirely surprising that there was quite a gathering, but not written into the scenario was thick fog at 11 o'clock! The cellar was soon running low so reinforcements were called for from numerous local pubs, bars and shops. Around midday, I was in the kitchen brewing up another potion, when a local foot-follower arrived to inform me that, "Old Fred from down the road, has just died."

I said, "What do you mean he's just died—where is he?"

"He's definitely dead and we asked a visiting doctor to have a look at him, he got off his horse and pronounced him dead. So we have dragged him to the back of the bar, (which was in the garage) and we have put a tarpaulin over him."

When I went out, sure enough there was the tarpaulin with people gaily stepping over it muttering, "Poor old Fred, what a good way to go!" I do recall thinking a second opinion might be prudent and asked the very competent horse vet, Bob Baskerville, to check him out. Bob got off his horse and then ventured that he did not think that he was dead, but just in a deep diabetic coma which together with a surfeit of whisky, was not a good combination. This was born out by the ambulance crew that arrived shortly after. "Old Fred" was out hunting again the following week!

Thank goodness the fog did lift at about 1 o'clock and it soon became apparent that we were on a flyer. Two fairly spectacular and fast hunts, each of about thirty five minutes ensued with satisfactory conclusions, but resulting in quite a number of loose horses! Denny Green once again, came up with the most complimentary remark about the hounds, "Best I've ever seen, like bloody Exocets, once they're locked on its game over!"

The last day's hunting that season, saw a large crowd gathered at Trafford House to witness George and Liz Thame handing over two delightful photograph albums depicting the last 12 seasons followed by an amazing party that night in their barn. Billy Evans who farmed locally, sang a song mainly orchestrated by Ann Mallalieu (now Baroness) with a chorus from the well refreshed guests accompanied by Ben Burton on the drums.

All Bicester eyes are deepest red
They cry all day, They cry in bed
What causes all this grief and pain?
The Master's taking Pammie-Jane.

Chorus
He's gone to hunt with Dukes and Earls,
Princesses, Kings and high born girls
He is taking with him more than half
The horses, hounds and hunting staff.

No more we'll see him draw the hounds
Or hear his funny hunting sounds
No longer hear him cross the ride
With swearing from the covert side.

From Stratton, hark the clipping sounds
From horses? No they're clipping hounds
The Beaufort want this pack quite bare
The hounds must have no surplus hair.

The Magistrates are in a state
For Farquhar's off, sad to relate
Nobody left to break the law
The Court will have to close its door.

Christmas comes but once a year
But not at Farquhar's house I fear
His Christmas cards can still be seen
All from Her Majesty the Queen.

He used to play a little game
With Heather T and Mrs Thame
Now he's gone to pastures new
What will the Bicester bitches do?

Our Master's loss will cause us pain
But most of all will Pammie-Jane
Missed by our Chairman most of all
Who will dance with him at the Ball?

Now raise the Bicester guarantee
It's far too high for you and me
It's our new Master we must thank
Let's hope he owns a Merchant Bank.

We must not weep, still less complain
The Bicester's loss is Beaufort's gain
We do not blame him, Princess Mike
Is not Kilkenny's look alike.

Oh thanks for twelve good seasons here
On every side we raise a cheer
And when your days with them are through
Let's hope they don't dig you up too!

George and Liz Thame had been the greatest of friends to us, and Liz had been tireless in her chairmanship of the Bicester Supporters' Club.

Bicester Hunt Panto—Sally Nicholson, Anne Mallalieu

Liz did not miss much, and I have always been amused by her report after she journeyed to London to attend a newly thought up MFHA Committee organised by Captain Ronnie Wallace to represent Hunt Supporters' Clubs. "Well, I would make three observations. Firstly there was a large man called Margadale who must be very important as he slept the whole way through and no one woke him. Secondly, nothing I was going to say was going to make any difference whatsoever. Thirdly Captain Wallace was a very clever Chairman, as every time someone asked him a difficult question he replied, 'Good point, very good point, I'm glad you brought that up. I will come on to that later,' but he never did!"

Our final swansong was the Puppy Show at the end of April. It has always been customary, should a master and huntsman leave a pack after a worthwhile number of years, that the annual Puppy Show should be held before the cut-off date of May 1st. Pammie and myself were very touched by the presentation of a silver hound, Bicester Farmer '76 (who else?) to match Portman Playfair '51 (previously presented to my father) for me, and a pair of delightful paintings of foxes playing, mousing and stalking hens for Pammie. With that it was back to the Mill to start packing up for the move to the Beaufort whilst still clutching the remains of the wonderfully hound decorated cake that Ros Boughton from Ashington had produced for tea.

ARRIVING AT BADMINTON

ANYBODY WHO HAS lived in the same house for quite a number of years will know that to up sticks and move everything is quite a magnum opus. In the first place, we had been so busy during the final season at the Bicester that I have to admit we had not fully concentrated on where we were going to live? Very important you might think! We had put feelers out for a farm, but nothing suitable had come up. In the back of my mind, I had always thought that maybe one end of my father's house at West Kington might be a possible stopgap. Quite rightly other members of my family were of the opinion that three small children, four large lurchers, three ponies plus Pammie's horses (mine were always planned to go to the stables at Badminton) might be a bit much for my father already in his eighties. Therefore, it was a brilliant solution when David Beaufort offered us The Cottage in Badminton where he and his own family had lived for some years. He was moving obviously into 'The Big House'.

'The Cottage' could well be termed a misnomer—how many cottages have a very grand library, drawing room, sitting room, lovely dining room, spacious kitchen area and some ten bedrooms looking out onto a delightful garden with for the first time in my life a swimming pool, tennis court and a croquet lawn! It all seemed too good to be true and if that was not enough, it was also only a 100 yards from the kennels, so very easy for early morning exercise, and stables for the children's ponies were also available only a stone's throw away at the other end of the village street. It was also entirely convenient therefore, that not only my horses could go to the main stables, but Mrs Farquhar's could as well. So everybody, as they say was catered for.

The other stroke of luck was that Sally Armstrong who had been with us at Twyford Mill also agreed to move down with us. Sally was, and still

Margot the Spaniel, Victoria, Pammie-Jane, Emma and Rose, Brassey the lurcher at The Cottage, Badminton.

is a brilliant. Her family continue to farm just outside the north end of the Bicester country. Years before, we had met at Hellidon one morning and as we moved off, a small girl on a black pony trotted past me and joined Bryan, spending the rest of the day with him. When we were boxing-up that evening I asked Bryan, "Who was the little girl who spent the day with you, was she your niece or something?" "No said Bryan, I've never seen her before, I thought she must be something to do with you!" Next time we were at that end of the country, once again a little girl on a black pony turned up and trotted off to join Bryan. Needless to say, she was all smiles, went jolly well and was in fact very helpful, so neither of us had the heart to order her back to the Field, and that was the way it remained. She obviously grew up a bit, and we didn't see her for a time until she turned up at a Bicester Hunt 'summer do,' brown as a berry, wearing hot pants, and looking a million dollars. As smiley as ever, she explained she had been in Australia for a year, was now back and looking forward to her hunting. When I asked her what her plans were, she said that she hadn't really got a clue, but was looking for a job

Sally Armstrong and IWF on Winnie, Charles and Nan Chafer—Yorkshire late 80s.

and didn't mind much what it was as long as she could get her hunting. As it happened, I had just lost my driving licence, Sally had just got hers and was happy to drive me and help with the children, so she started work that week! Subsequently Mrs Farquhar helped Sally to get a place on a Prue Leith Cookery Course and she stayed with us for some years before setting up on her own. Nowadays, she lives just down the road from our current home Happylands, hunts all over the place, still cooks for everybody and has done the Beaufort Puppy Show Tea for years. To my certain knowledge she has never spent a day with the Field in her life! Sally was soon joined by Sue, whose role was the children, plus Richard Rich one of the former resident gardeners who remained.

Before actually moving, of course two most important factors had to be dealt with, horses and hounds. In those days it was very much the responsibility of an amateur huntsman to find and produce his own horses and obviously those for his family. At the Bicester, a four day a week country and challenging to cross, we had just enough horses to cope. However one or two of them were getting on a bit and were what you might call 'hunting sound', but not 100% enough to take to a new hunt country and face the naturally exacting standards of the resident Stud Groom, together with a different crowd on the lookout to judge their new amateur huntsman. A fact of life, so therefore it was time to go shopping. Luckily, that last season we had already acquired two new ones from Tom Connors; a lovely quality horse that he had still owned but had been lent to the Belvoir huntsman, and another classy young Irish horse, called Black Jack, a five-year-old who made the grade, and who probably as a hunter could have had his photograph taken more times than most horses in England. In his first season, just over from Ireland, he did jump into the middle of a Bicester hedge with Pammie, he probably thought he could bank it. That genuinely was the only mistake he ever made. I hunted hounds off him for the next fourteen seasons, mostly two days a week and I always had him first for the big days, or visiting. He never fell with me once, not a bad record!

So shopping we went, and bought at least a couple of others from David Barker who was still dealing, but also hunting the Whaddon Chase hounds. As a former showjumper, David had won the 1962 European Championship at the Royal International Horse Show at White City on Mister Softee and had as good an eye for seeing a stride as anybody I have ever known, not that I know much about that sort of thing! I know at one stage he was placing horses with two well known Leicestershire huntsmen, one who could ride and one who could not. David schooled horses for both of them, teaching one to take off when he was right, and teaching the other to still take off when they were wrong, that takes some doing.

But back to the matter of the hounds. It was agreed that I would take around five couple of Bicester hounds with me and in return draft about the same number of Beaufort hounds back. Probably of little interest to anybody, but the ones that came with me were obviously favourites hunting wise, but also had fresh and new bloodlines that I wanted to use in the future at the Beaufort. Looking down the list age wise, the oldest was a North Cotswold dog, Stanley '79 out of Staple '76, the sister of the already mentioned North Cotswold Stanway '76, to maintain the best of the Carlow ST line. Then a brother and sister, Sailor and Salary both '80 and both by old Bicester Farmer '76 and from the same year Medley, but more of her later. Then of course the aforementioned Mortal. Another two sisters, Comma and Comical both '81, who were two more Vale of

Clettwr Fairy grandchildren, together with yet another young dog of that same line, Bicester Farrier '84. Farrier after only one season, before our move, had luckily already developed his own character before finding himself in the somewhat different environment of a more orchestrated pack of hounds and had the confidence to do his own thing—albeit with my backing, and soon alongside his Bicester brethren proved his worth as a trustworthy foxhound. At the time I had brought down a nucleus of individuals with an eye to the future not realising at the time how important they were going to be in the short term. To progress however, Farrier with his Farmer blood and his North Cotswold ST line through his mother was also in the long term going to prove a very influential stallion hound both at the Beaufort, nationally and subsequently internationally as well.

Master, Ronnie Dallas, Gerald Gundry

A friend once asked me, "Was it a big change moving from the Bicester to the Beaufort?" I could only reply, "Not really, hounds are hounds, horses are horses and farmers are farmers—of course there was just a lot more of everything—although on the whole, the country was a little easier to cross." In theory there should have been more country to play with, but in fact after the M4 had come through in the late 1960's a lot of country was lost, and like most hunts when it came to real estate the problem was too little, rather than too much. Obviously I was extremely fortunate having hunted and lived there in my youth, and I already knew quite a percentage of the landowners and farmers, many of whom were old friends and acquaintances, and I dare say I had a reasonable understanding of the topography of quite a lot of the hunt country.

The Beaufort country itself had of course been brilliantly administered. The 'Old Duke' as he was fondly referred to, 'Master' was King in his own country, indeed without a slight sideways move in the Plantagenet and then Tudor dynasties he could well have been King overall. His determination and lifelong passion for the sport of foxhunting had ensued for decades, even encompassing the effects of World War II; the well-being and passage of hounds and their followers within the boundaries of the Beaufort Hunt was paramount.

A number of other individuals come to mind, but on the organisation front two stand out; Major Gerald Gundry having been Hunt Secretary before the War, became joint master with 'Master' in 1951, hunted the doghounds until 1974 two days a week until Brian Gupwell took over full time. Gerald was tireless in his efforts to keep the country open and left a legacy of no stone unturned in his dealings with the farmers. Rather a nice story told to me by his daughter Jane; apparently when the 10th Duke advertised for a Hunt Secretary, his personal secretary arrived in his study clutching a telegram from India where Gerald was serving, "An application, Your Grace, for the position of Hunt Secretary, it is rather difficult to read, but I believe the signature is Gandhi?" At the Point-to-Point soon after, the word amongst the farmers was that the new hunt secretary was rumoured to be an important Indian diplomat!

It was on Gerald's watch as joint master that every effort was always made to keep up standards. In this respect, both incumbent masters were more than aided by the legendary Major Ronnie Dallas. Ronnie was Hunt Secretary when I arrived in the area as a teenager, and was still the current Secretary when I joined the mastership. There are few people I have ever come across that I have had more respect for than Ronnie. Small in stature, but with a mammoth heart. What Ronnie went through would have destroyed almost anyone. He was commissioned into the 3rd King's Own Hussars which as it happened was later commanded by my father, and indeed to become my regiment subsequently. Fast tracked as was usual for most officers in those early days of the war, as a young subaltern he soon found himself posted to Singapore. Having hardly disembarked, he was taken prisoner by the Japanese who had quickly advanced down through Malaya, the defences of the island concentrating on a coastal invasion rather than via the mainland. Like many others in that predicament, Ronnie found himself having to endure the appalling privations of life as a prisoner of the Japanese in Java for three and a half years. He was not alone in the fact that like others of his ilk he very seldom talked about it, but I do remember him opening up a little one evening, needless to say maybe after a glass or two. He told me one of the things that upset him most was that having survived and on returning to some semblance of normality that many former prisoners were left with a sense of failure rather than achievement. They had not died, but they had not won battles, nor been decorated or even promoted and had not had the satisfaction of liberating their fellow humans from the tyranny of others. I, like so many of my age group adored Ronnie. He strived to promote the young, and as Hunt Secretary, if a young student was short of a bob or two, a few hours' laying a covert or building a hunt fence would soon take the place of a subscription. He was also an intrepid horseman, shortlisted for the 1952 Olympics, winning a bronze medal in the 1955 World Equestrian Games at Aachen as well as competing in more than one Nations Cup.

His wife Sylvia, the daughter of the Hon. Guy Cubitt (former Founder Chairman of the Pony Club for 25 years) is without doubt one of the most delightful women one could ever be lucky enough to meet. Ronnie's stamina was unbeatable and working together I soon realised that although I was considerably younger, I had met my match. A remark made to me one day by a former fellow prisoner, "That Dallas he was so tough, we almost felt sorry for the Japanese." Part of my baptism of fire on returning to the Beaufort, and I laugh every time I think of it, is that because I made sure I had a driver, I often used to pick Ronnie up to take him to some of the many meetings that we seemed to have to plan endless hunt dinners and other functions, meetings that seemed to go on late into the night. "Just come in for a quick one," this said with only a limited amount of hours left before we had to be on horses for an early morning start. "Sylvia would love to see you." Sylvia, I might add had wisely been in bed for hours, but 'Sylvia would love to see you' normally won the day and by that time of the night as well! Of course next morning there was Ronnie as bright as a button having already sorted out a couple of problems that we had discussed tonight before!

So with David Beaufort senior master, Antony Brassey as Chairman and Ronnie Dallas as Secretary the hierarchy looked suitably supportive.

Fieldmasters

Before I start on the intricacies of overseeing a large Kennel and Stable complex, I thought I would touch on another problem that faces most changes of mastership, although David of course was still in office, and that is the question of Field Masters. Many hunts, especially two day a week packs have survived with just one or two individuals, who in some cases have gone on for years, thus providing that much sought after bonus of continuity. In larger countries with bigger mounted fields this was not so easy, and the Beaufort had for some time divided the responsibility along the lines of the days of the week. This was the system I inherited, although before too long we split the work load within those days, but always hopefully with the proviso, that if the same person did the same area, then a degree of trust could be built with the farmers.

Saturdays were easy as the incumbent Field Master, Toby Sturgis was happy to remain in office. Toby was born and bred in the Beaufort country, and was also more than capable on a horse having evented and competed at Badminton Horse Trials no less. He was also backed up by his wife Gail, who was herself more than impressive in the saddle. Like ourselves they had a young family of three children, a boy and two girls and all of them including ours were mounted on little grey Welsh ponies that whizzed about, mainly out of control. You could hear the expletives, "Look out, white mice on the right!" They are all great friends to this day and Rupert Sturgis has followed in his father's footsteps and is now himself a highly successful Saturday Field Master.

Mondays took a little more organising; Tony Keen who farmed just north of Tetbury and who had done it for some considerable while, decided it was time for him to retire, and so a replacement was required. Two volunteered, both eminently suitable, so we split the country.

Rob Ingall, Monday Field Master.

Left: Simon Tomlinson, Monday Field Master.
Right, John White, Thursday Field Master. (Photo by John Minoprio)

Simon Tomlinson took on the area around Down Farm, his home and farm in the north, and Rob Ingall, the more eastern ground around his farm at Doughton. They were both old friends of mine as well as being intrepid horsemen, although each had slightly different ways. Rob had point-to-pointed and hunted, whilst Simon's metier was polo and being married to Claire Lucas, was in the process of building up the Tomlinson Polo empire. Rob's method was to know his country backwards, and to be more of a purist following hounds, not interfering with the huntsman, at the same time giving followers a good ride, but only when hounds were running. Simon on the other hand having been a Master of the Oxford Draghounds, as well as polo later, was slightly more of the opinion that having a pack of hounds somewhere in the vicinity was a brilliant excuse to jump fences! Being a little bit gung-ho he was looking for any opportunity to take on obstacles regardless. On one memorable occasion hounds were running well and were followed in turn by myself, the Hunt Staff, and the majority of the Field, when we met Tomlinson accompanied by a few kindred spirits head-on coming in the opposite direction over Baber's hedges, needless to say, I did shout at him that perhaps he was going the wrong way, and all I got back was,

Saturday Field Master—Peter Sidebottom flying a hedge on horse Tory. (Photo by Ray Bird)

"Don't worry, I know, I've got two more (fences) to get in and then I'll come back and rejoin you!" However, they both did a great job. Simon gave members of the Field the greatest fun, and Rob became amongst one of the best Field Masters we ever had—I will add more to that later, anyway that was Mondays fixed. Wednesdays were a little more complicated. Before 'Master' died his heir apparent, David had been fulfilling that role, which was enormously popular. Again, he was a very able horseman and as previously mentioned had achieved glory in the early days of Badminton Horse Trials, coming second. However, having just inherited the whole of the Badminton Estate and also being very busy with his Marlborough Fine Art business in London, he did find it increasingly difficult to get the time to spend all day every Wednesday in the hunting field. Subsequently, he more and more asked Pammie to stand in for him until realistically, she was doing it full time—most successfully I might add. This she did for our first two years before handing over to Antony Brassey for the Sodbury Vale, and Richard Meade of Olympic fame—married to my first cousin Angela (or 'Tiddles')—taking care of south of the M4, whilst they both shared the area around Oakes Lane. Thursdays on the other hand was another natural progression. John

White continued to do every Thursday which he had done since 1978, only giving up in 2006 owing to a pulled muscle. He did it for thirty two years hardly ever missing a day, and largely overseeing the well-being of the whole of the Thursday country. John was always quite funny about taking on the Field Master role. He said he was never asked, but one day Dick Horton his predecessor was *hors de combat,* and in the middle of the day Gerald Gundry shouted at him, "John, for God's sake take control of the bloody field." So he did! John was another very capable horseman with point-to-point wins under his belt and both he and Rosie his wife, were a joy to watch crossing the country together. Rosie herself was quite frankly a racing legend, lady point-to-point champion and once even beating John Thorne who was riding Spartan Missile. I have an abiding memory of jumping a small rail on Robin Pocock's at Bremhill and looking to my left to see John and Rosie land together over a big hedge with a good drop, both laughing. Needless to say the two of them pulled up to let me pass as huntsman, that's the way they were. Not long after, Toby Sturgis retired, and Peter Sidebottom took over. He was another goer and rode like his father Derek who was still fearless well into his seventies. Derek, similar to my father-in-law Charles Chafer had been in motor torpedo boats in the Channel during the war, not a job for the faint hearted. So that had the Fieldmasters sorted.

Hounds and Kennels

I said earlier, that I found there was no great change in coming to the Beaufort, and that hounds, horses and farmers were the same whatever the country. Of course that was a very wide sweeping remark and obviously needs clarifying. I will start with the hounds. Without doubt, genetically the Beaufort was considered then and now as one of the most influential packs of hounds in the world. Although, before the Second World War 'Master' had always moved with the times not being afraid to go for new blood, since then he had been fairly conservative, and very much bred his own type. He had always been consistent in his desire for size as well as quality, and had maintained that if picking between two litter sisters he would go for the bigger one regardless, even if the other was a fraction better in her work. He would maintain that the genes as regards work were inherent in both of them, so concentrated on the purely physical attributes rather than just the hunting

IWF at the Beaufort Kennels 1987. (Photo by John Minoprio)

ability which would manifest itself anyway. Therefore, the hounds he left were indeed genuinely world-famous particularly for their size and also their stamina.

He himself had been a very capable huntsman, but when getting on in years (he was born in 1900) in the mid 1960's he had slowed down and took on Brian Gupwell to hunt the bitches, with Gerald Gundry continuing with the dog hounds until 1974. Jane, Gerald's daughter recounts another tale from when she was a young girl. Her father suffered from a perforated duodenal ulcer one day out hunting and had to be rushed to hospital. Gerald loved his dog hounds and they him, and she recalls that when they took them back to the horsebox without him the hounds just howled. Brian took over hunting both packs from then on. He was an amazing horseman, equally capable on a young horse or a made one and soon put a smile on the faces of the jumping crowd.

He was also more than able at producing hounds looking well and was a very methodical feeder. Without any shadow of doubt he was one of the best showmen of hounds in the country. Tony Wright, another top professional when it came to showing, having been well schooled by Captain Wallace, always said that Brian was the best man at showing hounds on the flags that he had ever seen. However, I don't think I am being unkind when I say that in those days latterly the performance of the Beaufort had slipped back a bit in the field. Never one to give up on anything, Master in his eighties was just as determined to go out every day he could, but obviously age was beginning to tell and so the days got shorter. This made things quite difficult for Brian who found himself having to gallop about somewhat to entertain the Field and make the best of the time available to him.

That first summer, like all huntsmen taking over a new pack, it was imperative to spend as much time as possible with them. So, it was up to the kennels first thing every morning to go out on exercise. I think it will always stick in my memory, the noise of the two large gas coppers in the feed house already fired up and hissing away, which is when I discovered Brian's method of producing the best gruel possible for his charges. One copper would provide the hot water for cleaning down the yards, and the other for the gruel that would be poured over the pinhead oats that had already been soaked to produce a cake. The gruel consisted of lumps of flesh boiled whilst still on the bone. The bones were then removed and the cooked meat was mixed with the cake and shovelled onto feed trays then mashed up and mixed with the gravy left in the copper. It produced the most palatable and nutritious porridge you could ever imagine! The hounds did not get this every day, but often enough to keep them in prime condition as the oats, although a very old-fashioned hound food were extremely expensive. In that vein it has always amused me that when the Duke of Wellington took a similarly fed pack of hounds to Spain during the Peninsula War to keep his cavalry officers up to the mark, a number of his foot soldiers complained bitterly that the hounds were great deal better fed than they were! The other thing that Brian changed my opinion on, was the regularity of feeding. At the Bicester we had fed only five days a week, all flesh, with a day off before hunting and then a blow-out the night after hunting. It seemed to work perfectly adequately, but I was soon a convert to a feed

Breakfast at the Portman Kennels, watercolour by FA Stewart.

every day, although only a light feed the day before hunting, preferably the porridge.

That summer was interesting in many ways, looking at the hounds and planning which shows to attend, still a major consideration in some quarters, plus steadily taking over the decisions in the kennels myself; understandably it was not altogether easy for Brian having been top dog for quite a number of years. He was enormously helpful in showing support especially on hound exercise when he was quick as a flash to gallop on ahead to warn a household, especially the local farmers, that the hounds were about to call-in and that sustenance would be required! A dangerous start to the day!

When it came to looking at the hounds, there were basically two levels; inspecting and practising with the young hounds prior to the Puppy Show to give them confidence, and looking at the older hounds, often with visiting masters from the other packs to quantify and discuss their hunting ability and their genetic potential. Two things that summer that immediately spring to mind are that firstly it was not difficult to select Wagtail '84 to take to Peterborough as she had an outstanding front (she duly won the Bitch Championship). Secondly, it always amused me that David Beaufort quite often came down to look at the young entry in particular in those days, and would be chatting away to whoever, apparently taking little notice of what was going on, when he would quietly turn round and say, "I know nothing about hounds, they are your department, but those two stand out." Of course he was a brilliant judge of quality in all things and needless to say he was always spot on.

The summer progressed as normal but with rather more Puppy Shows to judge all around the country. It might have been just the age we were, or the era we were in, but it meant that after judging and the serious business of the hounds that we seemed to have the propensity to partake in riotous dinners. We were also extremely lucky to still receive an annual invitation to stay at Milton for Peterborough, one that we had received since the 1970's, thanks I am sure to the fact that the Fitzwilliams had been friends of my parents and once on the list we seem to have survived the changes and were now being made welcome by Sir Philip and Lady Isabella Naylor-Leyland at that amazing house.

Another highlight that seemed to be written in stone in those days was our annual week in Corfu with Martin and Jilly Scott together with other various sporting acquaintances. The behaviour was a little reminiscent of a load of teenagers being let out of school with the days following a pattern of, get up, swim, breakfast, sun, then a trip down the coast in a small overloaded boat with an ineffectual outboard to a local taverna for a lengthy lunch. Back to the villa, more swimming, then sun followed by a prolonged dinner. There was the odd excitement. On one trip back after lunch when the wind had got up and although obviously it was not the Atlantic, it necessitated traversing out towards Albania, not daring to take the waves beam side on. Scottie, ever the gallant, kept the girls company in the bottom of the boat singing 'For Those in Peril on the Sea!'

I can't quite believe how honoured we were in those days to round off every summer with a week at the Castle of Mey, always commencing on August 11th to coincide with the opportunity to pursue an elusive Caithness grouse, (the aim each day being to shoot just enough for dinner that evening). I have already mentioned the regular guests Sir Martin Gilliat and Ruth, Lady Fermoy and other stalwarts such as Air Vice Marshall Sir Edward 'Mouse' Fielden. Past and present Equerries were often included, the most permanent being Ashe Wyndham often

Princess Anne and IWF judging Sir Rupert Buchanan-Jardine's Dumfriesshire Foxhounds.

accompanied by Queen Elizabeth's nephew, Mikey Glamis. All in all it was a very special week which was backed up with a couple of days on the way home with the children at Elleron Lodge, my father-in-law's lovely house in Yorkshire.

Returning to The Cottage, it soon become apparent that without doubt the ambience of the whole set up did pull in a happy band of kindred spirits to a fairly hilarious effect. One of the most permanent that had come down with us from the Bicester was the delightful Camilla de Ferranti. Camilla was soon fairly often living with us, initially keeping her horses with the Pelletts at Peter Sidebottom's yard, before moving them to the main stables at Badminton to hunt on a regular basis, plus keeping us all on our toes at dinner time. Camilla also has a charming brother called Hugo, who was a master of the Mid Devon for some sixteen years and is a remarkable man. He suffers from myopia and is almost entirely blind. When asked why he had elected to hunt on Dartmoor, he simply replied, "No trees. No jumping. Obvious." We took hounds down there for a very memorable trip in 1999.

Peter Lyster, Angela Meade, Martin Scott

The other person that elected to migrate south with us both as a friend and foxhunter, was Peter Lyster. I had first come across Peter when he was joint master and fieldmaster to Dermot Kelly at the Meynell and few men are more knowledgeable and passionate about their hunting than he. Not only did he go extremely well across the country when the chips were down, he was also a stickler for etiquette. When he joined us at the Bicester, a number of friends thought he was being unsociable to start with, as he would station himself away from the Field not joining in the banter, and would never dream of jumping a fence unless hounds were running. However they soon discovered that once off his horse, he was enormously good company. Although in fact always a perfect gentleman, he is a great one for chatting up the birds, and after a couple of drinks his, 'God you are a lovely girl' was an oft repeated catchphrase, accompanied by a cheeky grin. Peter was as relentless in the summer at the pursuit of fish as he was at hunting in the winter and now over eighty he is still driving on a regular basis from his home in Hertfordshire to Exmoor to ride to hounds but stating that now even he has retired from jumping fences.

HANDLING HOUNDS

ALTHOUGH THE MID 1980's are now only some 36 years ago, not long in the main scheme of things, it is sobering to look back to understand just how much has changed since then and not only with the bringing in of the Ban. At that time the sound understanding of the art of venery, i.e. the theory of hunting, in my case the pursuit of the fox, but in the broad picture any quarry, was still very much discussed and aspired to. A good pack of hounds and a good huntsman were much admired, and the achievement of that goal was something to be striven for. Even as far back as around 1868 the subject was remarked on by Henry Chaplin MP, (1st Viscount Chaplin and a Chancellor of the Duchy of Lancaster) who said, "It is easier to find a good Prime Minister than to find a good huntsman!"

Maybe not such an outdated remark. However, in that vein, regarding the neighbourhood in which we found ourselves, hunting was still very much the premier sport in the winter months. On an autumn morning, the lanes locally would be thronged with horses being prepared for the season ahead as indeed they still are.

In the main season a Saturday field of over 200 mounted was not uncommon, and the numbers out on an early mid-week morning even in September never ceased to amaze me.

At that time hunting—maybe not so in East Anglia and other enclaves—was definitely the main country sport in our part of the world. In the Beaufort for instance—most Midland counties would have been the same—a bag of one hundred pheasants was considered ample, and in total there were about ten to fifteen shoots mostly aiming for a mixed bag of twenty five to fifty birds per day with the requisite number of birds put down. Today there are over 60 shoots in the same area, with quite a number striving to achieve bags of 300 to 400 or even more. I often wonder what would be the total number of poults reared today in comparison to those in the past, literally hundreds of thousands, not always to the benefit of biodiversity, certainly not conducive to the well-being of the animal fox, and indeed quite a number of other indigenous species both living on the ground and in the air. To return to that era before the explosion of the popularity of shooting, hunting was just as important as it had always been.

In my mind therefore it was still necessary to get the standard of sport back up to scratch, but as always, the question was how to do it. Hunting a pack of hounds is very individualistic, and no one, least of all me, should ever be high-handed enough to dictate that they had found the answer. However, there were and still are a number of home truths that are worth considering, although at the end of the day a huntsman's personal input is overriding. Man's repartee with the dog has been going on for literally millions of years. The jury is still out as to whether the modern dog is purely a descendant of *lupus lupus* i.e. the wolf, or *lupus familiaris*; close cousins but a slightly different DNA, and therefore might be slightly more susceptible to domestication. The fact remains that the empathy between the two—man and dog—has always been paramount. Even in this modern age you have only got to witness a top-class gundog, regardless of whether it is a retriever or a flusher, or a sheep dog dealing with a limited number in-by (closer to the farm) or a team of dogs bringing in a whole flock from away on a hillside, to realise the understanding they have with their handler, and to begin to grasp the meaning of the word empathy. To go one step further, the degree to which dogs can be trained in their military roles and their staggering sensitivity of medical problems only brings home their ability, aptitude and empathy to their human companions. I use the word empathy—the propensity to sense the feelings of another being whether it be human or animal, and in this case the hound, and to appreciate them fully, has to me always summed up the magic link between a man and dog.

The degree to which a dog understands what you are thinking and their intuition as to what you are up to is quite frankly phenomenal. I always have had dogs and was very happily aware that we got on, but I must confess it was an eye opener when I had a lurcher called Beck whilst I was in Germany, and was on occasions flying back to England to chat up the future Mrs Farquhar for the odd weekend. I used to leave Beck with a brother officer Neville Anderson, another good doggy man, who said he always knew when I was coming back, as regardless of time Beck would be whining at his bedroom door ten minutes before I walked in to the Mess. Different flights, a taxi from Hamburg, different times, how the hell did he know? Yet he did!

In a round about way this brings us back to the empathy with a pack of foxhounds. I personally suspect that the inherent desire of the foxhound, and most other working dogs come to that, is to conform to the principles that they have basically been bred to concentrate on. The foxhound has evolved into a pack animal, but is still hopefully entirely loyal to its human handler. Single-minded in outlook on hunting, but also amazingly friendly in its disposition to life in general. It is the understanding of the fragile requirement of a dog or hound for the need for discipline, but also the physical and indeed mental need on the other hand for freedom, and the ability of fermenting individual genetic idiosyncrasies, that sets some handlers apart from others. This is where obviously handling comes in. Being logical, hopefully the massive genetic input of hundreds of years of careful breeding is tempered with a friendly environment of upbringing. The puppy lives with their mother at the kennels before going out to walk as a whelp, usually with a sibling, on an understanding farm. Meeting children, other dogs, horses, chickens, cows and the general clutter of country life, before returning to the kennels as adolescents to commence their next chapter, is overriding in importance.

If I had a pound in my pocket for every hour I have spent both on a horse and on a bicycle on hound exercise on the highways and byways around Stratton Audley and Badminton I would be a rich man; I expect many hunt servants and other huntsmen would agree. Hound exercise is of course the beginning of the link between a huntsman and his hounds. It is also the start of the delicate balance between control and freedom that should be pre-eminent. Control, discipline, whatever you want to call it, is obviously of paramount importance and the very clear understanding that if a hound is told that it cannot do something, then that is the rule, and any infringement could result in a serious reprimand. By that at times, I mean a serious reprimand. No one wants to be unkind to a hound or any dog come to that, but the judicious use of a whip and words of admonishment can be deemed as necessary with a serial offender. This is normally best done by a whipper-in or member of staff, but on occasions I found it beneficial to take the matter in hand myself. It did remind the pack who the boss was, and it was always interesting to note that after such an altercation, the culprit on sneaking back into the pack, could be further reminded in no uncertain terms by the others that he or she had let the side down. A lot of growling and hackles up. The power of peer pressure. The corollary to that however, is that the freedom of mind is just as important and that the lack of restraint in the educational process during the formative years of any enquiring mind must allow the ability for self thought. Once again the combination of insisting on pack culture, but not destroying confidence is the way forward. Too much freedom can result in chaos, but too much over handling can result in a lack of mojo—by which I mean self-confidence—and that in my view is just as damaging. I cannot stand seeing hounds being forced to keep in a tight group by the over indulgence of a whip. They should keep an eye on the huntsman because they want to, not because they are forced to. The old adage relating to hunting a pack of hounds is that it should be a love affair not a dictatorship!

One trick I personally found beneficial during the hound exercise training period was the use of just a touch of guile. When on bicycles and therefore mainly on the road I would let hounds run on unconstrained,—not into a village obviously—but when it was time to let them know who ran the show, I would do a quick about turn and pedal back in the opposite direction, leaving them behind with mainly the young ones looking about wondering where the boss had gone. In those situations I loved to see them come galloping back with written all over their faces, 'We didn't really mean to go missing and we do love you really!' On horse exercise I would often announce to the boys that we were off on manoeuvres now, and pick enough open ground to get the hounds galloping on in front until once again I would suddenly stop short and either turn 90° or even backwards when again the younger and more exuberant would suddenly realise you had disappeared and they would come storming back to look for you. The funny side of that was that the old hounds in most cases would still be with you, just looking up as if to say, 'Silly old fool he's at it again!' The really interesting outcome of all this was that later on in the season when it became important to move them about to cast or whatever, then you could do so without any fuss and without them losing concentration. Writers much more qualified than I, for many years have termed this empathy or the bond between hound and handler, the Golden Thread, but call it what you will, it is what the magic is all about and in my opinion every good huntsman must have it.

Despite the hours put in on hound exercise during most of that first summer, when we did get going at the end of August it soon became apparent to me that I was dealing with a pack of hounds that had a somewhat different outlook to that which i had become accustomed to. Gallop and look, taking the place of noses down and sniff! The small contingent of hounds from the Bicester were undoubtedly a great help, and I do recall on occasions some of them stopping and looking at me, practically saying,'Where the hell are they off to?' As the main body disappeared on a wild goose chase, each vying to get in front of the other on an imaginary line, before the Bicester crew put their noses down and carried on hunting. This latter behaviour did eventually start catching on and then slowly filtering through.

In the meantime on the breeding front, as always Ronnie Wallace had been extremely helpful recommending Berkeley Freshman '84 who was by Exmoor Freestone '81 full brother to Exmoor, Friar '81. This line produced a necessary orthodox influence on the increasing dominance of the Bicester Farmer/Farrier stuff which I was going rather nap on.

Continuing in the same vein regarding the handling of hounds in the early years at the Beaufort, slowly but surely the strategy outlined earlier began to show dividends. Gradually the pack on the whole began to concentrate on the job in hand rather than flying about. Naturally it took longer with some, especially with a number of the older hounds who were more set in their ways, but when the penny dropped it was very satisfying. I remember one dog hound in particular, Palmer '83 who had won the Championship at Peterborough in 1984. Brian Gupwell naturally thought he was the bees' knees and he had been paraded on every occasion when anybody came to look at the hounds, perhaps rather too good for his ego—Palmer's I mean! Palmer was a very well put together dog but wouldn't hunt. Brian was a little miffed when I told him to leave Palmer in the kennels. I softened the blow by telling him that if Palmer missed a day or two it might change his attitude. Anyway, he had a year off, then started on hound exercise the next season and coming out with a more focused pack he took to it himself, and in the long run was one of the best. In his sixth season I even lent him to Brian Fanshawe for a year to hunt as a stal-lion-hound. For certain I would not have lent Fanshawe a hound unless I really rated him. To some extent, Palmer making the grade illustrated what had already been drummed into me by Newton Rycroft and others, that handling and giving them opportunity is the basic requirement in the making of a foxhound. At the same time, the Vale of Clettwr and Plas Machynlleth bloodlines were making a notable impact on the sport and that in itself bore out the thinking that handling produced the well-being of the 'cake' and that judicious breeding adds the icing. I would therefore be so bold as to state that there is nothing wrong with a good cake, icing on top is definitely a benefit, and to go one step further a cherry or two on top of the icing is even better! For me the Bicester Farmer line certainly produced the cherry.

Stables

An improvement in sport brings me on to the other vital ingredient in a huntsman's armoury namely the horse and its management. The stables at Badminton, mainly through the medium of the Three Day Event are world-famous. How many other private establishments can pride itself on nearly seventy boxes that can all be inspected from the main House without the need of stepping outside. All the boxes are a decent size, 10'x 12' with a covered passage fronting them all. The nearly symmetrical main hunter yard boasts 45 boxes plus a feed wing and blacksmith's forge, with an adjoining 13 and a further eight which were originally built to house the hunters and carriage horses before the 8th Duke added on the main yard. The story goes that this latter yard was built in 1882 with the proceeds of the sale of the 8th Duke's commission in the Horse Guards. Fifteen more boxes can be found round the corner in the Portcullis Yard together with a few more in the adjacent farmyard, which means that eighty five or so contestants for the aforementioned Horse Trials can all be catered for. During the Second World War, these same stables were occupied not by horses, but by a company of soldiers billeted at Badminton to ensure the safety of Queen Mary, the grandmother of our late Queen, who being the aunt of the then Duchess of Beaufort, resided at Badminton for the duration. Queen Mary was reputed to loath ivy and would travel around the Estate in her old chauffeur driven car and upon spotting ivy climbing up a wall or tree would order the car to stop and the soldiers to start cutting down the offending growth, often much to the surprise of the occupants of the cottages. Another story that has always amused me is that one night a message came through from Buckingham Palace for Queen Mary from the then Queen, to say that Buckingham Palace had been bombed, but not to worry, all was well. Queen Mary replied thanking them for the message and adding that all was not so well at Badminton as a German bomber leaving Bristol, being pursued by a fighter plane, had let go of its bombs over the Estate and that 'Master' was not at all happy as he thought they might have landed on a litter of cubs!

Like all well run establishments, the day-to-day organisation is often the sole responsibility of one man who as head of department oversees the horse operation, and in this case that was the well-known figure of Brian Higham. On being demobbed from the RAF Brian had arrived in Badminton in 1959 on the recommendation of his uncle Bert Pateman who was Kennel Huntsman to 'Master'. Bert himself had hunted hounds two days a week on Tuesdays and Fridays for a couple of years, with Master doing Wednesdays and Saturdays, and Gerald Gundry, Mondays and Thursdays, hounds at that time going out six days a week! The Patemans were a very old Yorkshire farming family, great fun and most amusing. I knew Bert when we moved to Gloucestershire from Dorset when I was a boy. I then got to know his brother Matt after I married Pammie, as the Patemans hailed from Snainton east of Pickering, practically next door to the Chafers. Matt did a bit of work on local farms and also with horses but was best known for his penchant for poaching and his expertise with his long dogs. Old Yorkshire, every sentence was completed with a 'By 'eck' and a sucking of teeth. I was always fascinated how he trained his dogs. If he was out at night and thought the police or a gamekeeper were after him, he would just say to his dog 'Go home' and it would take itself off back to his cottage and hide in a bramble bush at the bottom of the garden. Whatever happened the dog would only emerge when he called them. "Me? Poaching? But I haven't got a dog as you can see!" Very clever. He often poached Charles Chafer's extensive farm, and being that sort of a man, Charles always turned a blind eye. One night Charles was doing some earth stopping when his old Land Rover slipped off the track, and whilst sitting there puffing on his pipe and wondering what to do, he heard Matt coming down

Brian Higham. (Photo by John Minoprio)

towards him so shouted out, "Matt it's you. Thank goodness! Come and
give me a push," but on hearing that, Matt had swiftly gone. They met
in Snainton next day, and Charles said, "Matt why didn't you give me a
hand last night?" "T'was not me Mr Chafer, not me!" Matt walked everywhere, his practice was to catch just enough to supplement his supper
and only ever used a dog, rather different to the poachers of today!

To return to Brian, he rode as second horseman to 'Master' for seven
years before being promoted to stud groom in 1966. At one stage in the
1970's, he was in charge of forty eight horses with thirteen grooms and
a strapper or two, and in those days, they were all male. He also had the
task of overseeing the stabling for the Horse Trials plus other numerous
horse related activities. Brian always had a way with horses and had as
good an eye for the right sort of anybody I knew. Although he never
rode competitively himself, he still somehow found time to do quite a
bit of dealing and seldom missed the opportunity of concluding a sale.

Like the rest of his family, he was Yorkshire through and through and I've always enjoyed the tale when one of his horses won a race, some-body asked him when he was going to run it again? "Nay, the next jump he takes is over't counter into Barclays Bank!"

When Pammie and myself arrived at Badminton, the Stableyard was still a full on affair with about 40 horses stabled, including the Hunt horses, David Beaufort and his family's, our ten (rather frightening!). In addition were liveries for Lord Patrick Beresford, Mrs Mary Hill, Antony and Susie Brassey, Camilla Taylor (de Ferranti), and Major Ronnie Dallas, the latter both when he was Hunt Secretary and then when he had retired. Oh of course and one or two for Brian himself...

Highly regarded by Pammie, Brian looked after my horses for nearly 30 more years and although we occasionally did not see entirely eye to eye on the amount of grub they were getting—I did not enjoy getting bucked off—his ability to keep condition on a horse was exceptional, "Just look at his bum—that's the secret." His knowledge of equine legs, gleaned as a boy, then subsequently with a vast amount of experience, was quite frankly second to none. At times we nearly fell out when I wanted a particular horse for a big day and then was told I could not have him. I would say, "But I saw him on exercise this morning and he was a sound as a pound."

"Well, you can't have him, them legs—they're not up, but they just don't handle right." And that was the end of the conversation! He rightly always maintained if you worked a horse when its legs 'Just didn't handle right' that was when you broke it down. The proof was definitely in the pudding, because in the long run very few of his charges did ever break down.

The expression 'selling coals to Newcastle' was certainly also true about Brian and he could see a buyer a mile off. One day we were out hunting, and there was nobody in the kennels. An American and his wife turned up unannounced asking if they could see the hounds. They bumped into Brian who immediately invited them down to the stables. The American husband had been a Master of Foxhounds in the States but was now retired. His wife announced that he had given up riding and certainly was not looking for a horse. Two hours later he had paid a fortune for what could be described as a fairly moderate cob but went away delighted. Brian retired in 2010, and although he and his wife

Sherry spent a lot of time in America, he was still able to keep his cottage in Shop Lane, Badminton, which he had been in for over sixty years. Universally known in the wider horse world, he remained, until the day he died, a fund of knowledge and famous for his amusing stories.

Another vital ingredient to the well-being of the horse is of course the ability of a top-class blacksmith. 'No foot no horse'. As to be expected Badminton had the finest. Bernie Tidmarsh must be one of the best known and respected farriers in the world. As an apprentice to his father, he started full time at the age of 15 in 1962 and has shod horses for over 60 years. He took over the Badminton yard in 1980 when there then 55 horses in full work and has trained nearly twenty apprentices. He reckons he has shod more Olympic Gold Medal winners than anybody! In his heyday he would start work at 4am making shoes and would often not finish until late in the evening. He told me that sometimes for up to three weeks he would not see his wife or daughter in daylight. They were in bed. On a personal note, he shod my horses and Mrs F's for over 34 years and I can say we very seldom lost a shoe. He was presented with a picture of himself in the Forge at Badminton painted by Tristram Lewis which he found delightful and was very pleased with the lovely composition, although a little disappointed to see as artist's licence a couple of shoes scattered on the floor. He said he could not condone that as a horse might tread on them!

***

In the doctrine of the art of venery, I think that the majority of huntsmen would agree that one of the most demanding periods that they go through is the first couple or so years in a new country. I am not just talking about the performance of the hounds as I feel we have already touched on that, but on the need for a thorough knowledge of the terrain in which they find themselves and this flags up different aspects. The understanding of the habitat, movement and location of the quarry, where it lives and the likely preference when pursued to find a safe haven. Another factor is knowing where you can get to on a horse without either losing too much time or breaking your neck! Both important considerations in the efficiency of the whole operation. In early days how many times have we all gone down an unknown route to find that we have let ourselves into jumping some horrific obstacle that was definitely not on the menu! More so than many countries, the Beaufort for the most part was eminently crossable, but there are still some pockets that took a fair bit of negotiating. The very nature of the farming pattern did not change as much as in some other hunt countries, and you could still get what was termed as a good ride if you went straight.

To hark back again to that first year, I think it took the country slightly by surprise when we ceased to follow the previous regime's practice of religiously holding up during the early autumn hunting. I myself have never agreed with it as I always felt that not only did it not educate the hounds, but that it was also detrimental to the fox population as well. If pre-Ban a farmer wanted foxes controlling because of lambs for instance, then it was just as effective out in the open rather than turning everything back into a small covert that would quickly become foiled. I remember one early morning when almost immediately hounds did pour out of a good covert called Cream Gorse; we had a nice hunt for a couple of miles jumping our way initially across Farleaze finishing up not far from Hullavington. When I looked round, I discovered that there was only myself, two whippers-in and David Beaufort, who luckily had happened to be on the corner when hounds had left. He was beaming from ear to ear and certainly his presence when we trotted back half an hour later to find an entire Field still standing by the covert, helped take the wind firmly out of the sails of any of the critics who might have thought that we had jumped the gun. It was not long I might add, before the punters began to enjoy this new approach.

On a more personal note, we had sold our house, Twyford Mill, in the Bicester country to Ian and Tocky McKie. They were, and are a lovely couple, and Ian became a very popular and able joint master and huntsman of the Bicester, before they moved north to join Martyn Letts at the College Valley where Ian continued to make his name. At the time we hadn't found a farm in the Beaufort country that suited, so I kept on the cows at Hillesden, but still struggled with the milk quotas.

GATHERING CLOUDS

Parading and Death of My Father

I DID DISCOVER that many other duties went with the position at Badminton. One of the more daunting to my mind was parading the hounds at the Horse Trials before the prize-giving in the main ring after the show-jumping on the Sunday to a packed crowd of over 20,000. Brian Gupwell, consummate showman that he was, had always done it brilliantly, not only often jumping a fence himself, but would also teach a hound to leap onto one of the fences, usually the wall, and would then lean down off his horse and give it a biscuit. The crowd as expected, loved it. It was a great relief therefore, that my first year I escaped as the event was held in the April before I arrived, the next year it was cancelled completely, and in the following year the mud was so bad after a sodden Saturday, that spectators were banned and just the last 20 horses jumped off for the placings.

So it was only at the beginning of my third year that we had to perform. Initially it was always the Beaufort hounds, their huntsman and two whippers-in obviously clad in green coats, but later we added to the mix a red coat from the VWH and a yellow coat from the Berkeley to add a bit of colour. Subsequently we also added four members of the Pony Club to bring to the fore the importance of the young. I briefed them all beforehand on what we were going to do. Parade hounds slowly, then faster and into a canter across the arena, back into the centre for the 'hats off' salute to the Royal Box. Then a final gallop around the ring to the tune of *D'Ye Ken John Peel* played by the band that were already formed up in the centre. I always advised that if you happened to fall off your horse, and it galloped off, just lie there rather than limping about horseless, you always get more sympathy that way! We would mostly get all the hounds out of the ring on leaving despite the band and the tremendous cheering, and then it was off to the Hunt Club Tent, followed by a visit to the British Field Sports' Society (later Countryside Alliance) Stand, before finally extricating ourselves. A gallop around the Lake was next, amazingly still accompanied by the majority of the hounds even though they had been surrounded by well-wishers, let alone the tempting aroma of hot dogs, kebabs, and burgers not normally on their menu. Talking of hound parades generally, one of the crowd pleasing tricks I enjoyed doing if more than one pack was parading—for instance at the Royal Show—was to let all the hounds get mixed up together for a gallop past the spectators. Then taking them quietly into the centre as one huge pack, to show how you could separate them back into their own individual packs by simply the different huntsmen moving to one side whilst calling for their own hounds before going out of the ring. It was usually a total success, with hounds returning to their own huntsman. Something natural to us, but it always impressed the crowd.

Returning to 1986, it was a year for me of personal change. In the summer my father died. He had not been well for some time suffering a broken hip through a fall, resulting in a spell in hospital which did not suit him. He then returned home, where he was very conscientiously attended to by my brother Mike and his wife Wong. They often went to sit with him in the evening, but as it happened, I was there the night he died. He was asleep and I was reading when he woke up, looking straight at me and said simply, "Monty was a shit wasn't he?" They were the last words he spoke. I often thought about that, no mention of my mother, his sons or even his hounds, but just a recall of El Alamein when he had advised Montgomery—as one of his cavalry colonels—to attack earlier to try and avoid the German 88mm guns against the 'popguns' that our tanks had in those days. Monty had told him, "I am fully prepared to accept one hundred percent casualties of your Regiment." This of course proved rather too near the truth. After the main part of the El Alamein attack, when the 3rd Hussars, or what was left of them (21 officers killed and 98 other ranks, 47 tanks out of 51 destroyed) had been relieved, Monty arrived asking Dad, "Where is your Regiment?" To which Dad replied, "Thanks to you, this is my Regiment." Shortly afterwards the New Zealand General, Freyburg arrived and declared that thanks to the 3rd Hussars, the tide had changed, and because of their

IWF—Badminton Horse Trials

participation with the New Zealand division during the battle he would like the Regiment to accept the honour of displaying the New Zealand Fern Leaf on their vehicles. In my day the fern leaf was still painted on every armoured vehicle of the Regiment.

To go one step further, Queen Elizabeth, the Queen Mother one day when we were discussing such matters stated that as Queen, she remembered the morning when she and the King were having breakfast and Churchill suddenly arrived, threw down some dispatch papers and simply said, "Sir I bring you victory." He was of course right. It was a turning point in the war, and I repeat the story as it is history.

Field Masters again and David gives up Riding

The remainder of the eighties saw the hounds improving steadily, and we began to achieve reasonable sport in all parts of the Beaufort country. Peter Sidebottom took over as Saturday Field Master, not only was he a brave and forward going horseman, but he was also great fun.

He was one of the first of his day who tried very hard to combine the ability of giving the Field a good ride, even on difficult days, without either getting in the way of hounds or of permanently 'cheating' and by that I mean skylarking and jumping fences when hounds were not running, which of course in those more purist days was a capital sin. We normally had enough going on for that not to become an issue, but it was still even then very frowned upon, both by our own punters and also by visitors. It was encouraged and indeed admired for a Field Master to swing a bit wide over a line of fences rather than just plodding through the plough straight behind the hounds, but only when they were running. Peter was working very hard abroad during this time, and would often only get back from America in the early hours of a Saturday morning when he would telephone for a situation report and we would go through the day ahead. He would often call again in the evening after he had religiously counted every fence that he jumped that day. Something I must admit I never did!

Richard Meade on Mondays, was a great planner as to where he was going which was probably part of his success as an Olympian. He definitely preferred a carefully constructed plan as to how the day was likely to go, quite tricky considering the vagrancy of the quarry and also the weather which were both out of our control. Richard was also painstaking in his relationship with the farmers and keeping them informed. My old friend, Antony Brassey conquered the formidable Sodbury fences with a grim faced determination reminiscent of when the Scots Greys crashed through the French lines at Waterloo, and I will always remember his delight in taking on gates and big fences one early morning from Mr Daniells's kale field in the middle of the Sodbury Vale. John White as ever, just carried on running the Thursday country almost single-handedly and as a Field Master just simply got it right. He was always charming, but tough when he needed to be, very steady when there was not much going on, but unbeatable when the chips were down. The same undoubtedly could be said for Rob Ingall in his share of the Monday country and also when he did a number of Saturdays later on. The others were very good indeed, but John and Rob were undoubtedly both brilliant Field Masters and as good as any huntsman could ever wish for. That only left the other half of the Monday country with Simon Tomlinson, whose penchant for looking for fences I have already mentioned. Often mounted on a polo pony, his bravery was unquestion-able and on occasions he would set off with great gusto together with any of the Field prepared to follow him, but not necessarily in the same direction as the hounds, the result however still produced immense fun. As a team they were all amazing and extremely able, and it was no wonder the punters turned up from far and wide to follow them.

Another pleasure in those early days was the fact that David Beaufort did I think quite genuinely enjoy his hunting, and not just for the ride, but also for the hound work. He had always loved horses and hunting *per se*, but became interested to a greater degree than perhaps he had been before in the pattern of a hunt, its outcome and the performance of the hounds. It was therefore a great sadness when in 1989 he had a nasty fall in the Sodbury Vale that exacerbated an already bad back. He never really recovered from it.

It was on a Wednesday. We found in Horton Bushes, and ran fast across the well fenced grassland towards Chipping Sodbury and onto the Common. I remember jumping quite a good gate going onto the Common and looking back to see David following me with a grin on his face. We swung right-handed surprising a game of golf going on (there was a small golf course on the Sodbury end of the Common) then back onto the pasture land heading towards the Bushes. The fence off the Common was quite frankly pretty nasty, quite big, but with a horrible gripe in front of it, not a clean ditch, but more a hollow indentation on a bit of a bank with a drop to the fence that took out any ground line. I was lucky, as I was riding Black Jack who was brilliant in a trappy situation as well as across a big country and of his own volition he came off the top of the bank and made the fence easily. On the other hand David was riding Clandestine, a lovely looking seventeen hand black horse out of Cuddle Up, that mare of David's I had ridden in point-to-points. Clandestine had been in training with Jeremy Tree and had won all of the three hunter chases he had been entered in, but he did not have much experience of hunting.

He got into the bottom of the gripe and turning a circle over the fence, and landed rolling on David. We got him into a Land Rover and taken back to Badminton where he soon recovered. He did ride again, but found it hurt too much to jump and rang one evening to say he was giving up completely. I pleaded with him to continue and remember

IWF and David Beaufort, Worcester Lodge. (Photo by Ray Bird)

suggesting that perhaps he could still come out, but not jump to which he simply replied, "And just trot round the road? No thanks!" Sadly he never did. Being the man he was of course, he kept Clandestine and Lord, his lovely grey for others to ride. I rode Clandestine myself occasionally later and he was as good as any over a big and uncomplicated fence, Lord was top class anywhere.

One day I remember in particular. We had had a fairly steady morning when about one o'clock we found in the Park, and ran to Hinnegar, then for the next hour and three quarters we traversed the top of the Saturday country before crossing the A46 to Bodkin and onto the Sodbury Vale, through Horton Bushes. We then went back up the escarpment to Lyegrove, on to Sherston and the Quarry. Twenty three miles as hounds ran with two points of more than five miles. Throughout, David was patiently following in his Land Rover before getting close to us and declaring how pleased he was that 'Lord' his horse was going so well. At least he did for the first 45 minutes before the euphoria began to wane somewhat. Then after over an hour it was, "Is he still all right?" When we finished it was, "Definitely time you got off!" The horse

Ronnie Dallas's Retirement Meet—Badminton House—IWF, Ronnie Dallas, David Beaufort, Sylvia Dallas, ca.1987.

actually had the most amazing stamina and strength and was still going within himself, but it was definitely time to take the hint! Twenty three miles with hardly a check was I think the longest single hunt that I ever had; I'm not saying that we never changed foxes, but not noticeably, and not often, however we might have done so at Horton Bushes. It was certainly a very memorable hunt.

A New Secretary and Brian Gupwell Retires

Nothing ever stands still and sadly in 1987 Ronnie Dallas retired as Hunt Secretary after an amazingly long tenure. He was adored by all and sundry, and I have already touched on some of his idiosyncrasies. He had always said he would do just a couple of years to see me in, and although it did not come as a surprise to me personally, he was a great loss. As a mark of respect David Beaufort gave a meet in front of Badminton House for Ronnie and his wife Sylvia, a special honour reserved for the very few. Life goes on however, and we were lucky to find John Mackenzie-Grieve to take over. I had known John when he had been Secretary of the Pytchley, and we had overlapped for a time when I was at the Bicester next door. He had then done a stint at the Animal Health Trust in Newmarket before electing to come back into hunting. John was meticulous and for the next 16 years proved to be an eminently efficient and popular Hunt Secretary. JMG as he was known, was remembered fondly for his use of a trademark dictaphone whilst hunting that would appear out of his pocket whenever a question was asked, or to note information that needed acting on, which were both immediately dealt with.

John was passionate about lurchers which at the time were becoming very popular in this neck of the woods and countrywide, indeed Pammie and myself had had them for years. John was very fond of his, but being a stickler for correct behaviour they were never allowed to run free on a hunting day. One day John happened to be following on foot and thinking the hounds were miles away he decided it would be safe to let the three of them off the lead with the result that they bowled over the hunted fox when unexpectedly it changed direction. John was morti-fied! I will confess I was not pleased, whereas everybody else was very amused and John got his leg pulled unmercifully at Christmas time with cards and cartoons depicting lurchers and foxes! As well as having had previous experience with hunting in his earlier days John had enjoyed a short career as a midshipman in the Navy, followed by a short stint advising on tobacco farming in Africa, all of which meant he was well prepared for the challenging times ahead dealing with the rigours of the fight to save our sport.

The next major change was the retirement also in 1987 of Brian Gupwell, with a final meet held in his honour at Worcester Lodge in front of a large gathering of locals and hunt staff from all over the country. The Duke made a presentation and Major Gerald Gundry in his usual inimitable style made the most amusing speech alluding to the fact that Brian had had to finish his days having to put up with an amateur. Gentlemen and Players as he put it! A good day's hunting ensued and Brian continued to hunt regularly, being made more than welcome by all and sundry, much of the time mounted on Seamus, a horse he had been given. As masters, David Beaufort and myself promoted Charles Wheeler to Kennel Huntsman, which although considered young for the job worked extremely well. He was joined in the kennels by Giles Wheeler, (no relation) as second whipper-in. He was ex-King's Troop

Brian Gupwell—"Guppy's"—Retirement Presentation, late 80's—DB, IWF, BG
& Major Gundry, retired Master. (Photo by John Minoprio)

and a good horseman. Obviously used to riding and leading gun horses, it was a slick performance to see him take one of my horses round a covert if I decided to draw it on foot (especially in the early autumn when the undergrowth was extra thick) and jump a fence or two with both horses. Charles and Giles made a good team, and it was an obvious one when I heard somebody extol that, "Things are going well now that the Captain has mastered a two wheeler!" In fact, in my opinion they were both extremely good. Charles was an above average and talented scout as first whipper-in, and Giles who I kept with me, soon caught on how to judge the tempo of the moment. He was as tough as old boots and I never saw him step out of line, although I had heard that his party trick in the pub was to do an impression of me. I persuaded him to give a demonstration at his farewell party and he had me and everybody there in stitches! He got the huntsman's job at the Isle of Wight and then later moved to the Fernie, where I always understood he was a good huntsman, both with the hounds and across country. I fear a two day a week country proved not challenging enough for him, as he then changed career and became a steeplejack. The last time I heard from him he was hanging from a rope in a howling gale on the top of the suspension bridge over the River Severn—not my cup of tea!

On a different tack, as touched on before, I was fairly regularly asked to either America or Canada to judge and this continued with Pammie and myself making some very good friends in both countries. The children were often home for half-term during the Virginia Hound Show and therefore on a couple of occasions I went alone, always staying with Jimmy and Sarah Young who lived in one of the earlier red brick 'settlers' houses. Sarah in particular prided herself on English standards as far as equines were concerned, and rode well bred thoroughbred hunters, whilst always immaculately turned out in a beautifully cut tweed coat. I always felt I let Jimmy down when I could not judge his final year as President of the Virginia Hound Show, then the biggest and most prestigious in the United States. We continued to visit and judge in Canada mainly staying with the Berminghams and the McDonalds.

As regards showing in England, the Beaufort Puppy Show remained a big affair. 'Master' had always loved people coming to look at his hounds and had taken delight in asking a mass of locals, as well as masters and professionals from all over the country to look at the puppies, and later partake of a prodigious tea. This was followed by a look at the older hounds in the early evening, rounded off with a drink or two in the Kennel-Huntsman's house. This format continued. Most hunts had different judges each year, a mixture of amateurs and professionals, but some had the same judge year on year, accompanied by A N Other. The Beaufort always had the same two judges, who often did twenty or thirty year stints. The thought behind that was that continuity in judging was a benefit and a guide as to whether the standard of an entry was going up or down. Captain Charles Barclay from the Puckeridge, and Captain Ronnie Wallace from the Heythrop—and later the Exmoor—had been officiating at Badminton for some years, and continued so to do. They were both of course good judges, and interestingly their after judging speeches were more individual, Wallace's being full of advice and politics, and Barclay's being rather more humorous and lighthearted. One of Barclay's trademarks was to appear as if he had finished before firing off again on another amusing tangent!

As regards breeding during those initial Beaufort years, I harked back strongly to my old Bicester blood, Fanshawe's North Cotswold ST line doubled up with Beaufort and Berkeley and before my day a touch of Puckeridge, before in the early 1990's returning to the more modern orthodox lines from the Exmoor and the Heythrop.

We now move on to the Peterborough Royal Foxhound Show, which then was and now still is considered the premier hound show in the world. Having won both the Dog and Bitch Championships in 1985, the next few years were somewhat leaner, whilst the Welsh influence came through,which was simply not to the liking of the hierarchy of the hound world at that time. We were enormously lucky to be still regularly asked to stay at Milton for the two days, and when I say lucky I mean lucky, because there was no better billet in the country. We still showed, and would pick up quite a few prizes, and personally I have never felt that showing is the be all, and end all—it was merely an indication that if you were in the shake up, then there was hopefully not too much wrong with the hounds' conformation, itself very important.

However, we did win the Peterborough Dog Hound Championship in 1992 with Ranger '90 who was full of the Carlow ST line by Cottesmore Starter '85, and again in 1995 the Bitch Championship with Peewit '94 who was by Exmoor Pewter '89. I had purposely used Pewter on the recommendation of Captain Wallace not only for his hunting ability but also because of his size. He was a big upstanding dog, and I was just beginning to become a little perturbed that we were losing size in the bitches through the increasing use of the Welsh. This in no way affected their hunting ability, and in fact had undoubtedly improved it, but the Beaufort had always been synonymous for their size and were a fountain head for other packs to come to. This slight tailing off in the size in the bitches was understandable as there is no doubt that the difference in size between the Welsh bitch and the Welsh dog is greater than the differential between the English bitch and the English dog. Peewit certainly came up to scratch and in that regard as did her sister Peanut. It was not surprising therefore, when in 1999 the urge to go back to Wales once again became compelling—this time to the David Davies—that Peanut herself was to feature with huge success.

Marlin '95 triumphed in 1996. He was by the striking looking Mostyn '92 who had been widely used, and whose progeny were to feature in the future. An amusing anecdote concerning Mostyn I cannot help but tell was that he had won certainly in Yorkshire and at Ardingly was considered highly favoured for Peterborough. It was the beginning of the era when we started to pick up Peterborough Championships fairly regularly, somewhat to the concern of the competitive Captain R. E. Wallace. No fool, he was overheard briefly talking to the Peterborough judges in the year that Mostyn was due to be shown saying, "Of course only a very good judge can see the faults in Mostyn." He hardly got a look in!

One of the observations that did become apparent was that in the past a number had forecast that Brian Gupwell would never be replaced as a showman. He was good, but so too was Charles Wheeler, and in the future Tony Holdsworth was up there with the best of them, past or present. As a boy I always remember my father standing behind his then Kennel Huntsman, Harry Colbeck, in the Portman kennels with a large thumbstick threatening to hit him over the head muttering, "Get low man, get low!" By that of course he meant mesmerise the hound in question to keep his head down, thereby showing off the length of neck, and also thereby accentuating the quality of the shoulder. This is as true today as it was then.

House Move and Our Girls Hunting

We had moved from The Cottage to West End Stud, Shipton Moyne in 1988, as usual accompanied by the three girls, the dogs, ponies, and Pammie's horses. It had been a generous gesture of David Beaufort's to lend us The Cottage and it was just unfortunate that the three years spent there as non-home-owners coincided with just about the biggest house price rise in history! I also at that time had doubled up in Lloyds, another none too brilliant financial move. West End Stud was a good sized house with plenty of extra accommodation and about sixteen boxes and paddocks. In the summer we rented out the boxes to an international polo patron who ran a team at the Beaufort Polo Club at Westonbirt and whose main hired 'assassin' (as leading semi professional polo players were often called) was Antony Fanshawe, youngest son of my cousin Brian. He often played in the Argentine in the winter, in England in the summer and is now running the polo at the Guards Club at Windsor. When the polo finished in the autumn, we had hunter liveries done by Mrs Farquhar with the help of a very experience head girl and other staff. Among the liveries at that time was a young Royal Agricultural College student, James Andrews whose father runs the Wales and Border Hound Show at Builth Wells. James later hunted the South

Three Counties Show, late '8os: Winning Inter Hunt Relay Team, IWF, Gail Sturgis, Tony Pellett and Mike Tucker.

Pembrokeshire (now Cresselly) for a time and the South and West Wilts. Before West End, we had sold up the farm in the Bicester country partly due to the problems with the milk quotas, and also with the difficulty of running a farm so far away. That had been a great sadness especially as the cows were generally making into a good pedigree herd, mainly I might add due to the expertise of the team, especially Richard Smith who was a brilliant and invaluable Jack of all trades. I'm glad to say he's done very well since.

On the home front horse-wise, the girls were going from strength to strength, not only beginning to enjoy representing the Pony Club, but more up my street, beginning to really enjoy their hunting and unlike some children to actually take an interest in the hounds. It was still a curious time as regards the political situation and the general outlook concerning the future in retrospect was a false scenario. It was full steam ahead as far as producing sport was concerned, but there were growing indications that the future might be more precarious. Generally speaking, this was still confined to a minority of left wing agitators and a

Emma, Victoria and Rose jumping (Photo: Charlie Sainsbury-Plaice)

number of passionate Animal Rights Activists. The British Field Sports' Society and the Masters of Foxhounds' Association still reigned supreme and most sportsmen in the countryside considered it to be business as normal, with the old guard still running the ship of the sporting state. At that time, despite the attention of people like Kevin Hill and Joe Hashman from the League Against Cruel Sports and an increasing number of anti-hunting anarchists who turned up on occasions there was comparatively little trouble.

On a more personal front, one's journey through life sometimes results in bumps in the road and suffice to say that at about this time I hit a big bump and entered a rather tricky patch to put it mildly. I had badly hurt those I cared about, which resulted in finding myself living a fairly spartan bachelor existence together with my lurcher Brassey in a pretty bleak cottage. It is not a subject I will dwell on. I would not have been the first huntsman to find himself primarily living alone, who discovered that his hounds were his greatest allies. I have endlessly discussed the empathy a dog holds for his boss if given the indication of his affection and they are just as supportive in a time of adversity as in a time of euphoria. All that they mind about is that your resolve in their direction remains total. So, despite other difficulties sport remained consistent.

Politics

Moving on, 1993 proved in retrospect to be somewhat of a watershed when Wiltshire County Council headed by a particularly pernicious Labour councillor (Labour did have an over-all majority at the time) brought in a proposal to ban hunting on all of the County Council farms, at the time numbering just under a hundred. The threat of a motion did spur me to write a poem in the summer of 1993 which surprisingly enough was published in *Hunting Magazine*!

Countryweek Hunting July 1993

Up stands a rural Englishman to have his say

And Captain Ian Farquhar MFH of the Duke of Beaufort's puts it in verse:

> At local council level the knives again are out
> 'Ban all forms of hunting' is once more the Labour shout.
> The Democrats divided—the Tories just hold true
> But how many of them contemplate what it means to me and you?
> Me and you seem not to matter—even less the rural throng.
> And the politics of envy can fast turn right to wrong.
> Will reason ever triumph and will common sense prevail,
> Or who will wag the countryside—the dog or just its tail?
>
> For years they've been agin us. 'You, the killers!' is their cry.
> Yet sportsmen that we know of would themselves much sooner die
> Than to break the rule of Nature and be the cause of needless pain,
> Balance is our flagstaff, conservation our refrain.
> But at local council level a more important issue stands,

The right of those affected—the men who farm the lands.
Is their opinion asked for? Is their counsel even sought?
Or are they worthless individuals and their feelings put at nought?

The tenant should be sacrosanct—the voice of freedom heard,
Not to listen to the tenant is a paradox absurd.
If his choice is so belittled and his view of no account
Then the view that surely governs, which no reason can surmount,
Is that man in a minor minority can forget the will to fight
And the proven English adage 'I am free, it is my right'
Will be turned into the gospel so favoured by the few,
'If I don't want to do it, then I'll ban it all for you.'

In an age when standards falter, with the world in disarray,
Can not the rural Englishman stand up and have his say?
Must we now be always governed by an urban-biased vote,
Jealous in its nature, and ignorant to boot
Of the way of life we stand for and the pleasure that we seek
Of horse and hound, of gun and dog, and fish in every creek.
Or will the countryside fall silent and the sound of horn no more
Echo round the hillside and reverberate the moor?

No thought of where it leads to, no conclusion to the theme
Of every home its castle, every passion its own dream.
It's a dream of hounds and horses and fellowship benign
A fellowship that's tempered across the march of time
When men of all compassions regardless of their creed,
Age, sex or social standing, have always felt the need
To partake in something dangerous within a common bond
Which benefits community—a feeling deep and sound.

But those men who try to stop us, and who twist the common cause,
Have a little else to live for but to start up local wars,
Wars against our monarchy and wars against the realm
And wars against society and those who man the helm.
All those in authority, no matter who they be
And no matter what they stand for—they will harass you and me

As long as we are sportsman and continue in our fight
To pursue our country pleasures—ours of birth and ours of right.

Do they ever pause to ponder, as they chisel on their way
To inflict their will on others, just who holds the moral sway?
What becomes of hounds & horses, foxes, game-birds, deer, & fish,
Or can you differentiate at just a whim or wish,
As to which you make illegal and how far down the chain you go,
Should we all become pure vegans with only oats to sow?
Should we license procreation—with a Ministry for Man,
Will bureaucracy take over in this headlong flight to ban?

But we must not let that happen and it's up to you and me,
You and me must grasp the metal, put the facts for all to see.
When demonstrations flourish and lawful men descend
To battle in the hedgerows—it is time to call an end.
Let reason beat the cudgel, debate rule out the mob,
Fists are not the answer—the pen must do the job.
Let all sportsmen stand united, for divided we will fall,
The Hunter and The Shooter and The Fisher—Hear the Call!

'Ban all forms of hunting!' is to them but just a start,
Disregard of tenant's wishes is only one small part
Of their long-term plan for countrymen, for what they can and
    cannot do.
And they care not one iota what becomes of me and you.

At the Beaufort Hunt we started a petition from the County Council
farmers themselves, stating that they did not support the motion and
that they did not agree with the landlords dictating to them on a moral
issue; one which they felt should be left alone. It was gratifying, and I
think my figures are right, that ninety seven of the ninety nine council
farmers signed at once, one was very ill in hospital, and another who
was in the process of renegotiating his terms was worried it might be
held against him. He elected not to sign but said he would let it be
known that he was supporting the Petition. Not a bad Mandate. As I
recall, we did reinforce the Petition with a well attended demonstration

outside the County Council offices in Trowbridge, packed with Council tenants, local farmers and hunting folk, when the much respected and charismatic head of the Tenants' Association, John Borras, handed over the supplication. The lack of Labour Councillors present did not go unnoticed!. We felt that our endeavours had made their mark when later the tenants received a letter stating that the Council had decided that there was to be no change in the present legislation.

There is often a bizarre twist in such matters and one Council tenant, who had always been a little reticent in allowing access to a large number of horses, actually rang me up before a big Saturday in his area, and very firmly told me, that it was his decision as to whether a tenant should allow the Hunt and not the Council's, and unless we took the whole entourage over his land the next day, he would himself ban us permanently!

Although this seemed a very satisfactory conclusion at the time, in retrospect it was more a pause before the gathering storm, there was certainly more to come.

Live Oak

However, in another direction the Gods were smiling. Having judged the cross-breds (American X English blood) at Virginia, I was asked to stay with Marty and Daphne Wood at their home, Live Oak Plantation near Thomasville on the Georgia-Florida border, before accompanying them to the other major American Hound Show at Bryn Mawr in Pennsylvania to stay with George and Sheila Hundt. Pammie and myself had met Marty and Daphne on numerous occasions in the past, but as Masters of the Southern packs, we previously had been more acquainted with the Hardaways and the Lamptons. I think it is true to say over those few days between shows,we struck up a friendship with the Woods that has never looked back. We seemed to spend just about every waking hour either looking at hounds or talking about them! I might add nothing much has changed to this day! I will confess that I did not think there were many individuals left in the world that could enjoy quite so many hours discussing the relative merits and weaknesses of particular hounds and hence their bloodlines. The Woods had been introduced to hunting (hunting in America generally speaking being used as a term for shooting, but obviously in this case we mean hunting in the English

*Visit to America, 1995. Back Row: Ronnie Wallace MFH Exmoor Foxhounds,
Sherman Haight MFH Litchfield County Hounds, IWF MFH Beaufort
Hounds, Thady Ryan MFH Scarteen Hounds, ???, Jake Carle MFH Keswick
Hunt. Front Row: Judy Greenhalgh MFH Blue Ridge Hunt, Daphne Wood
MFH Live Oak Hounds, Louise Humphrey MFH Woodfield Springs Beagles.*

vernacular) by Ben Hardaway at the Midland, near Columbus. It was not
long before both Marty and Daphne became passionate converts starting their own pack. They built kennels and stables a stone's throw from
their imposing colonial type house in the middle of mostly pinewoods,
which also sported some of the best quail shooting to be had anywhere.
The Live Oak are now probably one of the most influential packs in the
United States. They started with the basis of American Crossbreds from
the Midland, followed by a strong outcross of pure Modern English.
The Woods became disciples and great friends of Ronnie Wallace;
a meeting of minds that was to endure until his demise. Their early
(Bywater blood, pure American) put to an Exmoor female line then
produced Live Oak Drummer '89, patently a very able foxhound who
was to have an over-riding influence not only at the Live Oak, but also
throughout America and Canada and in time in England as well. Nearly
30 years later every time I have one of many endless discussions about

Rose, Emma and Victoria—IWF birthday meet at Nesley Farm circa 2005

past times with Daphne, it's not long before I get reminded of the brilliant influence of Live Oak Drummer! There's no doubt in my mind at that time there were already a few good pure English hounds in the United States but the increasing quality of the Midland and then the Live Oak began to dominate.

Family

During these early Beaufort years there was always a stream of interludes other than just sport. One instance that will always remain in my memory, is the day when our two eldest daughters, Emma and Victoria, then in their very early teens, both mounted as usual on their dun Connemara ponies, Wogan and Casey—the ponies I might add considerably older—were sort of with me on a fast Saturday. When I say 'sort of with me,' I always insisted that I was not responsible for, and therefore not encumbered by, the children. I had a different priority, but still loved them being about. So they were sort of with me, when we were going well towards Hebden from Scratch Face Lane. I jumped what I thought was really quite a big hedge before looking back to see where they had got to. I couldn't see anything the other side of the hedge until suddenly two little dun ponies appeared, the hedge being taller than either of them. Talk about out of the mouths of babes and sucklings. That evening at tea I did say to Victoria, who was about 12, "That hedge going towards Hebden, wasn't that biggest you have ever jumped?" She thought for a moment, and not trying to be clever, announced simply, "Actually Daddy, I think the one before, when you went through the gate, was bigger!"

Remains of the Day

There always seemed to be so much going on, and not just in the hunting Field. In the summer of 1992, the Beaufort Hunt were invited to join in for the filming of a hunting scene for *The Remains of the Day*. The story was based on the 1989 book by the Nobel Prize-winning author Kazuo Ishiguro. The plot explored the lives and loyalties, both personal and political, of those in a large country house at the time of the rise of Nazi power in Germany just prior to the Second World War The subsequent film, beautifully orchestrated by Merchant and Ivory, and shot mainly on location in major houses in the West Country— Powderham Castle, Corsham Court, Badminton House and for the outside shots, Dyrham Park just north of Bath which was to include in our case, the hunting scene. The cast was formidable, Anthony, now Sir Anthony Hopkins, as the butler Stevens, James Fox as Lord Darlington and Emma Thompson as housekeeper Miss Kenton, and the late Christopher Reeve as an American Senator, to name but a few.

We, the Hunt, did get paid a bob or two for producing a pack of hounds, some 60 or so mounted members, dressed as much as possible in pre-war attire, plus a good attendance of similarly clad foot followers. Regardless of the interminable waiting about, it was in fact quite fun doing it. Anthony Hopkins did appear to be the most senior actor present—if indeed actors have a pecking order. I was secretly amused when at the so-called 'Meet' James Fox turned to me as Master and huntsman to enquire, "What sort of thing would we usually say to Anthony?" As butler, he was hovering by my side with yet another stirrup cup of Ribena on a silver tray—pity not port, but probably just as well after numerous retakes! I replied, "Nothing. It's pre-war and he's just the butler!" James Fox at that, gave what seemed a satisfied smile! Anthony Hopkins was in fact delightful, and when Pammie asked if the girls could have his autograph—they had been both riveted and terrified by his portrayal of Hannibal Lector in *Silence of the Lambs*—he invited them into his caravan remarking, "Don't worry, I'm safe until after dark!"

We fielded a strong team of sidesaddle ladies, including Pammie, with Emma and Victoria on their ponies. Rose being the youngest was on the front of a pony and trap driven by Wilkie who I had known back in my own childhood. He needed nothing from the props department looking a suitably old-fashioned character who could have come straight from any previous age, in an aged frock coat and sporting his ancient bowler. He was a familiar sight at local weddings and funerals and would often be seen on his way home to Horton after generously partaking of a beverage or two, fast asleep, sprawled out across the seat of his trap, while his trusty pony trotted along the A46, looking right and left before turning off the main road heading for home.

The final filming involved bringing the hounds out of the stable yard, to coincide with Emma Thompson arriving on her bicycle, this did begin to pall a bit after about fourteen re-takes. I'm not sure who was more bored, the hounds, the horses or Emma Thompson!

One of the aspects of filming a period piece was the amusement of seeing everyone, ourselves included, dressed in the correct period fashion. Jack Windell, a very senior Beaufort tenant farmer for instance needed no additions to his attire, looking as resplendent and correctly dressed as ever in his traditional country clothes. Chris Casey, was sent off to Make Up and emerged with a very short back and sides much to his chagrin. When the redoubtable and elegant Mrs Cynthia Pitman (sister of Sir John Miller, Crown Equerry) still hunting side saddle on blood horses well into her eighties, glared at the waiting make up artists, announcing, "I am not being messed about with", all those present quaked in their shoes!

Following on in the vein of the children, it was only a year or so later that Emma then sixteen, showed a very firm inclination that she wanted to point-to-point. We were fortunate to be told of a Ledbury horse that would be just the ticket as the perfect schoolmaster. I went and saw him and we acquired a lovely grey who went by the name of 'Jack and Jill'. He turned out to be perfect, a total gentleman and a very capable hunter to boot. Tragically later he broke his leg jumping the only telegraph pole in the Royal Wiltshire Yeomanry Ride at Badminton open to ex-soldiers' families. This was very sad indeed as Emma was and indeed is not only a most capable horsewoman but is also very brave and conscientious, she certainly did not deserve that.

Back to the theme of being tracked by the children out hunting, Emma was with me one day and we jumped a fence near Alderton that had recently had a huge ditch dug out. Her mid-air scream of "F...king hell Daddy," did amuse the Field! Rose was also by then going well, and the pleasure I had of seeing them all having a real crack was untold, although I must admit it was orchestrated by their mother rather more than me.

As a follow-up to *The Remains of the Day*, by chance, not long after our encounter in Dyrham Park, Pammie and myself found ourselves in a lift in New York, staying in a hotel not far from Central Park. Who should get into that same lift, but James Fox, exclaiming, "Oh the Master is here!" We chatted happily on the way to the ground floor, which being New York took quite some time! We were there as I had been invited to make the speech at the North American Masters of Fox Hounds' Dinner and Dance, which was on the Friday night, and having flown over that day, with the different time factor, it meant speaking at around 5pm UK time. Quite a tester! On the Saturday evening we had dinner with Bill and Lou Bermingham in their suite at the top of the Hilton overlooking Central Park, and I vividly remember looking down at the skaters on the lake. From that great height they looked just like Lowry 'stick men'. We flew back overnight on the Sunday, just in time to host a Meet at Happylands on the Monday. Luckily in those days we had Lucinda Cursham helping with things at home so everything went off smoothly although somewhat exhausting!

Staff, Horses, Showing and PR

"A Horseman's Grave is always open" was a favourite saying of Brian Higham's, rather gloomy, but sadly over the years I have witnessed all too many accidents. Any horseman knows that falls and sometimes broken bones are inevitable if you are in the saddle on a regular basis.

It was not surprising therefore that occasionally members of the Kennel team were incapacitated from time to time (myself included!) The first casualty around that time was in 1989 when Charles Wheeler

'I must have been riveting'— Ben Hardaway listening to IWF speaking in New York, American MFHA meeting.

had a wicked fall over a gate in the Thursday country at Bremhill and broke his leg quite seriously. It was before Brian Gupwell had retired so luckily he was still going full gun and Nigel Maidment stepped in to the breach having on occasions already whipped-in as an amateur to Sidney Bailey at the VWH.

A couple of years later Giles Wheeler, who as I have already mentioned was second whipper-in with Charles, broke his jaw in a fall and then did the very same thing again the following season of 1991. By a stroke of luck at that time, there was a very capable young man working in the Estate Office at Badminton as an Under Agent by the name of Edward Knowles who was also very keen foxhunter and who had helped us from time to time in the past. I remember ringing David Beaufort and explaining we were a whipper-in down and that help on the big days could be beneficial. I went on to say that Edward would be delighted to help and that we had the horses available to mount him. David response was typical. "Delighted! He'll learn much more out with you than in the Office. Not sure what they do there all day anyway!"

Edward was an enormous help and it obviously fired him up as he

Myra Chappell, Nick Stevens and IWF.

promptly left his job at Badminton and became master and huntsman of the South Dorset. A role he fulfilled until 1998, when a wife and young children necessitated a more lucrative outlook. He did join the Waveney Harriers for a time, but not hunting hounds. Some years later in 2016, he and wife Kitty (daughter of the formidable General Kitson) moved to the Tedworth Hunt where he is to this day, fulfilling the role as a popular master and huntsman strongly backed by the local Guinness family. On two occasions, when I judged at Peterborough, Edward has been my co-judge and we got on as well in the ring as we did when he whipped-in. His move to the South Dorset Hunt precipitated another change at Badminton triggered by Robin Gundry's departure from Dorset to the Wynnstay, in turn meaning that Nick Stevens, his terrier man, was looking for a job. Until then that role had been assiduously carried out by stalwart, Fred Ind, on a mainly part-time basis also assisted by Tim Smith who farms on the Badminton Estate. They were, and are, two of the best and most delightful countrymen you could ever come across and it says a lot that both Fred and Tim now in their eighties are still out on a fairly regular basis. Thirty years ago, the priority was to concentrate on the best sport possible, hence the decision to replace the part-time terrier staff, however dedicated, with a full-time professional. Nick was one of the best qualified in the land. A very tough, but also intelligent individual who understood nature and quickly proved his worth.

In the early 1990s, Charles Wheeler continued to show the doubters that it was not impossible to follow Brian Gupwell as a showman, and we again won a Championship at Peterborough with Patience '98 taking the Bitch prize in 1999. This was followed by Foxham '99 taking the Doghound Championship in 2000. This raised Charles's score up to five Peterborough Championships—Ranger '90 (92), Peewit '94 (95) and Marlin '95 (96) being the others. To start with in those days we showed all round the country, often accompanied by a hardy band of puppy walkers and supporters—the South of England Hound Show at Ardingly, the Welsh and Border Hound Show at Builth Wells, the Great Yorkshire at Harrogate, the Royal Peterborough Foxhound Show and the West of England at Honiton. Not all in the same year though, as the MFHA stipulation was that three shows were considered enough. By the turn of the century, I had basically settled for Builth and Peterborough as being sufficient. This in no way meant that I did not attend the other shows which were just as well run and just as much fun, with the benefit of seeing a lot of the local hounds at all of them. Builth in particular became a real favourite, the Welsh Hound connection being a strong draw. Another joy for me there was the success of my Bicester bloodlines that had been nurtured first by Ian McKie and then by Heather Tylor assisted by their then huntsman Patrick Martin. It is probably fair to say that in those days the Bicester were our greatest rivals for the ribbons, and on more than one occasion I did laughingly say that I really did not mind who won, as long as it was one of us! I hope I was never a pot hunter, but for me to see good conformation come to the fore was important. This was before the North Cotswold arrived on the Builth scene and widened the competition.

Changes on the home front were also running apace, and in the mid-1990s we were beginning to see a build up of the saboteurs and ensuing Press interest. At that time for me, the most fortuitous consequence of this was the involvement of Jo Aldridge who had arrived in the Beaufort country as a great friend of Jo and John Mackenzie-Grieve, hence her

Jo Aldridge.

moniker 'Jo2'. The big breakthrough as far as her helping out with our public relations was concerned was when one day at a meet we were inundated with Press, mostly local, but some national who were busy interviewing many of the old and the bold, all perfectly well-meaning of course, but not the type of image we needed to put across in those days. I turned to Jo and said, "For Christ's sake Jo help find some normal people for the press to talk to and not all these bloody generals!" Later we put together a team of locals, farmers and their young daughters, livery yard owners, saddlers, farriers and feed merchants, vets and vicars, all a wide representation of the hunting community. Some received vital media training from the Countryside Alliance and the system I thought worked brilliantly and in fact stayed in place till long after the Ban. It was a fact that nationally the polls began to show a turn around in hunting's favour and was in my opinion largely due to increased awareness of image. It did not filter through to the Labour backbenches, but that is a different story.

Another change, but in no way politically driven, was that Antony Brassey retired as a Field Master after eight very popular seasons and Chris Casey took his place. Chris was a brave and capable horseman who soon won his spurs over the Sodbury Vale fences later also helping out on Mondays and major Saturdays, in addition to becoming an extremely beneficial member of the Hunt Committee, giving excellent advice on financial matters..

Talking about the Sodbury Vale, reminds me of a time when we met in the Vale and found ourselves jumping a big drop fence with a meandering brook on the other side. Three visitors, thrusting members of a well-known Blackmore Vale family and Charles Wheeler plus Beaufort farmer David Akerman who had lost his leg in a farming accident, all jumped the fence to my left where the brook was a long way out and all turned a circle in a line. David's prosthetic leg spun round and was facing backwards, and I recall hearing the consternation from the Doggerell family, "Help help we have never seen a leg so badly broken." This of course was soon sorted out by David who simply turned his false leg round and remounted!

Although not there at the time, John Minoprio later took a photograph of the set up which appeared in his excellent book *The Blue and Buff.* He was mainly a very able portrait photographer who came to see me in the late 1980's and asked if we could help him to take his dream picture of the fox, hounds, huntsman and the Field altogether, as depicted in so many sporting paintings, but never caught on camera. I rather dampingly told him he would never achieve it! Jim Meads had been trying for years, but without success. Not to be daunted, for a number of years John turned up regularly. We tried to position him in the best vantage points possible and although he never got his dream shot, he did produce for us the most delightful photographic book illustrating every facet of hunting in the Beaufort country you could think of.

Looking back on those pre-ban political years they were in fact very testing. There was a lot going on and we were still hunting four or five days a week. The farmers remained firm as rocks but the endless meetings, conferences, and discussions as to what to do and when did produce pressure. Being a major hunt, we were expected to come up trumps which I hope we did but it tested the administration. On that score we were supported on all fronts but I would hate for it not to go on record that undoubtedly an important lynch pin regarding internal organisation was David Beaufort's Secretary, Cherry Hollyhead. David had asked Cherry to become his personal PA on the retirement of Mr

Bywater her predecessor and she proved a brilliant choice. Cherry had always been involved with the Beaufort. She did the books for a number of local farmers and had helped run the Hunt Supporters' Club for a time. Whether it was looking after the Kennels account, or overseeing endless Hunt events including rather a major Puppy Show, she never missed a trick. We worked together for over 30 years. I relied on her so much she became known as Nanny! Later when Jo Aldridge took on the public relations, she too acquired the moniker of Nanny, but Cherry was always Nanny One and Jo was allowed to be Nanny Two! They did make an amazing team and we were very lucky. Back to Cherry, although never over the top, she had a brilliant and quick sense of humour hitting the nail on the head when going through the Puppy Show invitation list one year, we came across the name of a well-known master and I said we should ask his girlfriend and I would find out her name. I went back to Cherry to report she was in fact Dutch, had a title and she was a "Van" Oh said Cherry quick as a flash, "Does that make her Transit Van?"

In 1992 a sad occurrence that was to affect the steady flow of hunt horses into the Badminton stables was triggered by the premature death of Dr. Tom Connors. I know I have already eulogised about Dr. Tom as he was universally known before, and his demise left a large hole in the horse power of many hunts, not least our own. Always charming, and always straight, he had personally sold myself and Pammie horses at the Bicester and then the Beaufort where he had already supplied a good number of horses for David Beaufort and also the Hunt Staff. He was a great friend of Brian Higham's and together they made a formidable duo. Dr Tom was a hard man to replace and indeed it was a few years before any one individual even began to step into his shoes as it were. His son Derry had moved down to the Beaufort country and with his wife Alex later kept us going with boots and breeches instead of horse flesh. For a time we acquired horses from wherever. Shortly before Dr Tom had died I had persuaded him to relinquish one of his own hunters and sell it to me to give to Pammie for Christmas, hence the nickname we gave him of Santa, although in the stables he was known as Connors. He did fairly soon get generously passed back to me and was a very good one indeed, with noticeably lop ears. I had often been told that they were an indication of ability and temperament, I can't think why, but certainly in his case that was very true.

A humorous episode that comes to mind concerning Santa was at one stage he was beginning to get above himself, and I advised Brian Higham that maybe he needed less oats. To no avail. I then suggested to the delightful Scottish girl groom who looked after some of my horses that it would be a good plan to take out half his rations each day and dispose of them. A week or so later Brian grumbled to me that he couldn't understand why his own horse, that had always been so civil, had tried to buck him off and then run away. I asked the groom if she could throw any light on the situation when with a mischievous smile, she confided that the discarded oats were ending up in Brian's horse's manger! Her secret stayed with me.

Other horses did materialise: Andrew Parker-Bowles, the Brigadier came up with a cob who went by the imaginative name of Trooper. Trooper did have his place, although when he got cast over a tiger trap (I always thought they were rather nasty modern contraptions, although I suppose they did have their place in some situations) in a muddy bog in the Thursday country, he was re-christened by Gail Sturgis as Hippo. His 'street cred' did go down somewhat!

We also had a number of good ex-showjumpers from Graham Fletcher, one in particular called Geordie, who came to me on the advice of Tom Normington who was in charge of the horses at Highgrove at the time. Tom had been a professional huntsman at the Grafton when we were at the Bicester and he knew a good horse and hound as well as any man. Another really very exceptional horse that came my way, was Pip, a quality light bay that Mrs Farquhar tried from Vere Phillips who was dealing mainly in Leicestershire and was making a name for himself for producing some of the best. Mrs F rode Pip once and straight away announced that he was ready to hunt hounds immediately. I took her at her word and rode him for the first time on a big Saturday. We stood outside the Kennel gate and as the entire bitch pack flew past voicing their excitement in anticipation of things to come, he never moved a muscle except to just turn his head as they swept past. He then trotted across the Park to the Meet at Worcester Lodge as the hounds played round him as if he had just found his role in life, which of course he had. He was a lovely mover, completely brave, never made a single mistake, and it was a tragedy that after only a few years he suffered from navicular and eventually the amount of phenylbutazone that he needed made him unrideable.

Another major breakthrough as far as I was concerned at that time was the arrival of Paul Hardwick in 1995, he worked firstly as a groom in the stables, with the aim to enter Hunt Service. He did a year with us, whipping-in for a few odd days before going on to the Quorn as second whipper-in for one Season, and did not need any encouragement therefore in May 1997 to return to Badminton also as second whipper-in. He remained with me until I retired from hunting hounds in 2011. I would like to think that we understood one another and certainly had a very happy working relationship for fourteen years. It soon got that I very seldom had any need to admonish him over anything. He always accompanied me and regularly when a situation was brewing that needed nipping in the bud I would turn round to tell him to go and do something to find he'd already gone! More of that later.

Although on the general hunting front things were going from strength to strength, on the political front the storm clouds were definitely brewing. The number of demonstrators or 'antis' as they became known was definitely increasing and some ugly situations did become more commonplace. The inevitable press coverage did of course work both ways, sometimes in our favour and sometimes not, usually depending on the ideology of the paper concerned. The police generally speaking in those pre-ban days were sympathetic to our cause.

Harking back to the County Councils, in the mid-1990s we did get wind of a move also in Gloucestershire to ban hunting on Council farms. This in part had escalated when Labour came to power that spring with a Hunting Ban in their manifesto which precipitated Labour MP, Michael Foster to present a Private Members Bill to ban hunting with dogs. We had already started work on our own Gloucestershire Festival of Hunting, set for the 27th of July, when the recently formed Countryside Alliance announced it was going to hold a national pro-hunting rally in Hyde Park which was then scheduled for the 10th of July. This of course meant that we had two major events only about a fortnight apart, both of which required a considerable amount of organisation. The one nationally, but still putting a lot of pressure on us locally and the other obviously more in-house and therefore very time-consuming. Neither were short of support. The Hyde Park Rally has been well documented and was largely the brainchild of Robin Hanbury-Tenison who had taken over as Director of the newly formed Countryside Alliance and was undoubtedly a brilliant innovator. He was well backed politically by Charles Goodson-Wickes as Chairman and by Peter Voute as Administrator and the delightfully punchy Australian, Janet George running the Press side. They were further supported by Brigadier James Stanford, Captain Simon Clarke and Major-General Robin Brockbank, a former Director of the British Field Sports' Society and others. The 120,000 who turned up from all parts of the country at the time was considered an amazing achievement, although this of course was to be well surpassed the following year. Certainly what both Hanbury-Tenison and Voute in particular achieved was to unite a cohesive workforce from all over the country and from all sporting persuasions. As well as those already mentioned above, Bill Andrewes and Brian Fanshawe who together headed up the Council of Hunting Associations (formed to represent all sections of hunting), readily spring to mind. Bill had worked for Granada Television and his understanding of the media was a breath of fresh air. Working with Brian who in turn really did understand how hunts and hunting worked they made an effective pair. Brian always impressed me as in military terms he had been what one would have called a good Field Officer and then actually also became the equivalent of a good Staff Officer. I greatly enjoyed working with both of them.

As Chairman of the MFHA, Lord Daresbury, Peter, did enthuse the racing fraternity, but also backed Sam Butler from Warwickshire and Charles Mann from the VWH who together initially organised the Campaign for Hunting galvanising national teams of stalwart individuals. In particular, men and women, young and old, in three groups marched Jarrow style on London, from Cornwall, Scotland and Wales. Our eldest daughter, Emma joined the Welsh March, which set out from Plas Machynlleth under the inspiring leadership of David Jones, huntsman of the David Davies, making their way through Wales, across the Cotswolds and on to London. As it happens, also in that group was a young man, George Wade who although they were just good friends at the time was to be our future son-in-law. He was marching accompanied by a fellow Cirencester student, Rupert Sturgis, later to become an inspiring Beaufort Field Master.

I had been given the job of organising and getting together 50 assorted tradespeople from all over the country, each one representing a way of life that in some way was either very or totally dependent on

hunting with dogs to hand in a petition to Downing Street for the attention of Tony Blair. That obviously took up really quite a lot of time, so I
was unable to do the whole walk, which would have been very rewarding. I did go down to Plas Machynlleth for the first day, out of the town
and over the hills, with that motivated group. It was construed as a good
omen when we watched a red kite circling below halfway up the first
mountain. They were rare at the time, although now in places almost
out of control. Pammie, myself, and our two other girls did join Emma
and the Marchers, when they stayed with the Wills family, John and Liz,
at their home in the Cotswolds. Pammie then walked on for a few days
and we met them all again in London.

Standing on the dais with the 50 due to go to Downing Street, and
listening to the reception from the crowd that was accorded to Ann
Mallalieu, now Baroness, who as ever spoke brilliantly was memorable
and extremely moving. I do recall feeling very proud indeed when
Emma arrived with the Welsh contingent. There are always later recollections of course, one being the pain Richard Williams from the
Eryri was going through with his sprained knee. Refusing to give up,
he fortified himself with a painkiller (gin!) and rather like a Centurion
tank was heavy on fuel! Anyway we, the 50, then all trundled off in our
bus to pass on our message to Blair, who needless to say was not in. Only
one person was allowed through the doors. However, we hoped we had
made a point.

As has been well documented the Rally really did set the countryside
alight and left everybody with a good feeling. Many of the attendees had
gone to London by coach, and the logistical problem of parking was
solved by suggesting that the rest of the journey was completed by Tube.
That in itself did cause a certain amount of merriment in some quarters, as a number of the crowd had never been to London before and
certainly not been on the Underground. One much loved local farmer
of ours was overheard grumbling to his companion that he couldn't see
the sights and when being reminded he was underground, he replied,
"I don't mind where I am, I still likes to look out!" He was later heard
discussing horse management with a mounted policeman!

No sooner had we got home, it was as mentioned straight into
the Gloucestershire Festival of Hunting, which was very much a joint
effort from all the Gloucestershire hunts, although it was to be held at

Badminton. Those represented were, the Beaufort, the Berkeley, the Heythrop, the North Cotswold, the Ledbury, the VWH, the Cotswold and the Cotswold Vale, plus the Wick and District Beagles and the Clifton Foot and Mink-hounds. As well as the representatives from all the hunts, the home team were invaluable. Antony Brassey as Beaufort Chairman backed the whole idea completely and not only came up with funds, but also found Bron McLennan to act as my secretary. John Mackenzie-Grieve took over as Treasurer and Clarissa Daly was a great help from the Countryside Alliance—assisted by Jo Aldridge on the Press side. Mike Tucker manned the microphone. The whole day was run in conjunction with our annual Terrier Show organised by Anne Bye and the Beaufort Hunt Supporters' Club. The idea was to invite every councillor in Gloucestershire and every MP or MEP with local connections to come and meet representatives of all the trades or crafts that were in anyway related to hunting. The list was and is extensive. Huntsmen, kennel-staff, puppy-walkers, canine vets, equine vets, grooms, horse dealers, eventers, trainers of racehorses and point to pointers, feed and stable bedding merchants, farriers, livery yard owners, saddlers, sellers of horseboxes and trailers and 4x4, bootmakers, tailors, riding hat makers, event caterers, pub owners, butchers, Hunt Ball marquee companies, fence menders and fence builders etc. Provided by all the different hunts, you name it we had them there, and all giving up their own time to show their commitment.

The organisation of the day went off brilliantly except for one simple factor, despite offering every single invited guest lunch and drinks, hoping that they would be tempted by an informative and enjoyable free day, not one Labour Councillor or Labour MP turned up! Maybe this was because of the involvement and support of the local press. That was probably the first time when we really got an insight into the bigotry of the whole political move against us. Reason, common-sense and certainly animal welfare simply did not enter the debate. Looking back, I must confess that the timing and sheer number of Marches and Rallies that became an increasing part of our lives has in my memory almost melded together. I had forgotten that the first of the Countryside Marches in London on 1st March was so soon after the Hyde Park Rally. This again had an amazing turnout with over 275,000 starting on the Embankment to march past Parliament and onwards round Central

London. On a personal note, on this occasion I was again given the task of producing the leading 50 workers whose jobs were threatened, and who would readily be available to talk to the Press. Beacons had been lit two nights before on hill tops up and down the country, literally thousands of them. Locally, here in the Beaufort country, it was captivating to look out from Bremhill in Wiltshire and later the same night from Hawkesbury in South Gloucestershire to see the flicker of flames on the hill tops up through the Midlands, and then across to Wales and down to the West Country.

Other more localised marches soon materialised, Exeter in October 1999 and Edinburgh in December 2001. Every situation gives rise to different memories and that day I recall a party from Badminton flew up to Scotland for the day from Birmingham Airport. In the group was by then a very good friend and an increasingly important and involved member of the Countryside Alliance campaign, Lord Mancroft or Beano as he was, and is called by his friends. As we alighted from the plane, I must admit to strutting about muttering, "Scotland, I'm back home—did you realise we were Highlanders, I should have worn my kilt!" Not that I have one..! Beano with his normal quick wit said, "Oh do shut up, I don't make that sort of fuss when I land in Tel Aviv!"

Despite all this the Labour Party forged ahead with plans for a Ban fuelled by such remarks as that made by the then Labour Deputy Prime Minister, John Prescott referring to the 'contorted faces of the Countryside Alliance'. A formal Government inquiry into Hunting with Dogs, by Lord Burns had concluded that although hunting with dogs did seriously compromise the welfare of the fox, there was not sufficient evidence to suggest hunting was cruel. The continuing Labour attack did therefore precipitate the biggest of the Marches which at the time was the largest in history in Great Britain when over 400,000 from all over the realm and indeed the world. When I say the final count was over 400,000, this in fact was a conservative number as the tellers knocked off late afternoon, but buses were still arriving. This figure must also of course take into account the thousands who remained at home to look after livestock. All in all an amazing result and the press coverage once again did do it justice. At a planning meeting a few weeks previously I had mentioned that it would be very wrong to march past the Cenotaph shouting and hollering and blowing horns and banging drums and that everybody should file past silently to show their respect. "Quite right," was the answer, "Not sure how but if you feel strongly about it, you can organise it!" Hoisted on my own petard? Anyway, we put up a couple of plinths in the middle of Whitehall prior to the actual Cenotaph with two others further out and on all four of them we placed people with Silence Please on the tabards they were wearing, plus others on foot. I tried to recruit high profile individuals from the hunting world to help in this exercise, namely Antony Brassey, Luke Annaly, Jacky Thomas, Tony Holdsworth, Martin Scott, his daughter Milly, and myself. The amazing thing was that it worked.

I recall talking to a senior police officer in charge of that sector prior to the start and explaining to him what we were planning to do and all he said was, "Don't be daft, you will never quieten down that number we wouldn't even attempt it!" I remember saying to him, "We are a disciplined and respectful society. You watch." He was flabbergasted when it worked. You could just hear the tramp of feet as they went past the Cenotaph and as they reached a sign saying Silence Over, the shouting and blowing started up again. I also remember Richard Burge (Chief Executive of the Countryside Alliance) accompanied by Kate Hoey MP, Lembit Opik MP, John Jackson (Chairman of the Countryside Alliance) and other top brass going past giving us the thumbs up. Memorable stuff. Several of us had had dinner the night before with the American contingent, hosted by Marty and Daphne Wood who had by then become firm friends, and as a finale to the day we met up with them on Westminster Bridge.

***

Having moved somewhat ahead with tales of the Marches, I must now hark back to the hounds who had been going from strength to strength throughout the 1990's and on to one or two hunts that come to mind. A number of them seemed to go on for quite a distance. On one big Saturday we met at Littleton Drew. As it happened Ronnie Wallace was staying with David Beaufort for the Royal Wiltshire Yeomanry Dinner and was in a Land Rover with David when the first fox from the Withy Bed close to Ivy Leaze took off through Tim Smith's Alderton Grove, over to Cape Farm at Badminton, on to Withymoor, Warren Gorse,

Lyegrove and up the Seven Mile to be caught going into Swangrove, a five-mile point. Finding again in Centre Walk our next fox went to ground just short of Dunley, scoring another five-mile point. Two therefore by one o'clock. David was delighted, Wallace went home, and I was livid that the afternoon then went wrong, and we missed a third hunt. The staff got a rocket for being dozy which may have been a little unfair considering the morning! Around that time, we did have a number of surprisingly good days. One from Quarry Spinnies near Westonbirt, to Somerford was taxing. Lance Coppice on the edge of Lower Woods to the Quarry at Didmarton was very much a bonus, and fast from Oldown near Highgrove to Widleys at Sherston was testing on the horses, and again from Culkerton to Hyam was unusual—to mention but a few.

As I have said before, having Paul Hardwick riding alongside was always a pleasure and it was not long before he became known as my wingman or Wingy as his friends christened him. He went well and was brilliant at facilitating a passage across the country although was heard at times muttering to himself, "Oh Bloody Hell here we go again!" If we hit a stiff bit of country! One of his great attributes was that he noticed everything. Undoubtedly at times we hunted the same fox from the same area as we had before, and it became quite amusing to try and out guess each other as to where it was likely to go next if this happened. "If it is that same fox the hounds will swing right, up the next hedgerow," and so on. One day we were vying with each other speculating the next move when Paul suddenly turned round with a grin, stating that there was something wrong with that theory as we had caught that one last time! In fact, of course the chances were that we had indeed caught a fox on the last hunt in question but that it may well have been a different one. Foxes often run to the same pattern, perhaps the way that their mother had taken them as cubs but also to my mind because they remembered that it had worked before. I have always maintained that except for humans, the actual ability for coherent thought in animals is not part of their mindset. As one progresses up the animal chain the power of retentive memory seems increasingly advanced. The dog and the fox are perhaps therefore intellectually more advanced than the horse who in turn is more developed than the bovine and so on. In the past one of my cows fed itself cake in the milking parlour by banging the side of the dispenser. In my view she had not worked out that by banging

Paul Hardwick

the box she got an extra ration. She had banged the box by mistake and was rewarded and so learnt to do it again.

Death of Caroline Beaufort

Moving on to people, sadly it is a fact that nothing ever stays the same and in April 1995 the Beaufort community suffered the sorrowful loss of Caroline Beaufort. Quite simply Caroline was enchanting—extremely beautiful and always kindness itself. As time progressed and David her husband spent more time in London and abroad working, she very much took on a lot of the work at Badminton and became Patron of many of the organisations that in the past had been supported by the late Duke 'Master'. She had always been incredibly kind to both Pammie, myself and our children and was sadly missed not only by us but also by all the tenants and indeed the whole of the Beaufort country.

Back at Happylands family life continued apace. A well-known Australian huntsman, top class polo player and footballer by the name of John Goold was a fairly regular visitor. He was a great friend of Brian Fanshawe's and locally also of Sue Godwin who to this day runs a top class livery yard in the Beaufort country. John had been kind enough to recommend us to the daughter of a fellow huntsman friend of his to come over to England and help with our children. So, in November 1996 a delightful seventeen-year-old by the name of Renee Phelan arrived at Happylands. On a Monday shortly after Renee's arrival, Pammie lent her a horse. We drew a covert called Lady Violet's at Rodmarton and scored a six-mile point into the VWH country. Renee was later overheard discussing the day with Emma our eldest daughter saying, "If that is hunting in England I'm staying!" She's still here, still charming, still hunting and married to local farmer Anthony Tuck, together with two children and running another livery yard full of horses. At the time I doubt I would have had the foresight to envisage the little girl from Australia one day standing in to fill the gap of whipper-in. Even more surprising on the day in question her co-whip was also a girl, Jess Wheeler the then wife of Charles the Kennel Huntsman. Charles was off following a fall and indeed so was Paul Hardwick. It was late in the season and the hounds were settled but Jess and Renee had both spent a lot of time in the kennels and out hunting, both had brains and were capable on a horse. In those days it did raise a few eyebrows to have two females wearing rather oversized Beaufort green coats officiating! But a good job was made of it, and we had a first-rate day. I might add Mrs Farquhar filled the role as Field Master. Whoever said I was against promoting women!

Mentioning field mastering also reminds me that 1996 was the year Christopher Casey took over the Sodbury Vale. He again was a natural, with the ability to ride, plus an eye for the countryside, combining the element of competitiveness without creating jealousy making him popular in that role. He started with Wednesdays, then Mondays before finally progressing to Saturdays only retiring in 2012.

Hounds. Bouncer. Anti attack.

Despite the pressures on the political scene, the rallies, and the increasing presence of the antis, as far as I was concerned our hound breeding policy seemed to be going very well. Before elucidating on that however it is worth mentioning that in 1996, we did have a big hit in the Park when about ten vans carrying over 80 saboteurs caused a massive amount of damage, attacking Hunt Supporters, smashing car and lorry windows, and finishing up by throwing a brick through David Beaufort's Land Rover window which narrowly missed the occupants.

Getting more involved again with the likes of David Jones at both the hound show at Builth Wells and on the Welsh March, I found myself returning to the Principality for another infusion of Welsh blood, this time to the pack he hunted, the David Davies. I had been particularly struck by the quality and balance of their Benjamin '94. So, in the spring of 1998 we sent down two bitches, Peanut '94, who was by Exmoor Pewter '89 out of a strong bitch of ours Parsnip '89 together with another bitch Marble '95. Peanut, as I have mentioned before was sister to Peewit '94 who won the Bitch Championship at Peterborough in 1995 and was a very big upstanding girl, whereas Marble was a fraction smaller.

As it happened Benjamin didn't like the look of either of these smooth English girls (maybe he was racist) whereas luckily Bouncer his brother did, and we finished up with two good litters. Perhaps with the increasing Welsh influence, Marble's puppies, although they hunted well enough, on a fast day were struggling to keep up, whereas Peanut's litter being larger were mustard from the word go. One of that litter Bobbin '99 was naturally tenacious, so we put her to Gunshot '98. This produced Boycott '02. Gunshot was by VWH Guinness '92 bred by my old friend Martin Scott. Martin had been Master and Huntsman of the Tiverton for eight seasons, with a further ten sharing the horn with Sidney Bailey at the Vale of the White Horse. When he retired, Martin joined us in the hunting field at the Beaufort. He continues to breed the VWH and knows his pedigrees better than anybody. He is not known as 'Studbook Scott' for nothing. His ability for quoting pedigrees going back generations to my mind is exceptional.

For a long time, I personally fought shy of using the VWH stallion-hounds as undoubtedly, they were heavy shouldered, a trait that is hard to iron out, but Martin, by judicious and persistent breeding did so, producing many stars. Our Gunshot '98 inherited the best of the VWH/Portman blood and coupled with the Beaufort Mostyn '92 out of the Marble '95 lines was without doubt a quality upstanding stallion-hound. He in turn

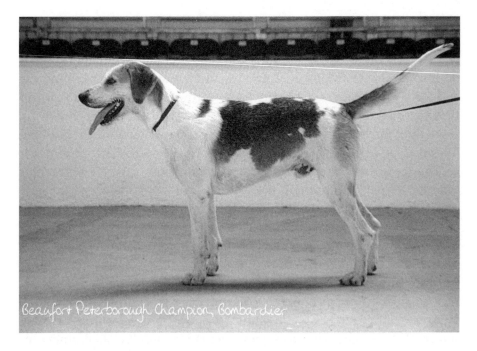

Beaufort Peterborough Champion, Bombardier

Beaufort Peterborough Champion Bombardier.

mated with the David Davis Bouncer outcross brings us back to Boycott.

I recall taking our dog hounds to Charnwood Forest in the Quorn country when hunted by Adrian Dangar MFH, as their pack was suffering from kennel cough. I pointed out Boycott and his brother Bowler, who that day as young dogs were cutting it out to catch their second fox above ground in thick woodland. I said to Adrian, "You want to watch those two, they will make their mark." Indeed, they did—Boycott in turn sired Bombardier '04, the first rough coated dog to be Champion at Peterborough, and his sister Boniface, who in turn was the dam of Bobcat '07, also a Peterborough Champion. More importantly though, they were as a family top class in their work. Bombardier was one of those hounds that you could hang your hat on, outstanding on a good scent and persistent on a poor one. His mother was Garlic '00 by VWH Gardner '95 who I had noticed doing a lot of work when we had a joint meet in our Thursday country with Sidney Bailey hunting hounds. In that vein I was able to use VWH sires again in the future with equal success.

Beaufort Peterborough Champions 2008: Halifax '06 and Bobcat '07. (Photo by Emma Farquhar)

Jim Barrington

Also, at that time a long running episode that was to have interesting consequences was coming to fruition. Way back in the Bicester days, I like, a great many others involved with hunting at all levels had come across one of the most capable of our opponents, Jim Barrington, the then Director of the League Against Cruel Sports. There had been other bright ones in the past, but none to my mind so well informed and articulate as Mr Barrington. He was passionate and intelligent and very capable both in court and with the media. A frightening adversary. The interesting thing about Jim though, was that unlike many of his brethren he was always courteous and always had time to talk sensibly and certainly not rudely even to the likes of me, a huntsman. We met on quite a number of occasions, court cases, meetings, media dos and the like.

One of the first times I met him was at Kenilworth and on that occasion, he was somewhat outnumbered, but we still had a chat. I think the reason we always got on was that it was apparent to both of us that our underlying passion was in fact the well-being of animals. Next, I remember in the early 1980's sitting on a grassy bank in London with Jim after a National Trust meeting discussing the overall question of culling and control not only foxes but of all wild animals. We debated the different methods of control and degrees of cruelty if there was any. After really quite a long discussion we found plenty of common ground which probably surprised us both! I recall saying, "You will join us one day Jim," to which he replied, "Over my dead body!" And off we went to have a drink in a nearby pub!

As time progressed Jim continued to be Director of the League but still enjoyed discussing the issues and he will say himself that he never changed his tune on the overall management of animals but found there was a moral middle way with wildlife. I also recall after a radio broadcast staged in Chippenham when Jim was taking on Janet George and a new voice on our side, Professor Roger Scruton (later Sir Roger) that we all returned to the bar afterwards and Jim and Roger had a very deep conversation. Associates of Jim's were not amused and began to call him a turncoat.

The upshot was that in 1995 Jim left the League and two years later in 1997 Roger Scruton held a memorable dinner party in his farmhouse near Malmesbury for Jim. Invited were Mark Davis the new Director of the League, Howard Hodges a former League Chairman, Brian Fanshawe, myself, Pammie-Jane and Roger's wife, Sophie plus the then new to us Charlie Pye-Smith who was at the time a neutral journalist who had agreed to write the evening up without bias. Sophie produced both vegetarian and beef, you could take your pick! This is not a political book but suffice to say that to my mind Jim went on to be the best speaker on hunting's behalf of anybody. He started and became Secretary of the Parliamentary Middle Way Group comprising Kate Hoey MP Labour, Lembit Opik MP Liberal, and Peter Luff MP Conservative. They, and Jim were invaluable in the Portcullis House Hearings on Hunting, and he got on famously with the likes of Professor Webster and the vets.

On a personal note, I also felt the Countryside Alliance of that time were basically suspicious of Jim very much to their and therefore our detriment. Had it not been for Bill Andrewes, Brian Fanshawe, and also Richard Schuster who kept the whole operation afloat together with Stephen Lambert, Janet George and to a small degree myself, Jim's expertise would have been lost. He did and still does stick to his guns as regards the importance of winning the argument on welfare. I would add that at various consultations about hunting I, backed by Fanshawe, would often point out that every time the Press questioned people at a hunt meet the subject of welfare would arise. This we felt needed addressing, only to be told incessantly that welfare was not an issue. Thank goodness Jim and Charlie Pye-Smith are still writing on just that topic and Pye-Smith's book *Rural Rites and Wrongs* is both thought provoking and logical and is about to be followed by another in the same vein. Jim does quite often come to stay at Happylands and I will always value his friendship and his faith that one day common sense will prevail.

A New Kennel Huntsman

Moving on to 2001 and again there were changes afoot on the home front. Charles Wheeler, who had been invaluable especially in the early days when we were getting the hounds sorted out, had developed a passion for big game fishing and had become restless. We discussed his going for a huntsman's job elsewhere, but he decided to take the plunge and set up his own fishing business in Vanuatu to catch the big game fish. It was something he was and is still I believe very good at. Tony Holdsworth, to me was an obvious choice as his successor. A friend of Charles's, he had been up to Badminton often. He ticked all the boxes. Good hound man, he had hunted the Tiverton professionally and with great drive. He made sure that the hounds were happy in kennels and in their work. A very brave and capable horseman and was as good a judge of the ability of a horse with the caveat that he would ride something that maybe others would not find so amenable! He was brilliant at finding the answers to a problem—"Don't worry Sir, I might know somebody who does!" And lastly, he was and is the most enormous fun. He arrived with his delightful wife Sandra and their then young daughter Katie. They settled in no time, although the spring of 2001 saw the start of foot and mouth.

The cessation of hunting that year was announced at the beginning of March just as we were preparing to leave to go to the Hawkers', Gardener's Farm meet at Hullavington. By May 1st, we were well into a lockdown. Limited hound exercise was the order of the day until just before Christmas. I'm not going to go into the horrors of foot and mouth. It got quite close to the Beaufort country and the funeral pyres of whole herds of cows below the escarpment towards the Severn were harrowing. It brought the whole countryside to a halt and in some areas, stock was decimated. In Cumbria the sheep cull was horrendous. Hunts throughout the country sent kennel staff there because they knew their job, to help the Army with the horrific task the cull entailed. From the Beaufort we sent Barry Strange (kennelman), who went for a long stint and Thomas Burton (countryman), a somewhat shorter time.

Not knowing when it was likely to finish, we still had to keep hounds and horses fit. We went on bike hound exercise locally but were allowed to go further afield with just the horses. So on Saturdays we started up organised rides across country, jumping fences just to keep everyone amused. Not surprisingly it got very competitive as I know to my own cost after taking on Rob Ingall across his own farm caused the worst torn riding muscle I've ever experienced, much to Rob's amusement!

A nasty accident with a bad-tempered stag in the Park in early December resulted in Paul and Thomas both in hospital, so when we did in fact start, we were a whipper-in down. By good fortune Luke Tomlinson had just left school and because it was shortly before the polo started up again in the spring, he was able to take time off to step in as whipper-in. Like the rest of his family, he loved his hunting and was a good rider and so was an enormous asset, having hunted the Eton Beagles. I think it is true to say that for the rest of that season things went surprisingly well. We found foxes everywhere and had some impressive hunts. One theory was that because the countryside had been closed, and there being no shooting, foxes had been undisturbed. In addition, sadly few sheep were brought in from Wales so there was no electric wire fencing and little foil. John White always maintained that it was the best Thursday sport he could remember, and I would agree that throughout the country we did score some memorable days. Another theory to add to no shooting was much less road traffic, so foxes had not been run over and had learnt to travel more.

Mentioning Luke Tomlinson reminded me that he went on to Newcastle University and whilst up north whipped-in to Frank Houghton-Brown at the Middleton which he really enjoyed. I do recall once saying to him that he ought to take a pack of hounds. I think he thought about it, but he was just beginning to make his name in the polo world follow-ing in the footsteps of his father Simon and his mother Claire, then the

Bruce Akerman's 90th Birthday Meet, 2015. (Photo by Ray Bird)

highest goal female player in the world. He stayed with polo which was undoubtedly the right decision as he went on to captain the English team. In my view, he would have been a very good huntsman indeed. As it transpired his younger brother Mark also played for England, as did his sister Emma.

While thinking about the young, I'm also reminded of two boys both then in their early teens who were passionate about hunting. Rory Akerman and Charlie Dando. On hunting days, they very often accompanied me up front and one morning I sent them off in the hills above St Catherine's to see if we could get along a bank below a nearby farm. Shortly afterwards I heard the following remarks regarding a gate, "I think we'll have to jump 'ee—'ee doesn't look like an opener," which they happily did. The Akermans farmed Kington Down Farm, West Kington and the Dandos, Plough Farm at Old Sodbury and both came from brilliant hunting families. Rory went on to hunt the Tiverton for several years before returning to the family farm and Charlie is now a farrier. Both whipped-in whenever they could at the Beaufort, and Charlie is now hunting the Monmouthshire as an amateur. Two other small boys from the hunting field in those days come to mind, Charlie and Rollo Deutsch. Their late grandmother Serena Henley, chief magistrate at Calne known as 'Hang 'em High Henley' was such a character as is their mother Richenda. Their after-hunting teas were the stuff of folklore. Practical joke after practical joke, a free range parrot and ferrets, cornflakes in beds, and at one meet a turkey plucking competition between myself as Huntsman, John White Field Master, Nigel Maidment Secretary. How wonderful it is now to see Rollo making a real fist as a sheep farmer, and Charlie now having become one of the finest young National Hunt jockeys in the business.

THE NEW MILLENIUM

IN 2003, THE first full season after foot and mouth, things did settle down to normality but with one big difference: John Mackenzie-Grieve retired after 16 years of unfailing dedication in the role of Hunt Secretary. He was always going to take some replacing and Antony Brassey as Chairman began to look around to find somebody suitable. After chatting to one or two locals myself, I remember saying to him, "I don't think we need to look any further, he's already right here." Nigel Maidment as previously alluded to had whipped in to Sidney Bailey on occasions at the VWH. He and his wife Val, who is a saint, had run the Hunt Supporters' Club and the Pony Club. He farmed, walked puppies and was heavily involved with the Malmesbury Young Farmers. With younger family help he could even work a computer! So, what more could you want? Nigel took over in 2003 and will take a back seat in 2023. What an innings and a hugely popular one at that.

The other change in 2003 was that my future son-in-law, George Wade took over as Field Master for the Wednesdays south of the M4 from Richard Meade, who was giving up after nearly 20 years. Replacing Richard, who was married to my cousin Angela, with my future son-in-law some might say touched on nepotism but both as it happened were rather good at the job!

On the hound front that year there were several factors worth mentioning. Undoubtedly the puppies from the year before took longer to settle than normal as obviously with no hunting they had not had the training the previous autumn. Nevertheless a 2001 litter by Cottesmore Fairford '95 had shown promise and in 2003 began to excel. Cottesmore Fairford was another ground-breaking stallion-hound for me. I had been sent him by Brian Fanshawe to hunt in the spring of 2000 and he had impressed me enormously. Rough coated and possessing a noticeable

Nigel Maidment

ability to keep going even in the worst scenting conditions. I remember him bellowing away in Lower Woods with his distinctive voice when most were at a loss. He was by Midland (USA) Hardaway '89 who had been given to Fanshawe by Ben Hardaway which brought in the low scenting American (July blood) coupled with English outcrosses to both New Forest Medyg and Bicester Farmer, hence the rough coat. Fanfare one of the best of that litter went on to produce Halifax '06 by our Bailey '03. The importance of July blood is often quoted by hound aficionados who know it's propensity in the American hound for their low scenting ability. Interesting enough the pseudonym 'July' stems from a couple of hounds Mountain and Muse that the Duke of Leeds sent to the colonies in 1814. They were believed to be descended from Northern Irish foxhounds reputedly crossed with collie and lurcher blood, hence the merle coat and wall eyes. A certain Colonel Harris in Georgia had hounds and bred a litter with this blood that were born on 1st July 1858. One dog hound puppy was named July and went down in history as a famous stallion-hound.

Continuing on the hound front, 2002 was the start of an amazingly successful run at the Peterborough Royal Foxhound Show. It was Tony Holdsworth's first full summer and we managed to pull off both Championships with Whipsnade '01 winning the Dog Hound Championship and Galaxy '02 the Bitch Championship. To be truthful, Whipsnade, I thought might have been lucky, whereas Galaxy was sheer quality. As it happened it was an added joy as we had walked her at Happylands.

2003, saw Palmer '02 by our Whitbread '97, take the honours and then in 2004 Bailey '03, by Heythrop Busby '96 was a very definite Champion. Gamecock '04 scored in 2005, and then in 2006 it was the turn of Bombardier who I have already mentioned. This made it five consecutive Peterborough Dog Hound Championships plus one Bitch Championship, adding up to six Peterborough Royal Foxhound Show Championships in five years. I'm proud to say this was a feat that had never been achieved before. I am lucky enough to have a wonderful painting by Neil Forster portraying the five doghounds' heads that the Hunt had given David Beaufort which he generously passed back to me.

Obviously, showing success on the flags is enormously gratifying, correct conformation and so on, but the name of the game is their ability in the hunting field, and I hope I never lost sight of that. With that in mind, talking to Rob Ingall, he did remind me of one hunt that illustrates some of the sport that we were getting in those days. Unboxing at Brokenborough by Lord Suffolk's corn dryer (I stopped doing so soon after as it was too near the main road) we had a circular morning. After changing horses we found on the old railway line near Tetbury and fairly flew through Larkhill Quarry over to Trouble House, Trull, Hazleton and on to Aston Down, left of the old aerodrome and into the Cotswold country where we came across some polo grounds. Luckily Rosie Vestey was with us. Goodness how she loves her hunting and as it happened was then a Master of the Cotswold. When I asked her whose grounds they were she simply replied, "They are ours, jump the rails and go straight across," which we did! Arriving the other side, we then ran down into the valleys by Oakridge where we caught our fox. Hacking back into the village of Frampton Mansell we were one hound short. Pausing to blow, a friendly local face appeared, and pointed out a stable into which we put the hounds, to wait for the lorry. I remember the hounds all lying on top of each other in the straw, I went in to give them a pat when Rosie looked over and said, "Isn't that magical?" I replied, "Yes. Wonderful! That's why we love them so much." The corollary to this story is that we did not get the missing hound that night but later heard that he had got the wrong side of some old security fencing on Aston Down. Finding his way out he returned to where we had unboxed that morning, something that hounds often do and was seen at first light having already covered twelve miles. Finding the horsebox no longer there, he set off to find his own way back to the kennels. Bearing in mind it was country that hounds always travelled to in a lorry, he still managed to turn up at teatime at the kennels right as rain having journeyed another twelve miles. Quite a feat.

To a great extent the support of the 2002 March fostered the growing commitment of so many country and indeed townsfolk that were involved with our sport not to roll over, and the resolution if necessary to break the law grew. 1st November 2003 was orchestrated as a Declaration Day when everybody was encouraged to even go so far as to sign up to say that they would actually break the law in defiance of the proposed legislation. The wording as it happened was drawn up by Roger Scruton. Twelve Declaration Day meets were held up and down the country with a meet at Worcester Lodge, Badminton allocated for the Wessex area. We put up pens for the hounds and hunt staff of each invited pack. A large marquee was added as a 'Declaration' sign up point, and food and sustenance were organised by Bridget ('B') Cross and Nigel Maidment, Hunt Secretary. A few weeks previously, Nigel as he trotted past 'B', as an aside called out, "By the way can you produce breakfast for around 4,000 people on Declaration Day?" In the end the numbers attending were estimated as at least 15,000! Speeches were made, and hopefully resolve stiffened.

Rallies, A Wedding and the Parliament Act

2004 was another fairly tumultuous year, some good, some bad, and some ugly. The good, undoubtedly was that Emma and George got married in the August, the bad was the storm clouds that were definitely gathering over the pending Ban, and the ugly was that for the first time at an organised Rally, the mood turned ugly, and a growing sense of frustration resulted in a fall out with the police.

When George asked if he could marry Emma (good old-fashioned stuff) we simply could not have been more delighted. We obviously knew him well by then, not only was he a thoroughly good guy he was also a very popular and capable Field Master. Not that this was of prime importance, but it was a good start! We also got on extremely well with his family. George's father, Peter Wade is a very go-ahead dairy farmer and happens to be a keen hunting man, an excellent horseman and a former master of the Blackmore Vale. Emma and George got married in Badminton Church and we had the reception at Happylands in a large round and colourful circus style marquee. The service was beautiful, and Christopher Mulholland, the vicar who also happened to hunt with us, was perfect. Thomas Irvine played 'When the Saints Go Marching In' on a trumpet with great gusto as they left the church. At the reception, Will Duckworth-Chad gave an amusing best man's speech. They had been contemporaries at Milton Abbey. The couple then made their departure perched on the back of an old open backed Land Rover loaded with dogs before returning for the night's entertainment of dancing, and lamb barbecued Argentinian *asado* style. It was one of the only sunny weekends that August and it could not have been better.

Then came the 'Bad,' the inevitable sinking feeling as the Labour Government looked like forging ahead with a Ban on hunting with hounds regardless of the scientific opinions to the contrary. This in turn began to breed a feeling of desperation in the minds of many of the hunting folk who felt they must do something. In the September the Alliance organised another rally in Brighton to coincide with the Labour Party Conference and so off we all set once again. This time as we tramped along the seafront many of the Beaufort contingent were waiting for news of how a young and local to us team who had managed to infiltrate the Labour Conference were faring. The newly wed George and Emma Wade, accompanied by Badminton farmer Philip Hall, Jamie Murray Wells, James Meade (a cousin), plus Tom Leeke the Ledbury huntsman, had all taken out membership of the Labour Party in order to attend the conference, and at the given moment when hunting came on to the agenda the group voiced their opinion. They did say afterwards that the speed at which they were forcibly ejected, and the vehemence that went with it was quite frightening. They were in fact relieved when the police arrived as things were turning nasty. The next organised Rally was in Parliament Square on the 15th of September, the day that Parliament was debating the Bill. Again, a team hit the headlines by actually getting into the Chamber when on this occasion they were more peaceably removed. Luke Tomlinson from the Beaufort, his future brother-in-law chef Nick Wood, plus David Redvers, John Holliday, Andrew Elliott all from the Ledbury, accompanied by Richard Wakeham, a York surveyor, Robert Thame from the Bicester, and Otis Ferry from the South Shropshire. I always thought it typical of the manners of most of our ilk that when Black Rod fell over in the melee, needless to say Luke Tomlinson helped him up!

Outside, however things were not so friendly. The police quite correctly realised that many of the crowd, especially the young were hell bent on making their feelings felt, and for a time it seemed that a full-scale invasion of the Commons could be on the cards. A barricade of police vans, riot police and metal fences was quickly assembled. Tempers were getting somewhat frayed, and the police resorted to using truncheons at the barriers, that sadly is when it got 'Ugly'. I'm sad to say it was the first time I had seen our supporters getting physical and fighting with the police, whereas both sides in the past had remained amicable. I suppose the answer is quite simple, you can push people just too far, and that is what the Government were doing at that time. The tempo remained nasty for some time, and it was a relief when George and Emma decided that it was time to go home.

Demonstrations of various kinds continued; it wasn't quite all over yet. A group of local Beaufort and West Country ladies chained themselves to the railings outside Parliament in November helping to raise the profile in the press. And indeed, on an earlier occasion we had taken some hounds up to Horse Guards, behind Downing Street to give Mr and Mrs Blair an early morning call. This manoeuvre had meant taking a horse box plus doghounds round to the nearest point at the back of 10 Downing Street at 6 am and beginning the day with a fanfare of hunting horns. I must admit that the reaction we got on arrival from a few of Metropolitan Police was interesting. One confided that he was quite sympathetic, another hunted, and we could take our time! What did however make us chuckle was that while we were on Horse Guards Mrs Farquhar suddenly pointed to the bushes on the edge of Green Park and said, "I think we've got a couple of flashers!" Two gentlemen were lurking in light coloured mackintoshes, with trilby hats and scarves covering their faces. It transpired they were friends, one a supportive member of the House of Lords and the other a senior member of the Countryside Alliance who had come along to see the fun, but did not want to be recognised. Flashers indeed!

However, on the 15th of September the Commons decreed that hunting would be banned. The Bill went to the House of Lords, then at odds with the Commons, but eventually, without any agreement being reached between the two Houses, on the 18th of November the Parliament Act was controversially invoked, and a date was set for the Hunting Act to become Law on the 18th of February 2005. The whole ridiculous debacle had taken over seven hundred hours of debate and at huge cost.

That winter we suffered another sadness when Rob Ingall had a fall jumping a fence going away from Horton Bushes. I was on my feet that day having just jazzed up the recurrent bad back. Talking to Rob he firmly stated that he was on a young horse and was going to go very steady. How many times have we heard that? Anyway, away go hounds, away goes Owen Inskip over a big fence with a good ditch, and away goes Ingall. Things looked dicey for time with the prospect of a serious back injury and the ground was too wet for an ambulance, so a helicopter was required. The outcome later resulted in rods being inserted into a couple of vertebrae with great success. These days he still insists on disappearing to Wales to walk the Brecon Beacons, but riding is ruled out. This left a vacancy for a new Field Master so Rupert Sturgis stepped in to do Mondays, and Owen Inskip took on some of the Saturdays as well as Wednesdays. Rob Ingall as a field master was a big loss but luckily the others all filled the gap brilliantly and so we went into the last few months of legal hunting with a powerful and committed team and a pack of hounds obviously none the wiser!

The actual enactment of the Ban was fixed for the 19th of February, a Saturday. We decided therefore to have a major day on the Friday and to stage a large meet at Worcester Lodge on the Saturday itself. The Friday was always going to be a big day, but once again my back had a bit of a blip at the beginning of that week, and I found myself car following with little prospect of hunting hounds for a day or two. On the Wednesday whilst I was following, by chance I stopped to talk to a friend who was a very well-respected Harley Street doctor. I mentioned my predicament and he replied, 'Don't worry I'll fix that'. Jumping off his horse he scribbled out a prescription on a scrap of paper I found in the car. I took it to Tetbury Pharmacy straight away. The chemist did say, "This looks like a pretty powerful concoction, but I suspect he knows what he's doing!" Suffice to say I took a dose and by Thursday evening felt no pain at all! Having hunting hounds all day on the Friday and again on the Saturday, I did ring Charles to thank him very much and I mentioned that it obviously was quite a strong concoction that he had given me, he laughed and said, "Yes that is what we give a certain famous rock star before he has a big gig!"

Going back to that last day on the Friday, hounds ran hard all day and rather spookily we finished up in the back of Badminton itself as dusk was falling. Trotting down into the middle of the High Street we discovered rather a fracas had started. A very anti-hunting left wing MP from Wansdyke Bristol, Dan Norris had decided to enter Badminton a 'hunting village' on this of all nights! Unsurprisingly he was not very welcome! He had come to be interviewed by ITV but by the time he'd been well covered with flour, eggs and chocolate yoghurt courtesy of the locals and ordered on his way by a very redoubtable and elderly lady resident shouting, "Get out of our village" her prodding walking stick reminding him where his rear end was, he decided it was high time to leave and departed to the sounds of both laughter and boos!

On the Saturday we were fortunate that Labour MP Kate Hoey had agreed to come down to speak to the crowd, which of course she did brilliantly. It was very fitting to hear her state that she thought the Party that she was a member of and represented in Parliament was wrong, and making a mistake. Her time-honoured remark to Mr Blair, 'Now is the time to govern for all of the people' sadly fell on deaf ears. Previously she had ventured that she had ridden a horse as a child in Ireland, and although out of practice would be prepared to give it a go and ride with us to the Meet. This she did, following for a time. Brave girl. We put her on Seamus who was generally quiet and in fact belonged to Brian Gupwell. Seamus, thank goodness, behaved like a gentleman. Mrs Farquhar accompanied her and then later took her following in a car until we called it a day.

The night before there had been a debate in the Bingham Hall,

Brian Fanshawe, Kate Hoey MP, Martin Scott, David Beaufort and IWF—
Badminton House gardens in the 90s, Puppy Show.

Cirencester, and Kate had spoken on behalf of hunting. Mikey and Fi Mitchell, great friends of ours who farm at Trull in the Monday country came to supper and despite the prospect of what the morning would bring, we all seemed to put a brave face on it. I do remember that at breakfast Kate asked, "What are you feeling?" Before I knew it, I had shed a tear and then felt rather stupid. We met with hounds in front of a large crowd. David Beaufort joined Kate and myself on a dray acting as a platform to give speeches. All I can remember saying was that I really could not predict what the outcome was going to be, or what precisely we were going to do. Then I reassured everyone that David Beaufort and myself would ensure that there would always be hounds at Badminton, and that there would always be some sort of hunting. Rather pushed for ideas, I recalled Churchill's remark in difficult times and said, "If in doubt, KBO"—Keep Buggering On! I was reminded of that remark in a lot of letters received which ended in just KBO!

Speeches over, we left the Meet, and went down the Diddle jumping some fences, and tried to hunt a pre-laid line. We hadn't got the strength of the smell right and so the action was somewhat intermittent, but things did improve. It was difficult to judge just what did happen, but we finished up in the Verge and called it a day. Simon Hart then Director of the Countryside Alliance was on his feet, and together with a few other huntsmen plus Jo Aldridge who had been dealing with the Press side, we all went back into the Holdsworths' kitchen. The mood was sombre, but the general feeling was that with practice and a different scent anything was better than capitulating and we were sure we could do something.

Later that evening I recall thinking how much I admired Kate Hoey and that she was of the same calibre as Ann Mallalieu. I had to smile to myself that despite being probably regarded as a committed male chauvinist pig and a dyed in the wool Conservative to boot, the two people I most admired in the whole of the political world—indeed any world come to that—were both Labour women!

The rest of that spring following the Ban was an intriguing time. Some hunts were torn between a decision of outright rebellion, or acceptance of mirroring the behaviour of the few draghound packs already in existence that just laid lines and had a tantivy over prepared fences with a few hounds trying not to get galloped on. The majority, I suggest were sceptical of both these options, but were not quite sure what the answer was. So, I might add were we. Outright confrontation was an attractive option especially when one looks back at the support shown on the 2003 Declaration Day. Against that, however, was the realisation that to blatantly give two fingers to the Law of the land was not necessarily our way of doing things, and there was perhaps a less black and white way ahead. Bearing in mind that the end aim was in the first place to safeguard the well-being of the hounds and in the second place to ensure our community remained intact, with the road left open to fight for Repeal without losing the structure so to do. Obviously, all that should be achieved without losing sight of the welfare of the fox or any of the other quarry species. Several of us came up with a strategy pioneering a new method of trail laying using in our case a fox-based scent and hare or deer scent for others in order to not entirely jeopardise years of careful breeding. The intention being to lay a trail in such a way that the tempo and manner of the operation was more consistent with the fluctuating flow of a hunt dictated by the varying conditions prevalent in the past. This would also help make sure that this new activity would still cater for the different capabilities of those taking part—the young and the old, the brave and the less brave, the knowledgeable, and the newcomer, all seeking different degrees of sport. There were of course other options or exemptions allowed by law, but this was the one that appealed to us, and by and large it was the one that seemed to carry the most favour with the majority of packs at the time. This obviously threw up difficulties. Firstly, hounds had to be taught to cope with the changed situation. The strength of the smell that was being laid had to be experimented with, as was the time element allowed between it being laid and being utilised which was also a factor. Every huntsman knows only too well the difficulties of judging how long the scent of any quarry lingers after it has been on the move. Fluctuation in temperature both in the air and on the ground, the rise and fall of the atmospheric conditions, the wind strength, and the proximity of foil, to name but a few. Scent can last for literally hours on the one hand, or become non-existent in moments on the other. This was and is true with a man-made trail just as it was with an orthodox quarry-produced trail, so this was another consideration that had to be taken into account to try to emulate the situation pre-Ban.

Another element that had to be considered of course was the logistics of explaining to everybody involved just how the new arrangements were to be conducted, and to leave them content that this new methodology was within the Law. A huntsman as a practitioner had to teach his hounds their new role. At the Beaufort we, as a recognised hunt, changed our own rules to comply with this and set about advertising that fact. This did not happen overnight and although we ourselves did start to put it into practice quite early on, a number of other hunts were understandably initially cautious of trying new methods. I think the overall evaluation of the Law was helped at that time by the recent changes to the hierarchy in the Masters of Foxhounds' Association who were obviously going to have to give guidelines as to the way ahead. Stephen Lambert had just been appointed Chairman and had kindly asked me to be his Vice Chairman. This in effect meant that the future of hunting, although it was banned, was back in the hands of masters who had, or who did actually hunt hounds themselves and who therefore understood the problems at the coalface.

I recall very early on, Stephen calling an impromptu meeting at his house for a number of experienced masters and influential hunt staff to discuss the way ahead. Some attendees seemed fearful of trying this new methodology, but soon realised that the future of the hounds was paramount and that a positive attitude was required. There was no doubt that the unswerving support of Tony Holdsworth for this policy helped carry the day amongst the hunt staff.

Although on the surface helping to run the immediate future following the Ban would seem to have been a thankless and complicated task, in fact it was more rewarding than it might have been. This was largely due in the first place to the personality of Stephen Lambert himself. He had a brain, undoubted charm and was fundamentally a negotiator, and not a dictator. When it came to hunting, he knew his onions having hunted beagles and then foxhounds finishing up at the Heythrop which was and is one of the major hunts in the country. It also helped that we got on! I was still hunting hounds myself and so could add input knowing first-hand the pitfalls that the new legislation had landed us with. Stephen always asked for an opinion and loved to discuss, which resulted in a healthy state of affairs. Straight away he produced what he called an 'Executive Committee' which comprised of Stephen and myself, plus Brian Fanshawe as Secretary of the Council of Hunting Associations, Alastair Jackson as Director of the MFHA, Joe Cowen as MFHA Treasurer, plus other representatives of related organisations co-opted if it was thought that further specialist advice was needed. For obvious geographical reasons it was understandable that at times we were referred to as the Gloucestershire Mafia but that was just the way it was! We often met at the Hunting Office to discuss particular problems, and mainly met in London the night before any MFHA Committee Meetings to clarify strategy. Another factor that undoubtedly lifted the spirits at that time was the enormous resolve throughout the country to keep things going and to plan for Repeal.

A strong team at the Countryside Alliance was permanently concentrating on that aspect, both legally and politically. Simon Hart was tireless, as was Beano Mancroft who was increasingly coming to the fore as a negotiator on hunting's behalf. The first port of call on the advice of many eminent lawyers was to challenge the validity of the Act under European Law namely Legal Challenges. In my humble opinion they were quite correct to throw money at this, and although in the end it did not succeed, it might well have done. From a local (Beaufort) point of view the initial upshot was to some extent inevitable that once again we were involved in a move to raise money, and quite a lot of it. Bobby Nicolle, who in the past had raised large sums for charity offered his advice which subsequently resulted in him running our effort. He came up with a simple plan which then became a yardstick throughout the country. Basically, it was a classic example of social blackmail! You split supporters ruthlessly into categories of wealth, sat them down in a room with some sustenance, explained the problem, gave them a form to sign and then when they had agreed, thanked them, and let them go! It worked by and large, raising a staggering £250,000 from the Beaufort alone. The format did nationally pay for the Legal Challenges exercise, which might well have proven fruitful.

Whilst on the subject of Repeal, the other avenue to concentrate on was the campaign to alter the balance of power in the House of Commons to be more favourable to our cause. Successive Conservative leaders had promised Repeal if we could help them with securing a majority. For that reason and for the perceived well-being of the countryside, the hunting world did campaign to this end. Being in fact a highly motivated and disciplined community it was surprising therefore how much could be achieved, and this we felt was understood and appreciated. Early on I do recall that we took the decision to move the MFHA Annual General Meeting back to London to allow the then Leader of the Conservative Party, William Hague to attend and to openly promise us his support in return of ours to him.

The work of Charles and Chips Mann plus Sam Butler running Vote OK at this time should never be forgotten. Many individuals were tireless, but those three really put their hearts into it. Vote OK was designed to be non-political as there were supporters from all political parties, a fact which should not be underestimated. Indeed, in the countryside generally the backing we received was amazing. Jumping ahead somewhat, on the home front undoubtedly Rob Ingall was pure gold. Although as a hunt we gathered a team, Rob indisputably was the driving force that put it all together. Over the 2010, 2015, 2017, and 2019 Elections the Beaufort Hunt delivered 432,700 leaflets putting in 11,500 individual hours which eventually in 2017 helped achieve a Conservative majority for David Cameron who had also always declared his support. This time it really did look as though we were going to get a change in the Law as regards the Hunting Act. As usual at the last minute the prejudice that we had continually come up against prevailed, and Mrs Sturgeon went back on her original promise not to vote on an English matter and announced that the Scottish Nationalists would vote against the Government thus tipping the balance. Another chance gone. When I agreed to put pen to paper to recount my own personal memories regarding hunting in particular and limited to subjects that just involved me, I never intended to go into too much detail with regards to politics. As it transpired of course, purely through circumstances I found myself near the sharp end and looking back it was both aggravating and interesting.

Hunting under the Ban

Returning to the main issue—hunting—as I have already said was in fact more rewarding than we had anticipated. Organising a day of trail hunting that as far as possible mirrored action pre-Ban did require much the same skill as before. Hounds still needed to be fit, biddable but capable of working on their own, and still needed to be schooled into having the determination to make the best of the scenting conditions that nature provided. A laid trail was just as unpredictable as the real thing. Too strong and it was like a steeplechase, too weak it was unworkable, and again it also differed from day to day and indeed from hour to hour depending on atmospheric conditions. Early on, experimenting with the different strengths of smells, I remember Peter Sidebottom setting off laying a trail from a fast horse with a stronger dose than usual on what proved to be a good scenting day. We caught him after only about ten minutes—and he wasn't hanging about! There was also the predicted possibility of hounds changing onto a fox which also kept the forward whippers-in on their toes. Tony Holdsworth was brilliant at this and was always reading the situation to constantly move ahead, and by constantly moving ahead was able to assess the situation, and pass back information. In the meantime, Paul and myself dealt with the hounds. Trails were laid on foot especially early in the year, sometimes from a quad bike but most effectively from horseback. A well mounted and knowledgeable rider could replicate the imagined route of a live quarry far more credibly than by other methods. It was how we, and the vast majority of other packs were able to go forward maintaining our aim—and here I repeat myself with no apology—of keeping our hounds and our community together. This being the case, the requirement of top class hounds and good horses had not diminished.

Hounds First

The winning streak in the show rings of the early 2000's missed a year in 2007 but in 2008 we came up trumps again, winning both the Dog and Bitch Championships at Peterborough Royal Foxhound Show. As it happened, it was the year that Sir Philip Naylor-Leyland had asked me to be President. A great honour. My father had been President in 1953, so it was doubly pleasing. To win both Championships that year was nothing short of amazing, but what was even more gratifying was that both were recent outcrosses and therefore very important for the future. The Dog Hound Champion was Halifax '06 who as mentioned had the Midland American blood on his female side and the Bitch Champion was Bobcat '07 who had the David Davies' Bouncer line on her female side. Both were by our Bailey '03. In my own mind both were outstanding.

Roddy Bailey assisted by Charles Frampton judged in the morning and Martin Letts assisted by Adam Waugh in the afternoon. Martin Letts, sadly no longer with us, I always thought one of the better judges of hounds and I was very gratified when he said he thought very highly of Bobcat. In my President's statement in the catalogue I was delighted to be able to point out that we all owed much to the Fitzwilliam family and now Sir Philip and Lady Isabella Naylor-Leyland.

2009 for me was another triumph when Farrier '07 won and I could not help but smile to myself thinking back to the bloody-minded little Welsh girl, Fairy that my father, Sir Newton Rycroft, Pammie and myself had picked up from the Vale of Clettwr over thirty years previously. Farrier, I must mention was by the Martin Scott bred VWH Darius '04 an influential stallion-hound who in true competitive spirit I always jokingly referred to as the 'beagle'. In fact, although he was smaller than some it was only relatively. Crucially this brought back to the kennel the top line of Duke of Beaufort's Palmer '59—not only a Peterborough Champion but a stallion-hound of great note and working character—and thence the Portman blood, Meynell Pageant '35 so greatly cherished by my father.

There followed a couple of milestone victories with two litter brothers—Doublet '09 and Doynton '09—taking the honours in 2010 and

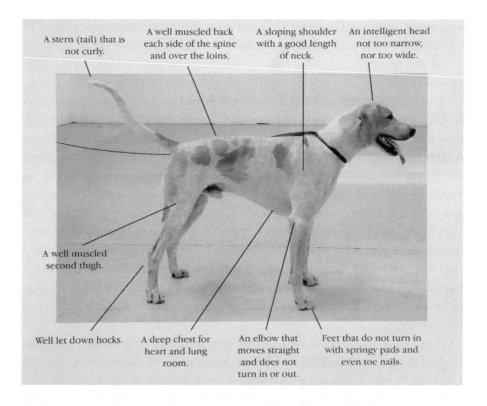

A stern (tail) that is not curly.

A well muscled back each side of the spine and over the loins.

A sloping shoulder with a good length of neck.

An intelligent head not too narrow, nor too wide.

A well muscled second thigh.

Well let down hocks.

A deep chest for heart and lung room.

An elbow that moves straight and does not turn in or out.

Feet that do not turn in with springy pads and even toe nails.

Farrier '07—Dog Hound Champion Peterborough 2009.

2011. Surprise surprise, they were both also by Bailey '03 which meant that not only did he win the supreme prize himself, but he then in a comparatively short span managed to sire no less than four other Champions. In retrospect, he was maybe overused, siring ninety nine litters before going to Canada, by which stage you could pick out his progeny all over the country. At the risk of boring everybody to death concerning championships, we did win again in 2013 with the bitch Rapture 12, this time by another VWH dog Rancher '09 who was also beginning to make his mark.

There is no doubt at that time the VWH were coming to the fore and so were the North Cotswold. Nigel Peel, another good friend, had a useful hunting pack. He had originally found it easier to stay just with bitches but had eventually branched out with some doghounds to mean-ingful effect. I may have been guilty in the past of observing that as a pack they were perfectly formed but a little on the small side similar to their Master, and an infusion of Beaufort female genes had not done them any harm.

On the horse front, Tony Holdsworth was always on the lookout, and with friends like Dermot Considine in Ireland plus several other dealers he always seemed to have a horse up his sleeve. He was also never jealous and would just as happily recommend a horse for somebody else, and not necessarily for himself. Andrew Richards from Cornwall also entered the picture and to my mind as far as I was concerned, he began to fill the shoes of the late Tom Connors. A very different character and indeed type of horsemen, Andrew is big in stature, a keen hunting man with a busy livery yard not far from Penzance who also produces good horses and is totally straightforward to deal with. When I say big, in the past I have often noticed that some fairly substantial men ride lighter than their weight, but also in some circumstances lighter men seem to ride far above their size. Andrew supplied me with a number of good horses, probably the most recognised being a grey called Spotlight. I was trying him at West Littleton one day, and when he had proved himself very easy, and perfectly capable, I was asked by my daughter Emma what I thought of him. "Perfect," I replied, and Emma trotted back to the Field and announced in a loud voice, "Marvellous, Daddy has found his Zimmer frame!" So poor old Spotlight was known as Zimmer forever more!

One of the best I had from Andrew was a real quality lighter boned black horse called Rubic. He was one of the kindest and bravest horses I had ever come across and also one of the most comfortable giving the most beautiful balanced ride you could ever wish for. The girls also loved him. He never put a foot wrong until one day he had a touch of azoturia and hit a gate badly. It was the first mishap he ever had, not his fault and it sadly destroyed his confidence. Andrew came up regularly to hunt with his girlfriend Emma, now his wife, who schooled a lot of his horses. He then joined the mastership of the Four Burrow and still keeps in touch—I owe him a great thank you.

Harking back to Holdsworth's flair for finding horses, his friend Dermot in Ireland did send over some pretty good ones. One in particular springs to mind. A grey with strawberry streaks known as Pinky. Together Tony and Pinky made a formidable pair. Pinky had a lucky escape one day when he slipped off a narrow bridge over the River Avon

Thomas Burton

below Foxley and was cast with a leg through the planks and suspended over the water. It looked a dire situation until thank goodness, Thomas Burton jumped into the river to see if he could help which maybe caused Pinky to have a last final heave that freed him, and he turned over falling into the water missing Thomas by inches. Thankfully they both climbed out. Thomas was good at that sort of a situation. On another occasion a hound got spiked trying to jump rather nasty iron railings round a reservoir in the Bath hills. Thomas lifted her off and carried her draped round his shoulders for a good mile or two up a steep hillside where she was put into a Land Rover to be taken to a vet and patched up. She was right as rain again surprisingly quickly.

Charity

One of the less publicised accomplishments performed by hunts generally is the raising of charitable funds. Collections to support local churches, village schools, and farming charities, for example with occasionally a more major collection for something such as the area's Air Ambulance service or local hospital coming to the fore as and when the need materialised. This was so before the Ban and remains very much part of the community spirit that prevails after it. In the early 1990's at a dinner party with Owen Inskip he suddenly announced that he was thinking of running in the 1992 London Marathon for SANE and would I join him. Being an absolute idiot, I thought that since I had run a bit at school, and thinking I was fit, I could just wing it without training. I did wonder why when we lined up for the start, me wearing an old pair of cotton long trousers, my old tennis shoes and smoking a fag why eyebrows were raised. Being over forty and never having run a marathon before, we started quite a long way back. I must confess to feeling somewhat demoralised when after running for about twenty minutes and feeling a bit puffed, we passed a large notice saying 'The Start'! Suffice to say at about the twenty mile mark my legs gave out and the last six miles were excruciating and very slow. It was quite a struggle to keep in front of the County Council team clearing the road picking up the litter! However, I did finish and joined up again with Owen who had trained and therefore was sort of okay. I will admit it took about two days before I could even walk!

The outcome was that Owen got enthusiastic about the fact it was a good money spinner and volunteered to become *chef d'equipe* of a British Field Sports Society team to try and raise some serious money pending the gathering storm. Being rather miffed that I had done so badly the first time, I bought a proper pair of running shoes, trained pretty seriously and joined the team, which also consisted of Frank Houghton-Brown, Adrian Dangar, Robin Gundry and myself as the amateur huntsmen, Martin Thornton, Patrick Martin and Barry Todhunter as professionals, backed up by Marcus Armytage representing racing. We all stayed at the Turf Club which was in fact closed for the annual spring-clean but luckily, they opened rooms just for us. When I booked in the day before, who should arrive in my room clutching a bottle of whisky but Barry

The London Marathon team 1992: Adrian Danger MFH, Marcus Armytage,
Frank Houghton-Brown MFH, Martin Thornton, Robin Gundry MFH,
Patrick Martin, Owen Inskip, Barry Todhunter, Ian Farquhar MFH.

Todhunter which rather set the tone of the evening for the two of us.
He did mention that it was the first time he'd ever been to London, and
he wanted to buy a bar of chocolate at Harrods to give to his wife. The
others all drank water and had pasta, whilst Barry and myself had a steak
each and stayed on the whisky which was rather contrary to the training manual. Next morning, we all lined up and it was not long before
they all left me behind—aged forty-five, the old man of the team—the
others calling out 'See you later'. I had to admit I had a wild card up
my sleeve or rather in my pocket—a couple of morphine pills left over
from the car smash—and not wishing to repeat the previous excruciat-
ingly painful episode, down one went at about twenty miles, and a super

charged Farquhar, pain free, stormed past the team down the Mall, except of course Barry Todhunter who was the first professional home with myself, amazingly, the first amateur! Frank needless to say twigged, and ran another Marathon himself three years later after managing to get one of the last pills off Mrs F. No fool Frank!

The next departure from the usual local good causes was a charity meet for the Intensive Care Unit at Frenchay Hospital in Bristol. The unit had successfully brought Mechelle Lake back from the brink after a serious bout of meningitis. Mechelle was and is the most charming girl, who had worked in the Badminton Stables for a number of years until moving in with her partner Michael Bell, a highly competent Scottish farrier. The said Charity Meet, was to be the first of many hosted by the Milsom family at their small farm at Sopworth. Leslie Milsom cut the hedges for most of the farmers in the area and his son Roger had been the hunt fencer for several years. Their annual meet raised literally hundreds of thousands of pounds over the ensuing twenty or so years. One of the biggest being Help for Heroes which also gave rise to the notion that the hunting world across the board should front a major fund-raising effort for them. Backed by the MFHA office, basically Jo Aldridge and myself put together a scheme that raised a total of £76,000 with contributions from many of the hunts. With the help of the Cheltenham Racecourse hierarchy and pushed by Mike Tucker as the commentator it was agreed that we handed over the cheque in the autumn at the Countryside Race Day. I travelled up with Jo and was grumbling about a having a bit of a cold only to meet the two soldiers who had been designated to receive the donation to find neither of them had legs and one had also lost an arm. How humbling was that? It made one feel very small. Jo told me later how moved she was to hear the crowd up in the boxes and grandstands suddenly start clapping and calling out, "Well done boys" as they caught sight of the young Marine and young Paratrooper being wheeled across the lawn to receive the cheque. Brave men all.

The Hunt continued and still continues to this day raising considerable sums for worthwhile causes at not only the annual Charity Meet but also from the yearly highly successful Badminton Horse Show run by Gill Brack and her sister Jenny Minney, and also from the popular Badminton Ride, together with other events.

Overseas

One of the greatest diversions after the Hunting Ban that helped in keeping spirits up waiting hopefully for a change in the law and at the same time dealing with the idiosyncrasies of a badly drafted law, was to many of us the fun and friendship that was so readily forthcoming from overseas. For Pammie and myself, this in particular came from the United States but also from Canada. It was most uplifting to hear overseas friends expostulate how unbelievable it was that the British Parliament of all Parliaments could outlaw something so intrinsically British!

Visiting the States in those early days I recall a really very good hunt with Mason Lampton at the Midland in Georgia with Ben Hardaway's cross-breeds in the woodland north of Alabama. The first day he gave us an example of the antics of the grey fox, not as adventurous as the red and in this case to its detriment. On the second day we were to witness the other extreme with the 'catch me if you can' attitude of the coyotes that were then moving into most of the Eastern Freeboard. They thought that they had the drop on the foxhound and so just kept lolloping along. In the past I had sometimes thought that our growing friendship with the Woods had produced a touch of artistic licence when it came to stories about the length and speed of their hunts. But having seen the coyote in action I realised they were if anything, under playing events. Moving from the Midland to the Live Oak the hospitality of Marty and Daphne seemed to know no bounds. Not only did we stay with them for their Southern Hound Show on more than one occasion, three at least, but we also joined them on two memorable trips. The first, to shoot doves in the Argentine and the second to spend a week with them in Zimbabwe. The Argentine visit was amazing. I had always shot as a boy and in Scotland later and had continued to have a day or two each season, but the Argentine doves were something else. We all flew to Chile and over the Andes to Cordoba to stay in a comfortable shooting lodge and for three days concentrated on the doves. The doves are wild and appear to be in plague proportions, so the farmers are delighted that somebody wants to reduce their numbers. When I say plague proportions, it may sound as if that is a justification for shooting so many, but witnessing them devouring a maize field, the density of doves is mind blowing. Anyway, the answer is that we were issued with twenty bores as the kick is less than a twelve bore, shoulder pads, ear defenders, and charming local Argentinian loaders (who also had click machines to record every time you scored a hit). Believe it or not we were also advised to tape up our nipples, the girls certainly, because the friction of so much shooting could actually cause blisters! The long and the short of it was that in three days seven of us shot 21,000 doves! Unbelievable, but remember they were regarded as vermin. They were also incredibly good shooting, flighting out in the morning at first light providing steady shooting in the maize fields until midday. Then lunch, the best Argentinian beef steaks you could ever imagine, the secret being they were entirely grass fed. A short siesta in a hammock before more serious shooting, flighting the doves back into their roosts. Each evening started with a massage. Even only shooting with a twenty bore your shoulders were bruised. We were presented with a baseball cap if we scored more than a thousand hits in one day. Marty Wood with two guns and going for it did actually top the two thousand mark. Then it was into bed exhausted. On the last evening flamenco dancers arrived from the nearby town and gave a rousing performance and somehow Mark Phillips, one of our team sitting in the front row, managed to sleep happily throughout the whole display.

The Zimbabwe trip was also huge fun. Marty in particular had always had a fascination for the big game in Africa. He organised and funded a spectacular complex on the banks of the Zambezi that had an impressive clubhouse and subsidiary chalets overlooking the expanse of the river giving a unique opportunity to see at first hand the magic of that troubled but captivating country. Surprise surprise, our fellow travellers from the UK had a common denominator, the foxhound. Martin and Eildon Letts, Alastair and Tessa Jackson, Nigel and Sophia Peel, Martin Scott, Pammie and myself landed in Harare before flying down to our destination over the ruined farmland that had once been known as the bread basket of Central Africa. From our light aircraft you could pick out what had once been cultivated acres with adjoining dams to supply irrigation. As we disembarked the locals seemed amused to catch sight of a ruddy-faced Martin Letts, still in his flat tweed cap, wielding a shepherd's crook, stiffly alighting off the plane. The whole week at camp was special. The fun and laughter coupled with the ambiance of a common fellowship was enhanced by the wildlife. The crocodiles were bigger and more numerous than I had ever imagined. The hippos, so long as you didn't come across them in the early hours of the morning on their way back to the river or interfered with their families when you were in a boat, seemed just like large cows underwater! The tigerfish were really good fun, and if you landed a good one, the local ghillies would call out "IDB, IDB" which roughly translates as "in da boat" and judged as very good fishing indeed. For me, one of the greatest pleasures was early one morning to witness a pack of African wild dogs, very rare indeed now, trotting back to their day quarters in the jungle having caught a buck the night before not far from the camp. Their freedom of movement was spectacular. Another morning, I also had to chuckle when at an "Eton and Harrow" cricket match on the banks of the Zambezi I managed to bowl out Scottie with an exploding mass of hippo poo!

I've already mentioned that we had also enjoyed many trips to Canada. Firstly, to the Berminghams, Bill and Lou, when Bill was Master of the Hamilton and also President of the Master of Foxhounds' Association of America, which as an organisation encompasses Canada as well. At that time, and very much continuing today, the McDonalds, Jack and Sue from the London Hunt were in the same position of trust now continued by their daughter Charlotte who like her father is an eminent doctor. More recently we have added the Byrnes to the list of true friends. Mike, an Irishman with all the dangerous charm that country produces is big into bloodstock and spent ten years as Chairman of the Jockey Club of Canada. His wife Laurel is a Master of the Toronto and North York Hunt and herself a leading light in the MFHA over there. The Canadians have a slightly different system in the organisation of hound shows, moving them from year to year to be hosted by a different pack. Considering the climatic difficulties that Canada faces, most years a complete lockdown due to snow and frost from mid-November onwards until maybe March, the enthusiasm of the Canadian packs is laudable. Judging the Canadian Hound Show more recently I had to smile to myself as I turned to my co-judge Marty Wood whilst we were scrutinising the two options for a Grand Champion, a quality Midland dog that had triumphed at Bryn Mawr (USA) the previous year, but now a bit on the leggy side, against a Toronto and North York dog, when I turned to Marty, "I've got to come clean, I have to declare an interest here, the Canadian dog is top line all my breeding." Marty smiling replied. "Female side all mine, Live Oak Drummer through and through!" We both laughed and the Canadian dog won, he was undoubtedly the best of them.

Returning to Live Oak Drummer '89 (USA) I must confess; Marty and Daphne had sent over three puppies in the nineties. They had to go into quarantine, two came to the Beaufort, and the third to Ronnie

Wallace at the Exmoor. Sadly, the two that we had did not impress me. These days I would not advocate sending puppies into quarantine. I don't think it enhances their ability to grow to their full potential both mentally and physically. At the time, I was aware that we were in danger of losing size at the Beaufort. Not that size worried me hunting wise, but I knew the importance of keeping the Beaufort stallion hound lines intact as regards size, so that other hunts could come to us to grade up genetically for that size and quality if they felt it necessary. I admit therefore that we did not use the Drummer puppies here although thank goodness Ronnie did at the Exmoor. That line later moved onto the Heythrop. Beaufort Matchbox '16 by Heythrop Magnum '11 produced Beaufort Matchless '19, who just to confound the odd critic went forward to win the online International Virtual Hound Show held during the Covid pandemic in 2021. The Live Oak Drummer line is now established at Badminton.

Staying with the hounds for a moment, during Tony Holdsworth's tenure at Badminton both as kennel-huntsman and then huntsman, our friendship with Wales certainly flourished particularly with the Pembrokeshire. Gary Barber the Pembrokeshire huntsman and joint master had always been a mate of Tony's and indeed a good friend of the Hunt and when he produced a little woolly person called Gwyneth the whole country fell in love with her. Little Gwynney as she was known was quite a character. When she didn't win a Puppy Show prize the groans and even discreet boos could be heard all around the ring! She managed to dodge the roll call as to which hounds went hunting each day on a regular basis, so was out more often than not! She had a very good nose and great determination and being small and rather woolly was also easily distinguishable. I recall a day when Gwynney had cut a pad and was just a touch lame but soldiering on resolutely. If one member of the Field, but even more so, one of the many foot followers observed, "Captain have you seen poor Gwynney, she is lame, you must pick her up," if there was one, there must have been a hundred. Gwynney had a litter, and it was one of nature's tragedies that sadly the line did not continue. However, we did get given another Pembrokeshire dog called Farrier who excelled in the field and his progeny, now with the prefix PE, are thriving in the Beaufort kennels.

Welsh Foxhound Bitch Gwyneth—Beaufort Puppy Show—IWF, David Beaufort, Martin Scott, Tony Holdsworth.

Builth

One of the more memorable features concerning Hound Shows in the last two decades or so was without doubt the Beaufort Hunt's increasing input into the jollifications post the judging at the Wales and Border Counties Hound Show held at Builth Wells. It was a show I had always gone to and much enjoyed. I had judged there on occasion in my turn and also shown there consistently with I must admit surprising success. Being asked to judge in the Welsh Hound ring, the only Englishman to do so was to me a considerable honour. In the 1990's however, the after-Show singing, led by the Welsh of course, that had been so much a part of the Show previously seemed to die a death. But one evening a few of the Welsh decided again to have a little singsong on their own. I don't know why I joined in and as any member of my family knows I cannot sing! But anyway, I did, and quietly one or two others came over and joined us. The idea grew and three years later we were back where we had been in the 1970's with about two hundred Welsh voices gathered round our Beaufort lorry belting out everything from the time honoured 'Land of My Fathers' to a more recent Tom Jones style 'Delilah' usually starring the inimitable Jacky Thomas. Perhaps a cheeky rendition of 'My Threshing

240

Machine' from the legendary tenor 'Corky', some rousing hunting songs, with the Fell boys vying for a slot against the Welsh and of course the mournful yet beautiful songs from a talented Dylan Williams. We even got my daughter Rose there once who I proudly say was as good as any. It was all such fun. All hound shows to me are enjoyable and well run. Builth, run by Jonny and Sarah Andrews is no exception, but the singing just added a different dimension. I was thrilled by the compliment, "the Beaufort have brought the singing back to Builth." I often wondered about the hounds still hopefully asleep in the lorry and if Farrier said to Fanfare, "That was a bum note, not as good as us when we get going!" Visits to Builth were always hilarious and often finished with rather a late drive home, normally with a long-suffering Jo Aldridge at the wheel who had to cope with the demands from myself and Tony Holdsworth for the traditional stop for a pee, when Tony would always try and convince us that one day, he was going to reach the River Wye about hundred yards away!

Away trips have always been enjoyable and without doubt our forays to the South Pembrokeshire, now the Cresselly, are seared in the memory. Whether it was taking the hounds in the season to hunt, or later in the year to judge their Puppy Show, often with Pammie-Jane. The hospitality shown by Hugh Harrison-Allen and his fiancée, the ever-smiling Ros, with suppers in the huge Cresselly kitchen, usually ending with laughter and dancing round the table to the sound of Hugh's ghetto blaster belting out Rolling Stones rock, are memorable.

***

Returning to the Beaufort, I continued to hunt hounds on a permanent basis with the help and top-class support from Tony Holdsworth as Kennel Huntsman and Paul Hardwick as whipper-in. We continued to achieve some really very enjoyable days. This was also greatly helped by committed and imaginative trail layers and a continuing team of hard-working Field Masters. To recap, Rupert Sturgis and Owen Inskip on Mondays, Bobby Faber and John Gardner on Wednesdays, John having replaced George Wade in 2007 when he and my daughter Emma moved to Dorset. Percy Lawson and David Maidment having taken over Thursdays, Percy replacing his renowned father-in-law John White who had sadly had to retire due to riding muscle fatigue. The ever-demanding Saturdays still pulled in a large hard riding crowd where Chris Casey and Owen Inskip held the fort.

MFHA-wise we now saw a major change as Alastair Jackson retired after a very popular stint as Director with Major Tim Easby stepping into his shoes. Tim is a good friend, he had hunted hounds himself at the South Shropshire, the West of Yore, and then the Middleton, whilst still a serving soldier, an example I feel of good organisation. As it happened, he had been in my Regiment, but I must admit, I had left before he joined! Tim was painstaking in his approach to hunting matters and amongst his other sidelines was his skill and humour as a mimic often to my and Stephen Lambert's cost! He joined the Executive Committee and we all continued fighting away with at least a smile and the odd laugh.

Writing on the Wall...

The hounds were in good nick, and I was still enjoying the challenge, but in reality, the writing was on the wall and the old bad back was beginning to catch up with me. Quite simply it was starting to hurt. I discussed things with David Beaufort and as ever being very supportive he said he understood and would welcome Tony Holdsworth hunting hounds with myself staying on as Joint Master. My last season as huntsman therefore ended in 2011, having completed six years under the Ban.

The Hunt arranged a Meet at Sopworth on the Friday before the Point-to-Point, which historically had always been the last day in the main country before going to the Hills. A good crowd turned up. David Beaufort spoke and presented me with a painting of the five consecutive Peterborough dog hound champions by Neil Forster. I thanked everybody and announced that both David and I were delighted that Tony Holdsworth was going to carry the horn next season. With many visitors, luckily, we had a good day. A jolly party in the village hall for everybody followed hunting with again a few speeches. The most poignant moment was when Peter Sidebottom as Hunt Chairman read Will Ogilvie's poem 'The Luckiest Man in England'. I know I found it extremely moving.

My last actual day hunting hounds was a fortnight later. We met at Peter Isaacs', Lower Chalkley Farm. David came, and not being as sound as he had been, and the Meet being held on rather undulating ground, he held on to the side of my horse who then sadly struck out catching

David on the leg quite nastily. David needless to say was big hearted about it blaming himself. However, I did say that after 26 years together as joint masters without a cross word it was rather unfortunate to suffer a kicking on the last day!

It was dry and sunny, and we did have a busy day, but nothing to write home about. We boxed up at Kingsmead, Didmarton with Bobby Faber. I couldn't bring myself to put the hounds in the lorry as usual, something I had always done, patting each one on the head and telling them how well they had done—occasionally leaving out an individual if they had been naughty. They always knew! Instead went straight home. Other huntsmen who had hunted hounds for a number of years would tell me that giving up was rather like losing a member of your family—a bereavement. They were right.

When I gave up hunting hounds, Pammie who had not hunted for some years decided to take it up again to keep me company which was very thoughtful of her, but it did mean that I got a five hour riding lesson each day!

Tony Holdsworth hunted hounds for five seasons, from the spring of 2011 to the spring of 2016, still with David and myself as joint masters. I personally not only enjoyed his company, but also thought he made a good job with the hounds. Things were undoubtedly more difficult, and maybe huntsmen all over England were relying more and more on the mobile telephone as a means of communication, not only to keep them abreast of any misguided antis but also to keep them in touch with the trail layers. Paul Hardwick continued to whip-in and was joined by the newly appointed Neil Starsmore—son of Ian Starsmore himself a respected huntsman in his day. During that season Paul had another bad fall, landing on a tree stump and so decided to call it a day. Paul was enormously popular, and the country showed their appreciation with a generous Testimonial and a good party in the village hall to see him off. His place was taken by Freddie Morby who had been at the Warwickshire and he soon proved himself as a hard worker and quick across the country. I continued to still enjoy going out on a horse and did go most days on bike hound exercise accompanying Tony. In fact, in Tony's final season I took the hounds for most of the August when Tony had a bad stomach infection. I greatly enjoyed it of course but after the first autumn morning hunting hounds myself I had no illusions about carrying on and was relieved when Tony returned. My old patent safety Zimmer was definitely coming to the end of his career and finding a suitable replacement with manners proved impossible. Slowly it dawned on me that it wasn't the horses that were no good, it was me! I finally gave up when going down the Avenue to Worcester Lodge in December on Zimmer who was on so much bute (phenylbutazone) he proved unstoppable and I rode slowly back to the stables, got off and never rode again. Sad, but that's life.

The family had organised a 70th birthday meet at Nesley just down the road from Happylands a fortnight later to which they all came but I remained on my feet! Pammie kept going and hunted here for a couple more years, before taking Bailey, her much loved horse down to the Portman to hunt with George and Emma and the grandchildren, which she enjoyed greatly, getting on well with Tom Lyle their new young amateur huntsman.

The Death of David Beaufort

David Beaufort died on August 16th, 2017, and was laid to rest in the family plot. His funeral was held at Badminton and David being the man he was had organised the Service himself with the help of Miranda, his Duchess. It was typically low key. Just a Service of Thanksgiving, no Memorial later, and no Eulogy, just readings by members of the family. I thought the two poems that were included in the service were quintessentially David: 'The Life That I Have' by Leo Marks and Rudyard Kipling's, 'A Smugglers Song:'

> "Five and twenty ponies,
> Trotting through the dark—
> Brandy for the Parson, 'Baccy for the Clerk.
> Laces for a lady; letters for a spy,
> Watch the wall my darling while the Gentlemen go by!"

Daughter Rose sang Vera Lynn's classic, 'We'll Meet Again' beautifully and although held at short notice, the Beaufort country was strongly represented, as well as by many from further afield.

Another milestone that year was the loss of John Berkeley. I often thought the demise of both David Beaufort and John Berkeley not far apart was a bad year for Gloucestershire. They were both great

*Badminton House Gardens, 2015: left to right, Tony Holdsworth Huntsman,
IWF, 11th Duke of Beaufort.*

benefactors to the County generally as well as very supportive Masters of
their own packs of hounds.

Winding up—or down!

So, on a personal front it was also a time of change. Stephen Lambert
retired as Chairman of the MFHA in 2014, his successor being Lord
Mancroft. Beano Mancroft came in as a political heavyweight which was
badly needed at the time. I remained as his Vice Chairman until the
spring of 2017 having completed twelve interesting years. We never actually got a change in the law, but we had helped to keep the ship afloat
and although often frustrating there had been exhilarating moments.

Peter Sidebottom also retired as Chairman of the Beaufort in 2015 to be
succeeded by Bobby Faber. Peter had been a friend and a compatriot from
way back. His occasional forays into Latin in his missives to the subscribers
and farmers may have mystified a few, but he had been very popular and at
one with the local community. We had always been able to discuss things.

As already recalled, Tony Holdsworth retired from Hunt Service and
hunting hounds in 2016. I have already made plain my regard for Tony,
and it was not surprising that his Testimonial and farewell party were

Chris Casey, Tony Holdsworth and IWF at Tony's retirement presentation.
(Photo by TTL Videos)

well supported. David Beaufort I knew had always got on well with him. He admired him as a Huntsman, and a horseman, and to boot, also as a good shot. He also found him, as I did, good company and made a cottage on the Estate available for him and his wife Sandra, where they both are still.

The other change that year was that countryman, Thomas Burton also decided it was time to move on and to return back to Cumbria where his son Michael was whipping at the time to Michael Nicholson at the Coniston, and where he was later to become huntsman to the North Cumberland. So yet another farewell party, and this was held at The Ship in Luckington which some might venture had been Thomas's spiritual home for a number of years! Thomas was extremely popular and gave a very moving speech outside the pub to a great gang of locals.

Matt Ramsden from Yorkshire was offered the post as Joint Master and full-time huntsman. He had hunted the Royal Agricultural University Beagles and then the Bedale and his family were long established hunting Yorkshire landowners. He took on Nick Hopkins from the North Cotswold as his Kennel Huntsman. I stayed on as joint master to see Matt in, taking a backward seat and retired in the spring of 2018 concluding 46 seasons as a Master of hounds, 38 of those carrying the horn four days a week.

I certainly do not wish to dwell on retirement arrangements. Suffice

John Hatherell, IWF and David Hibbard: IWF leaving do at Badminton House (Photo by Ruth Parker)

to say the Country and the locals were overwhelmingly kind. In front of Badminton House, a dray had been stationed on the grass with a loud speaking system. Antony Brassey who had been Chairman when we arrived, and indeed for our first 24 years, made I thought a generous and amusing speech incorporating a couple of humorous remarks sent to him by the Prince of Wales. This was followed by another kind address from Baroness Ann Mallalieu, going right back to the old Bicester days, and then the political battles, as well as tales of the hunting side. In response, I simply said a thank you to Antony and Ann for their kind words, going on to say how supportive David Beaufort had always been, what a special person he was, not only as a joint master but also as a friend. Thanks, also in no small measure to the farmers in both the Bicester and Beaufort countries without whom none of it would have been possible. Also of course a nod to the hounds for producing so much happiness and fun, and finally to my wife and family for putting up with me, sorely taxing at times!

However, that wasn't quite the end as three months later, Harry Beaufort now the 12th Duke and recently married now to Georgia, very kindly held a dinner party at Badminton House mainly for my family and a few locals who had been involved throughout my tenure, plus special friends who had come over from America and Canada. Marty and Daphne Wood from

IWF Testimonial Meet, Badminton. Pammie-Jane, IWF, Harry 12th Duke of Beaufort, Baroness (Ann) Mallalieu, Duchess of Beaufort (Georgia), Miranda Duchess of Beaufort, Antony Brassey. (Photo by Ray Bird)

Live Oak in Florida, Jack MacDonald from Canada, whose wife Sue sadly could not come, and Mike and Laurel Byrne also from Canada. Marty gave a speech majoring on the hounds that they had had of ours and their influence in the States. The finale the next day, a drinks party in the House and stunning gardens at Badminton, organised by Michael Baines and team, where unbelievably I learnt that they had run a well-supported and generous Thank the Captain Fund. Pammie and I received a specially bound and printed album of recollections and memories from far and wide organised by Mike Hawker and Julie Morrison, which we treasure. Myra Chappell who had painstakingly kept the accounts of the Fund also compiled a personal album of the amazing notes, letters, and anecdotes that she had received. To cap it all we received a magnificent painting by Tristram Lewis, myself on Black Jack surrounded by a mythical pack of hounds going back to the Bicester days and up until the present day. The picture portrayed a mixed pack of influential or old favourites, major stallion hounds, and quite a number of Peterborough winners. One glance at this, when it was presented to Pammie and myself and the depiction of so many old friends, probably not helped by a drink or two, cracked me up completely and when asked to speak I just spluttered, "Thank You," and burst into tears.

Back in the dog-house!

And That Is The Way It Is!